THE DARK ROOM

Rachel Seiffert was born in Oxford in 1971. Her first novel, *The Dark Room*, was shortlisted for the 2001 Booker Prize. In 2003 she was named as one of Granta's Best of Young British Novelists. Her most recent collection of stories, *Field Study*, was largely written while Seiffert was living in Berlin; she now lives with her family in London.

ALSO BY RACHEL SEIFFERT

Field Study

Rachel Seiffert

THE DARK ROOM

VINTAGE

Published by Vintage 2005

2 4 6 8 10 9 7 5 3 1

First published in Great Britain in 2001 by
William Heinemann

First published by
Vintage in 2002

Vintage
Random House, 20 Vauxhall Bridge Road,
London SW1V 2SA

Random House Australia (Pty) Limited
20 Alfred Street, Milsons Point, Sydney
New South Wales 2061, Australia

Random House New Zealand Limited
18 Poland Road, Glenfield,
Auckland 10, New Zealand

Random House (Pty) Limited
Endulini, 5A Jubilee Road, Parktown 2193,
South Africa

The Random House Group Limited Reg. No. 954009
www.randomhouse.co.uk/vintage

A CIP catalogue record for this book
is available from the British Library

ISBN 0 09 948349 1

Papers used by Random House are natural, recyclable
products made from wood grown in sustainable forests.
The manufacturing processes conform to the environ-
mental regulations of the country of origin

Printed and bound in Great Britain by
Cox & Wyman Ltd, Reading, Berkshire

HELMUT

Berlin, April 1921

Birth. His mother cuddles him and cradles him, and feeds him his first meal. Happy to hold this life she has felt within her all these months. He is a little premature, but not too small, and his miniature fists grip fast to her fingers. She knows him already, and loves him. The midwife takes her husband aside when he arrives home from work. Heads him off before he reaches the bedroom door. Unlike his wife, he never gets to look at his son and feel him perfect: to love him prior to knowing his fault.

The clinic is busy, the doctor brisk but sympathetic, recommended by the midwife. The new parents are told it is a congenital condition, but not serious. Put simply, their son is missing a muscle in his chest. Provided he is given regular physiotherapy he will certainly be able to write, and do all the tasks required in everyday life. He will never have full use of his right arm, of course, and manual labour will be impossible, but the absence of a pectoral muscle need not be a significant hindrance. He might even be able to play sport in time, though they are not to raise their hopes too high.

At home they watch their baby closely while he gurgles and kicks in his drawer-for-a-cot. His curved limbs and long toes, creases of new skin. He is beautiful, and the new parents smile at each other, each ready to laugh if the other will. They remove their son's little vest and inspect his chest and his right armpit as he moves. He is thinner on one side than the other, it is true. But both arms pump just as vigorously when he is fed or tickled, and he is robust and lively.

Mutti cries: There's nothing wrong. Papi puts his arms around her, still watching his son. They sit together on the bed for a long time, breathing, while the baby sleeps. And they name their tiny boy Helmut, bright nature, because that is how they see him. Perfect enough, and that is just fine.

—

Life between wars is harsh: food plain, luxuries scarce, living space small.

Helmut's father is a veteran, and still coughs in the night and in the autumn, when the weather is damp. He is older than his wife and grateful for his chance at happiness, so he leaves the house early, every day, finds work, again and again. The flat he comes home to is always clean, with at least one of the two rooms kept warm. And since Helmut's mother is a clever housewife, there is always something on the table.

Both parents are very happy with their one child, and take precautions against having more, showering their love on Helmut who laughs much more than he cries. The mattress the three of them share is wide and warm, and though he is now talking and walking, a separate bed for Helmut seems extravagant, uncalled for, a shame. Mutti grows herbs on the windowsill, and flowers, which she lets her son tend: and if Papi is not too tired when he comes home, he will sing a bedtime song or two for the boy. The morning and evening exercises are a game Helmut plays with his parents. He is to think that all boys do this, to be strong like their fathers. That all families are as happy as this.

In the hot summers of early childhood, Helmut's Mutti takes him on the long journey north to the coast while his father works on in the city, at whatever he can find. Helmut is brown as a nut within a week, and his hair sunblond. He plays naked in the shallows with other children, and Mutti makes friends with other mothers on the beach. She never draws attention to her son's chest, to his arm, and when the other women don't seem to notice, Mutti chats more freely, relaxes, lies back and enjoys the company and sun.

Summer nights in hostel rooms full of whispering mothers. Bedtime stories for sleepless children, confidences and shared cigarettes by a window open to the hot dark sky.

Helmut feels his mother climb into bed, smells the fresh smoke in her hair. Closes his eyes again, falls asleep again. Thumb in his mouth, sand under his fingernails, salt beach taste on his skin.

—

Helmut's father has found regular work with Herr

Gladigau, who owns the photography shop at the station. Three or four days a week of assured income. Papi cleans the darkroom, changes the chemicals, and minds the shop when Herr Gladigau has appointments to attend. Gladigau likes his new employee, trusts him. He is childless, a widower, and enjoys the contact he has gained with a young and happy family. He can't afford to pay as much as he would like; as much as Helmut's family needs. To compensate, he offers to create a photographic record of family life. A portrait sitting every six months is the initial agreement: while the boy is young and growing quickly. Mutti is excited, Papi slightly embarrassed, but also pleased. They arrange the first session for the following week.

The print Papi chooses has Helmut standing on his father's knee, pointing with his right hand towards Herr Gladigau's decorative palms which are on the left hand side of the picture, next to his mother. Both of his parents are looking at him and smiling. A blond boy, growing out of babyhood, his right arm at full stretch, at shoulder height, perhaps just over. A normal pose for an inquisitive, active child, but unconventional for a portrait.

Gladigau favours the more sedate pictures taken earlier in the session, in which all the sitters face the camera and have their hands folded in their laps. But his employee is quietly adamant, and Gladigau can find no reason to refuse his request. He chooses a simple frame from the middle price range and wraps the portrait neatly.

—

The carefully patched clothes and prominent cheekbones in this and the following portraits are painful for Gladigau to see. Papi is with him almost daily, with the same face, same jacket and shoes. But on the prints, alone in the darkroom, it is all too plain, sharp, clear: the cabbage-and-potato diet, the mend-and-make-do of the man's life, his wife, his son with the crooked arm. As soon as he can, Gladigau makes Papi's job full time.

There is enough money now to move into a better flat. The tenements near the station are well-maintained, light and clean, and Helmut, now grown out of his parents' bed, can have a small room of his own. Their new neighbours are friendly and house-proud, and there are plenty of local children for Helmut to play with. At first he is shy, preferring to watch the trains pull in and out of the station. Long mornings spent gazing out of the kitchen window, while his mother sings behind him as she cooks and cleans. Soon, though, he takes to watching the trains from the landing, and then the back steps. Before long he has forgotten the trains and runs round the back yard with the other children, playing riotous, overlapping games of hide and chase and catch.

Mutti looks for her son in the flat, on the landing, out on the back steps, sees him running. She spends an afternoon at the kitchen window, watching him play. Mutti can see how her son's right arm lags behind him as he runs. How his right shoulder hangs lower, and the way he introduces a small skip into his gait every so often, to help his right side catch up with the rest of his slight frame. She can also see that Helmut is unaware of this. Shifting her attention to the other children, she sees little feet without shoes that limp as they run over the rough ground. Pale complexions and eyes ringed dark with hunger, bitten nails and straggly pig-tails. Of course, shoes can be bought, and so can food. Certainly, bad habits can be dropped and hair can be brushed. Helmut cannot be cured by prosperity, by nourishment or by discipline. But none of the neighbourhood children mock him or even stare. And though she never gives up the habit of watching, checking, Helmut's Mutti does allow herself to feel relieved.

—

With school, though, there comes a change. The sports teacher orders a full inspection of his new charges. Vests off, they stand to attention in order of height. Those deemed in need of special treatment are pulled out of line and assemble in a raggedy bunch in the corner of the school yard. Helmut finds himself among the fat boys and the weak boys with bad teeth, and doesn't know why. Once it is established, in front of the silent eyes of his class, that unlike the others, he cannot raise his right arm above his shoulder, Helmut knows there is something wrong with him.

—

At home Mutti cries, and later Papi rages. He goes to the school with Helmut the next day, and demands that his son be allowed to take sport with the healthy boys. He has never had problems out in the back yard with the neighbourhood children, or on the beach in summer.

Papi is asked to wait in the wide lobby. There is no chair, so he stands near the door, on the edge of the parquet with its high wax shine. A class ends, another begins, and Papi is now very late for work. In the silence he remembers Helmut's birth. The clinic they took him to, with the same corridors; same wide, swinging doors; same stifled, shameful feeling about his son. He resents the midwife, the doctor she sent them to. Blames them for coming between him and his child. Resents the headmaster, too, though he does not argue when he is finally sent word. The school will not reverse the decision. Helmut will take gymnastics to supplement his daily physiotherapy, but no team games unless his condition improves. Papi reads the note, picks up his hat and coat, and leaves.

At home that evening, Helmut's father takes him on his knee. He is a strong little man, loved by his Mutti and Papi, and he will work hard to prove himself to the school. They will do it together, all three of them. The strength of the family will prevail.

But Helmut is still with the fat boys and the weak boys with bad teeth, and he still can't catch a ball thrown over shoulder height. At home, the twice-daily exercises become more vigorous, less fun, especially when performed with his father. In the toilet down the corridor, he scrutinises the thin twist of muscle below his right collarbone. In the wide, sleek bakery window he sees how his right arm hangs: low and crooked, crowding his narrow chest.

———

Helmut still plays in the back yard with the neighbourhood children, but Mutti also frequently catches sight of him standing at the high fence at the far end of the tenements, staring through the slats at the trains pulling in and out. It is not a large station, but most days there are two or three passenger trains arriving from other cities, going to places far away. Dresden, Leipzig, Stuttgart, Munich.

Helmut does not concern himself with engine numbers or types of carriage. He likes times and destinations, arrivals and departures. He likes to watch the people, in groups and alone, with trolley-loads of baggage, or carrying nothing. Judging by their other-city walks and clothes, he likes to guess if someone hasn't been to Berlin before.

Helmut is not always alone by the high fence. His encyclopaedic knowledge of the timetable impresses many of the other little boys. He also makes friends with the guards, quizzing them on arrivals and distances through the turnstile bars. Soon he is allowed on to the platform where he collects the punched tickets from the passengers as they disembark. Those who notice his arm and his carefully patched clothes sometimes slip a *Groschen* into his hand. Helmut is faintly embarrassed by these gestures: certain his parents would disapprove, uncertain as to why. But he never refuses the strangers' gifts: the ability to buy sweets is a powerful weapon in the war for friends. He uses his access to the railway station and his small bags of liquorice well. As favours bestowed, not pleas for acceptance. The neighbourhood children often come calling, clatter down the stairs behind him, across the back yard to the tracks.

—

The family photos show a healthy boy, already quite tall, standing between his parents, both seated slightly in front of him. He has a sailor suit on, the regular uniform for boys on Sundays and holidays. His right arm rests on his mother's shoulder, and he is standing so that his left side favours the camera slightly. The combined effect is to minimise his lopsided chest, to mask the crooked hang of his arm. For three or four years, the family adopts a similar pose, variations coming in the clothes, Helmut's height, and the gradual greying of his father's beard. The family looks content, healthier, cheeks plumper than in previous years. For all the artful masking of a son's disability, they are relaxed. Still proud, still a unit, gradually growing into a kind of prosperity.

—

Puberty and the Third Reich arrive simultaneously. To Helmut's shame, not only does he grow hair on his body, but the fluff that should be under his right arm grows higher, more visible, under his collar-bone. The strange sinew-twist below the skin on his chest becomes more pronounced as his muscles become more defined.

All boys do gymnastics now at school, but that only makes Helmut's restricted arm movement more conspicuous. He wears a long-sleeved vest, not a singlet like the rest. Some stare at him as they change, still others push into him as they pass in the long school corridors. Most of the time, it is not discussed.

Helmut is good at his studies, and has a few friends at school. At home, he still spends most afternoons at the station, usually alone. Some evenings he finds the neighbourhood boys in the back yard on his way home. Helmut stands with them a while as they wrestle and joke, and they ask him about the trains, but only half-listen to his replies. They have joined clubs to which Helmut is not invited, have grown more interested in the gangs and streetfights, and liquorice isn't the draw it once was. Occasionally one of the neighbours' girls will join him on the platform. Edda Biene, waiting by the mail sacks, sucking her long plaits, watching Helmut greet the disembarking passengers, gathering his tickets. The hang of Helmut's arm has become more pronounced with puberty, and increased prosperity has made the passengers more generous. Helmut knows if he saves for a few days, and takes Edda for an ice cream in the shop next to Gladigau's, then she might let him hold her hand, or even show him her legs in the stairwell on the way home.

He knows he is fit, feels he has a strong heart and good lungs and swift legs to offer his nation. He also knows he is imperfect.

—

Helmut has left school now. Other boys go to work, learn trades, but Mutti persuades Papi to let their son stay at home. Just for a while, he's not ready yet, still just a boy. Helmut's Papi sighs and agrees.

Mutti takes in washing now, and Helmut does a share of the folding and carrying, but for a year or so, his days are largely spent drifting between station and home. Quiet and content, his head full of timetables. Eating the warm lunches Mutti cooks for him, gazing across the kitchen table to the window with his daydreamer's faraway eyes.

Papi is irritated by his son's idle behaviour. At Gladigau's, business is good. He has new cameras, better film stock, and needs an extra pair of hands. Papi knows this, takes his son aside, suggests he make himself useful. Helmut is eager to please his father and come the autumn, he seizes his chance. Out before breakfast to greet the first train, Helmut finds the pavements glittering with a thick frost of glass. The early crowd pick their way carefully through the shards to the station gates, past Gladigau, whose windows are unharmed, but who stands and stares, pale in the November light. Helmut takes his keys, finds a broom and sweeps without saying a word, and Gladigau appreciates this. The boy is now the obvious choice.

Papi persuades this time, and Mutti relents. He can work Monday, Wednesday and Friday afternoons, and also Saturdays, if there are errands to be run. Employer, father and son work alongside one another: quiet, busy, efficient. Gladigau likes the boy and treats him well, teaching him, nurturing him, though never indulging him.

—

Helmut likes the darkroom. The soothing sound of the gently running tap, and the alkaline smell of the chemicals. He only has the light on when he is cleaning, likes to mix and load in the red of the safelight or the deep, rich dark. The portraits taken with the big studio camera are Gladigau's forte, and neither Papi nor Helmut are allowed to touch the sheets once they have been exposed. However, Gladigau also experiments with the new cameras and their long spools of film, and because Helmut is thorough and methodical in his work, he is allowed to process these negatives. He winds the long rolls off patiently, fingers working skilfully without the aid of eyes. He times the baths well, after discussing the exposures with Gladigau, and the old man is pleased and proud of his apprentice's understanding of the work. Although his employer always makes the prints himself, he does allow Helmut to do experiments of his own with leftover chemicals and discarded negatives. On slow afternoons, when the darkroom is free, Helmut teaches himself to print on scraps of thick photographic paper, which he seeks out of the darkroom shelves and drawers.

In the cupboard in the small back toilet, under the bottles of developer and fixer, Helmut uncovers the American magazines that Gladigau has kept neatly folded in brown paper. The bolt has a screw missing, so Helmut sits with his boot wedged tight against the door. Black and white photos of women, draped in veils, in half-light. Helmut does not understand English, but he does understand the references to stocks, to F-stops, cameras and lenses. German film and German cameras are the best, he knows, but these American women are very good, too. Rounded stomachs, small breasts, long, wide thighs. Some of the photos have been taken outside, and the women are swimming, their bodies rippling water and light.

When he is not working, Helmut daydreams about his job. The subdued lighting, the running water, his rigid right leg. The white skin of the American women, and the loose bolt on the toilet door. At night he conjures the images against his bedroom ceiling as the long, slow goods trains clatter below, a soothing rhythm of sleep.

—

To the east, new land is found; old land found again. So

many things are better now: brighter, healthier, cleaner. Helmut sees it in his parents' faces, knows it is enshrined in law. He feels it in his legs as he strides to the station; the freshness of spring and promise of summer tell him: larger, wider, stronger.

He could be called and carried by it, and perhaps even cured.

—

At eighteen, Helmut goes with three of the neighbours' boys to the draft board. All of their faces tight, and eyes bright with the adventure that lies ahead. Despite his flushed cheeks, Helmut has a cloud in his belly which he cannot shift. The doctor is not unkind, and Helmut is glad of the private room, the two minutes' grace he is given to blink back his boys' tears. The other boys slap him hard on the back, tell him he'll be in with them next time round. Perfect officer material. They don't ask him to come and share a schnaps.

He walks home, fast and by the back routes. Imagines each man he sees is on his way to the front while he is going home to his mother. Helmut locks himself in his box room, stares out of the window, up at the sky over Berlin. He musn't cry: that would be further humiliation. He knows Mutti is sitting tight and still in the next room, listening, guessing. His fists are balled tight in his blankets, and the windowpane swims shapes before his eyes.

—

His father is silent for a long time. Helmut listens at the door, and hears no sound from either of his parents, hands growing clammy in the dark. When Papi finally speaks, it is a relief. No more wasting time at the station, in day-dreams. He is not a child now, not a girl, he needs to start earning his place in the world. Helmut's father stopped exercising with his son a couple of years ago, and now he tells his wife to stop, too. The ritual has become embarrassing to mother and son. Too physical and too pointless. Mutti feels the loss of daily proximity, but repeats to herself that it is for the best, until she believes it.

Helmut's parents join the Party; the *Führer* joins the family portraits on the wall above the sofa. In the first days of war, Helmut's father finds a well-paid job managing the floor of a new factory on the outskirts of Berlin. Helmut gets a full-time job with Gladigau.

—

The last family portrait is taken. Helmut is now an adult after all. Gladigau jokes with Mutti as he sets up the camera. The next pictures will be of a wedding, and the christenings which will follow. Mutti flushes, Papi says nothing, Helmut busies himself with shutting up the shop and closes his ears. The moment passes.

For this last photo, both men stand, father and son, and their wife and mother sits proudly in front of them. Both have one hand on each of her shoulders, and Helmut has his left arm around his father's back. The encircling warmth of the family.

Since this is their final sitting, Gladigau also takes an individual portrait of Helmut. Captured from the chest up, left shoulder angled towards the camera, his gaze directed up and right of frame by Gladigau's outstretched finger. Helmut has the trace of a smile around his slim lips and the downward tilt of his chin makes him look shy, girlish. Though his hair is dark now and combed down with water and some of his father's pomade, it still has a boy's curl about it.

Gladigau is pleased with this individual portrait. He props it up against the till as he takes his evening schnaps. Examines the heavy brows, and the pale eyes set deep in their sockets; remembers the boy with the sharp cheek-bones and brittle-looking wrists; approves of the calm young man he sees in front of him now. Gladigau selects a plain frame, but one from the top price range, and wraps Helmut's likeness ready for his mother to collect.

Mutti sits on the bed and holds the photo on her lap. Stays still like that for half the afternoon, heart beating unexpectedly fast. She covers her son's right eye and looks only at the left, the eye nearest the camera, and finds the root of her uncertainty there. She thinks it might be the muscles of the lower eyelid, tightening slightly at the moment of exposure. Or perhaps just a trick of the light: the two sharp, white pin-points in the eye, creating the illusion of pain. Closer inspection of the family picture reveals no such information, so it could simply be that her son, a shy young man, was nervous of sitting by himself, for his employer. It was an extravagant gift, after all, and unexpected. And the frame.

The picture is not displayed in the living room where visitors might see it. His mother keeps it on her bedside table, and later lays it carefully away in a drawer.

—

War has everyone bound tight with purpose. Helmut's mother and father spend long evenings talking on the landings with their neighbours. Coffee and schnaps, leaning against the doorpost. Voices raised and lowered again, opinions offered. What is to come, what might be.

For Helmut, this is a lonely time. Not many young men have gone yet, but still he feels the shame of being at home. He keeps out of the way of neighbours whose sons are fighting, keeps himself to himself more and more, and his mother and father allow him his silence and his solitude.

He still goes to the station, before and after work, and sometimes at lunchtime, too, but he no longer collects old tickets. The passengers' charity is humiliating now, and the risk of abuse too great. Helmut hides his arm as best he can, folding it over his chest, or leaning his right side against a pillar. In place of the tickets, he notes times and destinations, arrivals and departures. He has a small leather-bound book, the kind Gladigau uses to note his exposures. The timetable has changed quite a few times since the war began, and Helmut uses this little book to keep track. At home in his box room, he sticks his ticket collection in a scrapbook, and writes the pre-war timetables out from memory.

—

Gladigau has not used colour film before. One of his regular clients has persuaded him to use it for her daughter's forthcoming wedding, and the first samples have arrived in the early post. Employer and apprentice examine the accompanying leaflets over a morning cup of coffee. An hour later Gladigau steps into the darkroom, announces he will shut up shop at lunchtime, invites Helmut to go out with him to test the new stock.

They take a tram to the heart of the city, Helmut gripping the tripod between his legs as they round corners, Gladigau peering out of the windows, looking for the most colourful street. It is a clear autumn day, crisp and fresh. Helmut watches the sun and shade on the buildings they pass, thinks the photos must surely turn out well with light this good and strong.

Once in the centre, they get out and walk until they come to a wide street lined with red banners. This is it; Gladigau is certain now, and Helmut can't help but agree. Smiling, smiling, looking up and around: he has never been so far from home, and has never been in a street so broad and bright and long. The cold wind has weakened his fingers and so setting up the camera takes longer than usual. Gladigau is excited, fussing with his light meter. The banners beat like sails above their heads and to the horizon, and Helmut is dizzy with light and cold and colour and joy.

The slides come back in small cardboard frames from the lab. Alone in the shop, Helmut holds the last and best one up to the window. The luminous street held between finger and thumb. Bright swastikas burning out against the sky, and the wind caught in the scarlet folds on the photo.

—

Close inspection of his notebooks confirms Helmut's suspicions. The station is being used more frequently. He imagines the whole country on the move: people, goods, places. At the same time he feels, fears, Berlin is emptying. He hasn't seen any of the boys from school since he started work, so imagines them at the front. A sudden rush of deaths and departures shocks Helmut's mother into pale silence, and her son absorbs her mood. Frau Biene on the next landing has lost both sons in Poland, and moves back to Bremen taking Edda, Helmut's one-time platform companion, with her. Herr Maas from downstairs leaves for the front, Frau Maas takes the children south to her sisters. Two weeks later, another neighbour, another soldier is killed, and another of the shops next to Gladigau's is boarded up, the owners gone without warning.

Business at Gladigau's is not as brisk. Some of their regular customers have become irregular, and there are fewer one-off jobs coming in. There is enough to keep Gladigau busy, but Helmut has more idle time to himself. While his boss is working, he goes through the order books, making lists of people he hasn't seen for more than four weeks, crossing them off again if they come back to the shop. Every week new names are added. Helmut is worried. He decides to keep a rough tally of arrivals and departures at the station. To monitor comings and goings, keep a check on the slow drain of people out of Berlin.

—

Evening at the station. Helmut stands with his notepad and a troop of soldiers hurry past him on to the platform, a sudden wash of grey. Most of them are older than him, but Helmut is acutely aware of each young soldier, youthful faces passing his own. He steps back, three, four paces, stands with his weak shoulder against the tiled station wall. Ashamed of his own lack of uniform, ashamed that he is standing still, going nowhere, he buries himself in his notebook and scribbles numbers that mean nothing, names of cities without reference to trains.

His notebook is snatched, his arm pinned to the wall. He is asked questions, but sees only the uniform he lacks. The voice and the shock blend with the grey soldier's coat, and Helmut is confused. Passengers stare in silence, and he thinks perhaps he should stay quiet too. He looks away from the shouting face, turns to the tiles on the wall he was leaning against, is being pressed against now.

The guard is there. The shouting stops. He is explaining to the officer about Helmut's hobby, the officer is loosening his grip on Helmut's arm.

Helmut apologises, though he isn't sure what for. The officer lets him go, but keeps hold of his notebook, and Helmut keeps his hot cheek pressed to the cool tile wall. The guard whispers something to the officer as he walks away, pointing at Helmut. The officer stops and turns back, explains to Helmut loudly and slowly that his notes would be dangerous in the wrong hands, and the passengers watch the scene. Some are drifting now that the officer has finished shouting, but Helmut feels their eyes still fixed on him, combined with the officer's glare. In the silence, he braces himself for the slap, kick, punch which never comes. The officer walks away along the platform, with Helmut's notebook in the pocket of his uniform coat. The guard pats Helmut gently on his crooked arm, still aching from the officer's grip. The passengers disperse as silently as they stared. Helmut walks home across the back yard, down the alley, up the stairs and writes everything he can remember of his notes into his scrapbook before it is too late.

—

After this he tries to work from memory. It isn't difficult for him to make mental notes of train times, arrivals and departures. He knows the timetable patterns so well that alterations are memorable. The difficulty comes in tallying the people. He knows he will never get exact numbers, but even rough figures are impossible without making notes. He begins carrying a scrap of paper in his sleeve and a pencil stub in the palm of his hand. He can jot notes quickly, concealed behind the mail sacks, or even slip into the toilets between trains and add his scrawled columns up. The problem with these hasty notes is accuracy. Helmut doesn't trust them. The figures reveal an increase if anything in the numbers arriving in Berlin. He reasons that some of them might move on from other stations or may only be visiting, but still, they do not concur with Helmut's impression of an ever-emptier city. Frau Steglitz and Frau Dorn both have husbands and sons in the army now. Their flats are empty, lonely, so they move out of the city, nearer the munitions factories where there is work. The lawyer who handles Gladigau's unpaid accounts has also gone, without leaving a forwarding address.

—

The first spring of wartime. Helmut's birthday has come and gone again, with a kiss and a cake from Mutti, after Papi has left for work. Helmut has not been back to the recruitment office, and has received no letter requesting him to return. His father sorts through any post that comes in the morning, and Helmut always feels a twinge of guilt that there is nothing for him. Sons in every block around them are leaving or preparing to leave. Fathers, too, if they are young enough and not doing essential work. Helmut starts doing exercises again.

Alone in his box room, he lifts his arm out in front of him, as high as it will go: just below shoulder height now. He steps forward and presses his palm against the wall. Steps forward again, pushing his hand up the wall with his good arm, and so on and so on, forcing his arm up above his shoulder. The ligaments in his elbow and shoulder strain, the skin around his shoulder blade burns. Everything resists. Without the wall, without his good arm, he gets no further than his shoulder. There is no pain, it is simply as if the air is too heavy.

Helmut picks stones from the back yard and hangs them in a canvas bag from his outstretched arm. Each day another stone, each day for two, three, four turns of the egg-timer. Still the air is too heavy. Still he cannot face going back to the recruitment office. Still he cannot look his father in the eye.

———

Papi brings wine home, has a surprise. A promotion; more responsibility; better pay. He fills his pipe after dinner, explains his news to wife and son. The eastern expansion, he says, has been swift. Helmut watches as the smoke climbs over their heads, waits for the blue-soft smell, and hears his father tell of the new workers, come to the factory from all over Europe. Papi is to have a week's holiday before he starts his new post. Helmut is to ask

Gladigau for leave. They are to go to the coast as a family for the first time ever.

Helmut refuses to take his shirt off on the beach. The most he will do is roll up his trouser legs and walk in the shallows. He has become fat. Soft and white. His right arm and shoulder are strong from his exercises, but he knows the rest of his body is weak. The extra layers of flesh do not fill out his chest. They hang in shameful, dimpled creases around his armpit, no muscle to give them shape.

It is a hot spring, and sweat shines in his hairline, on his eyelids and his neck. He is always flushed, and the sweat quickly turns stale in the armpits of his shirts. His mother washes them each night, but the smell lies deep in the weave and the seams, and Helmut is ashamed.

Gladigau has lent Helmut one of his new folding cameras: about time, he said to Papi, that the boy learnt to take photos. Privately, over his evening schnaps, Gladigau imagines Helmut a suitable heir to his modest business empire. In the light of day, he does not entertain such fantasies, but he still lends the boy the camera, and in so doing, saves Helmut's holiday. His parents take walks, and he struggles behind them, damp and pink. Taking photos gives him an excuse to stop and rest. It absorbs him, distracts him. Exposures by light meter and by instinct. Views, grasses and shells. He tries alternative framings, keeps the sun behind him, and strives always to maximise depth of field.

Helmut is happy, the holiday a success, his parents' worries about his usefulness eased: he could be a photographer like his boss.

—

Helmut returns to the news that the station is to be rebuilt. Gladigau is pleased with his apprentice's holiday photos, and sets him the task of capturing the construction work on the station. Gladigau hopes to be able to sell these photos as postcards.

Helmut is nervous under the weight of his first assignment, and feels conspicuous setting up his tripod on the corner opposite the station gates. Trams jangle past, and he imagines the passengers' eyes on him. Pedestrians seem to linger, casting their eyes in the same direction as the lens. Helmut cloaks himself in activity, busying himself with exposure calculations and adjustments, squinting and frowning as he has watched Gladigau do so many times before. He holds the light meter in his left hand, his right jammed on to his hip to prevent it hanging in front of his chest.

Nerves give rise to miscalculations, and Helmut's first set of professional photos are underexposed. No great tragedy, Gladigau consoles his protégé: under is better than over; they can coax the detail out in the printing; he will show him how. Helmut, however, winces at the grain in his prints and begs his employer to let him have another go. Gladigau is pleased by this enthusiasm and allows him one hour's photography two afternoons a week until the station is finished.

Progress is swift and by midsummer a new platform has been added and the expansion of the station-house has begun. Helmut becomes bolder, taking photos openly, and with a variety of cameras and stocks. He also begins to take photos inside the station. The guard grumbles at first and reminds him of the angry soldier, but Helmut promises he won't focus on trains, only construction work and people. He begins to explain his project, but the guard quickly loses interest. Helmut doesn't tell him the full story. This he keeps to himself. In his photos he is documenting the expansion of the station, but he is also monitoring the exodus. His method is simple: he remembers the sequence of trains in an afternoon and memorises how many exposures he has taken of each arrival and each departure. Then he counts the people on the prints. The complicated equations he calculates in his room at night confirm his deepest suspicions. Berlin is slowly losing people.

—

The army recruits heavily from Helmut's neighbourhood and the surrounding areas. There are plenty of young men here, all willing to die for *Führer* and *Vaterland*, in the service of the next one thousand years. Helmut still counts himself among them, aches and yearns for uniform, active service, *Kamaraden*. But he knows, he knows. Because of his arm, his fault, his flaw, he is left behind, while everyone else moves on into the *Lebensraum* beyond.

He withdraws further, speaking less. Gladigau trusts his steady, quiet boy: takes on more work outside the little studio, leaves Helmut to mind the shop alone for long periods of time.

Paris falls and the *Führer* returns triumphant to Berlin. Helmut's parents go to the centre to watch, without asking Helmut, leaving him behind. He spends the evening at the station, watching the crowds flood in, off the trains and on to the trams, into the city centre. A few quiet, solitary hours later they pour back through again, alive and glowing, off to their homes in the suburbs and outlying regions of Berlin. Helmut waits at the gates until finally he sees Mutti and Papi step off their tram and make their way to the station to collect him. They are both smiling, tired but joyful, like the rest of the crowd. Linking arms, the family walks home, Helmut in the middle, Papi on his good side, Mutti on his bad.

He feels their pride, knows he isn't part of it, turns away from their faraway eyes.

—

The first bombs fall on Berlin. A single attack, and for Helmut the novelty is frightening but thrilling. After the deep, distant thumping in the earth subsides, the sky to the south is lit a brilliant orange. Helmut's bed rattles gently with the explosions, but far less than it does when the trains go by. His parents wake him. Berlin burns on the horizon, the fires clearly visible from Helmut's bedroom window. Mutti and Papi sit with him on his bed and watch. Mutti asks if he is afraid, but Helmut shakes his head, glad of the quiet company, the warmth of his father's legs so close to his own cold feet.

—

Gladigau is displeased with the amount of film that Helmut is using on the station project. He tells him to concentrate on the construction work and stop taking so many photos of people. Helmut starts stealing occasional rolls of film, and sneaking out two cameras at a time. The weather is colder, and Helmut wears his old overcoat again. By checking in the mirror in the back room, he confirms that he can carry a second camera secretly under his coat by positioning it on his right side. The hang of his arm disguises the slight bulge made by the lens. He has to hold his right shoulder more stiffly than normal to stop his arm swinging too much. But in the back room and the alley on his way home, Helmut practises walking with his arm at this angle until he develops a more natural gait.

In the cold, dull days of late winter, the station is finally completed. The little row of shops, including Gladigau's, are spruced up for the grand reopening. The two empty shops have their boards torn off, their windows replaced, and new displays put in. Helmut spends an afternoon helping the other apprentices make the faked shopfronts presentable. In the months since their owners left, no one has paid them any attention. Helmut doesn't like their dark and damp interiors, the black graffiti, and the broken glass grinding underfoot. But he does not complain because Gladigau has entrusted him with his first major assignment: photographing the opening.

The light is not as spectacular as on the day they caught the banners on the wide city boulevard. But it is a bright day for the time of year, and Helmut is confident about his framings and his exposures. The dignitaries arrive and make their speeches to much cheering, and Helmut finds an excellent position in the heart of the crowd for the opening of the new station gates.

This last set of photos are really very good, and both Helmut and Gladigau are pleased. Although the station-house façade is in reality rather square and plain, on Helmut's photos it looks almost elegant, and full of the energy of the flag-waving crowd. The stationmaster orders postcards to be made and displays them in the station kiosk. Gladigau receives a percentage of the sales, and Helmut gets a modest pay-rise and the promise of more assignments. For his birthday, Gladigau gives him the folding camera, and his parents buy film and chemicals from Gladigau at cost price. Helmut now has his own shelf in the darkroom store cupboard. All four of them eat ice cream in the café by the station and toast Helmut's future career with the chopped nuts and whipped cream that are becoming more expensive with every passing week.

Unaccustomed to conversation, Helmut is exhausted by the company that afternoon, and is little more than monosyllabic once the food arrives. Gladigau is used to comfortable silence with his apprentice, and so he thinks nothing of Helmut's behaviour. But his parents are embarrassed by what they see as rudeness; his mother by his lack of table-manners and his father by his son's large stomach and pasty cheeks.

Gladigau suggests a photo of the birthday meal. Sets up a camera, instructs the waiter, and sits himself next to Helmut on the left of frame; mother and father are on the right. When she finds a space for it on the wall, Mutti notices that this is the first family picture in which Helmut is not between his parents. Gladigau looks cheerful, Papi a little tired and serious, and Mutti thinks she looks shy. A touch embarrassed, perhaps. Helmut still has his hand on his spoon, and his napkin tucked into his collar. It is difficult to tell with his soft round cheeks, but something in her son's expression suggests to Mutti that he has not yet swallowed his last mouthful of ice cream.

—

The war is not even two years old, but it reaches into every aspect of daily life. People are minded not to waste food; extravagance is frowned upon; resources must be conserved for the common good. In the family portraits which Helmut frames and wraps, there is often a woman in black. In the wedding photos the groom is usually in uniform. New babies are brought to the shop, the pictures to be sent to fathers at the front. And soldiers come in to leave a portrait behind for mothers, sisters or sweethearts to cherish.

—

Helmut sees more of Berlin now, out on assignments for Gladigau. He still goes to the station every day to count the trains and keep a watchful eye on the comings and goings, but he also ventures further afield with his camera in his spare time.

The late spring days of 1941 are cold and largely dull. Not great weather for a photographer, but Helmut is keen to improve his skills. He saves what he can from his wages, managing enough for a roll of film each week. Gladigau allows him long lunch breaks, and even occasional half days out, if his duties are done. On Sundays, with Gladigau in the darkroom to guide him, Helmut spends hours printing up his precious rolls. Rows and rows of tiny experiments on Gladigau's leftover paper: all strips and scraps.

Almost all of the prints have people on them, usually considerable numbers of people, too. Helmut gravitates towards crowds, busy streets, enjoys capturing the milling, moving mass. Gladigau admires Helmut's photos, squinting and nodding at the prints pegged up on the lines across the darkroom to dry. That's Berlin, he says. All that life. He points out the sense of movement in the pictures, clears his throat and tells Helmut he has a true photographer's eye.

The compliment is heartfelt, jealous and not easily voiced. Gladigau's chest feels tight in the chemical dark. His apprentice, however, shows little sign of hearing the praise: standing silently next to him, running his pale, critical eyes across the prints with a frown.

Later, after Gladigau has gone home, and Helmut has finished cleaning up, he lays out the dry prints on the counter and looks at them again. Next to him is a new notebook, begun six weeks ago, and already almost filled with his cramped script.

Helmut's project has moved out of the station and into the city beyond: not just photographing, but also counting, cataloguing, monitoring. Any street with no people on it is noted in one column; streets with between one and ten people in another; between eleven and twenty in another; and any street with more than twenty people is photographed, and then tallied from the print.

Week by week, the empty street columns get longer, the busy street columns slowly shrinking away. Each time he goes out, Helmut seems to find fewer crowds to photograph, can spend more time, more exposures on each busy street. Composition, detail, content have become important; the photos no longer simply documents. Helmut prefers the pictures, no longer enjoys his notebooks, finds them eerie and strange.

That's Berlin, he says, hand on his notebook. But his eyes rest on the prints. He can see the war in the queues outside shops, and the ever-present uniformed figures. But tonight he can also see the photos through Gladigau's eyes. An ordinary, busy city. Lively and full. He enjoys the pictures as Gladigau does: the faces, arms and legs, the many hats on many heads. He doubts his notebooks, and enjoys that, too. Feeling safe in his city again. His Berlin, his home.

—

By midsummer, Helmut has amassed a significant portfolio. One morning when he gets in to work, he finds Gladigau smiling in the studio, and his Berlin prints lined up on the broad table against the back wall. Gladigau has trimmed the paper scraps neatly, selected his favourites, and laid them out in chronological order. Hand on Helmut's shoulder, he walks his protégé along the table and points out his steadily improving photographic skills. Better and better, every week. They leave the shop closed and talk through the morning. Gladigau is proud, and Helmut is too. Especially when Gladigau selects his favourite photo, and asks him to make a new print for the window display.

—

Inspired, Helmut starts to think about depth in his

framings; foreground and background; throwing the focus; leading the eye. He experiments, using longer exposures to convey a sense of activity, figures blurring in their workaday haste. Over the next few weeks, Helmut also becomes more adventurous with his angles and elevations. Come September, he thinks nothing of climbing buildings, lamp-posts, lying on the ground, and taking pictures through the windows of moving trams.

It is a glorious autumn morning, and Gladigau has a wedding to do. He presses a roll of film into Helmut's hand as he leaves. Go out for an hour or two, he says. Fill it all. A shame to waste a day like today.

The magnetic pull of crowds takes Helmut to the market places, school playgrounds, the busy shopping streets. He takes a photo or two, moves on, the shop forgotten now, the light so beautiful, drawing him further afield. He wanders a series of mostly empty backstreets, and then picks up and follows the sound of voices. Loses himself in the alleys between tenements, finally tracing the source to a piece of waste ground.

There are trucks and uniformed men, shouting and pushing. There are a hundred, perhaps a hundred and fifty people, some milling, some striding, some standing still. Helmut crouches behind a low wall and begins to take pictures. Through the lens he sees possessions scattered; clothes, pots, boxes, sacks, kicked and hurled across the earthy ground. An officer stands by a jeep screaming orders, sharp voice frightening Helmut further behind the wall. He wipes sweat from his palms on to his trousers, fingers weak, he rests the camera on the bricks and looks quickly around.

There are more people watching. Gathered in the entrance of a tenement on the far side of the waste ground. They are much closer to the crowd than Helmut, but he is afraid to cross through the rushing and pushing, to join them. The shouting is louder now, the truck engines firing up. Helmut reaches for his camera, frightened, but also afraid that the scene will pass him by.

The gypsies are divided and loaded into the trucks. They shout back at the men in uniform, gold teeth bared. Children cry on their mother's hips and hide beneath their wide bright skirts. Girls bite the soldiers' hands as they pull the jewels from their ears and hair. Men kick those who kick them and are kicked again. Women push away the hands which push them, and one runs but doesn't get far and is soon unconscious and in the truck with the rest of her family.

Helmut is afraid, exhilarated. His hands sweat and shake. He clicks and winds on and clicks again, photographing as quickly as the camera will allow: not quick enough. He reloads, curses his fingers, feeble and damp, fumbles and struggles with the focus.

In the viewfinder, his eyes meet the eyes of a shouting, pointing gypsy. Others turn to look; frightened, angry faces in headscarves, hats, and in uniform, too. Helmut's heart contracts. He remembers the soldier in the station and hides his face with his hands. He hears a shouted order to stop, stand up, but he can't, he can only turn and run.

The camera drops to his chest, lens jarring against his ribs, strap tugging hard at the back of his neck as he twists away from the angry eyes and voices. The ground his foot finds is broken. Helmut's knee gives way and he stumbles, hurtling forwards, one arm flailing, the other hanging loose, useless and heavy, pulling his right shoulder to the stony ground. He holds the camera up and away from his falling body to protect it.

The landing comes swift as a razor cut, and with the same bright shock, then pain. Helmut is on his feet again and running, not daring to look behind. Back through the mostly empty alleyways, along the back-streets and across the market square. He runs to Gladigau's, too scared of standing still to stop and look for a tram.

The cobbles shift below him, walls, windows spinning away. Terrified, he vomits, jerking to a stop. Retching, coughing, hauling air into his lungs. No one shouts, no one follows him, but Helmut has the pointing fingers, the pushing, screaming pictures behind his eyes, and the panic drives him on again. Back on to home ground, behind the station, through the alley, arm throbbing, camera inside his coat, thudding against the fat of his soft white stomach with every heavy step.

Back in the shop, there is no knock at the door and no questioning voice. Just cameras, frames, the darkroom, the till. Safe and familiar, and all still there. The sweat turns cold and slowly dries on Helmut's back and legs, and the vomit forms flakes on his coat and chin. He sits quiet and still behind the counter until Gladigau returns. In the half-dark his employer nags him for leaving the closed sign up all afternoon.

They work in silence together well into the evening, unloading the cameras, cleaning, processing and printing. Although his arm still aches, Helmut's hands have stopped shaking. He develops the pictures but does not print them while Gladigau is there. They share a glass of schnaps and Helmut stays on after his employer goes home, printing and reprinting long into the night.

—

At first he can only cry. Angry tears: the panic of the day turned to rage. Turned against the photos, against himself, his failure to capture the scene.

Then he reasons with himself. Switches on the light and lays out the photos on the darkroom floor. He crouches and examines the prints again, imagines Gladigau with him, hand on his shoulder, guiding words in his ear.

Helmut remembers the scene, but with Gladigau's eyes, and he sees that the photos are unclear. That these photos could easily be passed over as a few people milling about on waste ground. That they convey none of the chaos and cruelty which had his hands shaking and sweating, and which had spurred him to fill almost two rolls.

Helmut tells himself: he isn't used to taking photos of frantic activity like this. Crowded streets, station openings, all of these things he is good at because he can take his time, find the right spot for the camera and do multiple exposures of similar compositions. He also concludes that black and white stock was really not suitable for the subject-matter. The bright skirts of the gypsy women are just drab rags on his photos and don't swirl and dart like they did that afternoon. The dark SS uniforms blend into the soot-black walls of the buildings, making them almost invisible. Helmut knows he was too far away to capture details. He blows the image up, but the grain evens out the angry lines on the face of the officer who was screaming orders by the jeep, and he barely looks like he is shouting. Helmut remembers the crowd calling and crying to the people inside the trucks, who in turn called and cried to the crowd. On the photo, he sees a still, silent, and oddly calm group, and the arm reaching out of the truck window is just a small blot on the picture, only distinguishable as an arm when he examines the negative under magnification. The woman who was knocked unconscious hardly looks like she is running on Helmut's photo of her attempt to escape, and he didn't manage to include the soldier behind her in the frame in his hurry to get the shot. He thinks he must have been reloading while she was being dragged back to the truck, and the shot of her being bundled inside is so badly out of focus as to be indecipherable.

Helmut searches and searches, but the shot of the gypsy looking into his lens, pointing and shouting, the shot which scared him into running away, is not amongst the photos. Nor is it among the negatives, which are uncut. He doesn't understand it, rages again, throws the long strips of negative to the floor, before picking them up and looking through them for a third, and then a fourth time. Finally, he reasons with himself. Got to the end of the film and didn't know. Panicked. Ran away before the shutter released. Coward.

Helmut stuffs the prints and negatives into a paper bag, not caring about creases and scratches, just wanting to go home. He knows he should keep the pictures for Gladigau, show how he made use of his time, but he is ashamed. He stands for a while with the bag in his hands, and then decides. An error in the processing. He will lie and say that he fogged the roll. Pay for it out of his wages, make up for it with other pictures, another time.

On his way home across the back yard, in the dark, Helmut throws the bag and its hated contents into the bin.

—

The army is victorious. Again and again: beyond Poland now, spreading south and ever further east. Claiming the good, dark soil of the Ukraine, the oil in the Caspian, the vast expanse of the Steppe.

Gladigau buys a radio, and he and Helmut listen to the triumphant broadcasts as they process and print and clean. Helmut smiles with his employer under the red darkroom light, eyes on his work, ears filled with news, shouting voices, the bombast and the drums. But he never turns the radio on alone.

Helmut takes photos. Fills the spring and summer months with experiments, adjustments, improvements. Pleasing his employer, enjoying the praise, seeing with his own eyes how his photos get better and better.

At home he retreats from the table as soon as his plate is clean. Sometimes his parents go out, to neighbours' flats, to meetings, but mostly they sit up in the evenings, Mutti knitting, Papi smoking, reading aloud from the newspaper or the Party magazine. Helmut climbs into bed when the sky darkens, leaving the curtains open, watching the night spread across the city, waiting quietly for sleep to come. From behind his bedroom door, Helmut can't make out words, just the sharp, insistent tone of his father's voice. He marks time with the passing trains, drifting away with their familiar clatter, and is usually asleep before Mutti comes in and pulls the extra blanket over her son. In the morning, Helmut rises early, often before dawn. He eats a hurried breakfast alone by the kitchen window, his back turned to the room. Avoiding his father's eyes, his parent's conversations, the clipped, saluted greetings of the neighbours on the stairs.

With Gladigau, he feels secure. Even when his parents' talk turns to whispers, when the neighbours return his silences with angry stares. Even as the autumn chill deepens and the word Stalingrad is no longer spoken with pride, only hushed, bewildered fear. Even during those long, strange months, Helmut learns to enjoy the afternoons with Gladigau and the radio voices. The certainty of victory, the comfort of routine.

The year turns, and in the dead of winter a surrender changes everything.

—

Spring comes and Helmut is not surprised to see people leaving openly, having sensed an exodus all along. But he is shocked at the numbers; the slow drain now a haemorrhage; crowds at the station, more and more familiar faces leaving every day. Over the dinner table, Mutti passes on goodbyes from friends who have left, and Papi nods firmly, says it is right that they go, the women and their children, says that they must be kept safe, and that the ones who stay must be brave. The neighbourhood gradually empties of children and the back yard is unusually quiet in the summer months. The young families are all gone before the bombs begin falling in earnest, and one dark autumn morning Gladigau reads aloud from the newspaper that over a million people have left.

When people speak of leaving, opinion is divided. Helmut listens to conversations as he photographs, on the station platform, on the ever-emptier market streets. Some are fiercely loyal to Berlin, and Helmut enjoys their rhetoric. Others fear for their lives, their children's future: voices tight and quiet, eyes watching for listeners, whispering predictions of the horrors to come. *Go.* Helmut hears them in snatches. *As far as possible from the capital, from the Ruhr especially, away from any city.* They fall briefly silent as he passes. *All of Germany is a target. For the British, the Americans, too.* Helmut lists the murmured names, already hit or sure to be soon. *Aachen, Krefeld, Duisburg, Oberhausen. Regensburg, Dortmund, Gelsenkirchen, Mülheim. Essen, Wuppertal, Jena, Münster. Köln, Kiel, Rostock, Kassel.* Fingers pressed white against their lips, the people whisper death in Hamburg, firestorms and bombs. Closing their eyes, they breathe their fears. *Everything gone.* Helmut listens. *It will be worse the next time.* He doesn't believe them. *Leipzig or Dresden.* They must be wrong. *The bombers will come for Berlin.*

—

Gladigau returns late from Herr Friedrich, a regular client. He comes into the darkroom where Helmut is mixing the chemicals for the baths and sits down on one of the high stools. Gladigau watches his apprentice work for a while, and Helmut becomes confused and self-conscious under his employer's eyes; spills on the clean worktop and has to measure everything twice. He is grateful when Gladigau finally speaks.

Herr Friedrich's sons fell in Russia at the beginning of the year. Gladigau knew them both, watched them grow up through his lens. Friedrich's daughters-in-law have left Berlin now, with his grandchildren. Out in Mecklenburg at the moment, they may go down to the Schwarzwald soon. In any case, Friedrich wants to join them. Gladigau recounts the story and speaks absently of shutting up shop before the winter sets in. Business is poor. The customers still in Berlin have other things on their minds. Gladigau plans out loud while Helmut wipes the surfaces down, ready to start printing. He can have his job back once things get better, of course, and hasn't his father perhaps spoken of arranging for his wife and son to go somewhere safer for a while?

Helmut stops working, and stares his employer full in the face. Gladigau is shocked into silence by the direct gaze, and still Helmut does not drop his eyes, insulted, ashamed to hear his employer suggesting such cowardice. He is not a child, he is not a woman. He does not want or need protection. Helmut returns the insult by questioning Gladigau's loyalty to the *Führer*, and the two of them stand under the red bulb, in the sulphur smell, and print the day's photos without exchanging another word.

———

Helmut is in bed when the second wave of bombing begins.

His parents go out for the evening. Mutti comes in to kiss him goodbye, but she doesn't tell Helmut where they are going, nor does he ask. He can see his father through the half-open bedroom doorway, standing half inside the flat and half outside in the stairwell, impatient to be off. His mother closes the bedroom door behind her and though it is still early, Helmut turns off the light.

He dozes for a couple of hours, then lies awake and listens for the rattle of a goods train to carry him off to sleep again. Instead, he hears the faint beginnings of a noise he can't identify. Distant, persistent, and now that he has heard it, he can't block it out again. Without knowing what the low drone is, Helmut lies still and listens to the hundreds of Lancasters carrying their lethal tonnage into the sky above Berlin.

Moments after the siren sounds, the tenement comes to life. Mothers bundle children out of bed and old people pull on their thick socks. The stairwell is full of people. Helmut can hear them rush to the cellar: sharp voices, quick feet. He knows he should go with them, but doesn't want to be near their fear and their hurry, so he stays in bed. He has heard people describing the incendiary bombs, Christmas trees falling from the sky, lighting the bombers' path to their target. He watches from his window but there is nothing to see yet, just a black sky above and a dark Berlin below. The block warden pounds at his door, but Helmut doesn't answer because he hears the clattering boots of the *Flackhelfer* on the stairs. The boy is only fourteen, and yet he works with the anti-aircraft gunners on the tenement roofs. Both hammer at the door now, and shout, but Helmut will not suffer the humiliation of a fourteen year old's orders. He pulls the blankets tighter round his legs, and only when he is sure that both the warden and the boy have gone does he put on his shoes and his coat and venture out into the stairwell.

Helmut hears the drone under the siren now. Becoming louder, becoming a roar. He stands with his hand in his pocket, fingers firmly wrapped round the camera, makes his way cautiously down the empty stairs.

The first bombs hit when he gets to the second floor. They are not very close, but the impacts tear into his legs. The building shifts, and Helmut is hurled off balance. Plaster falls on him in chunks and dust, and in his mind's eye a thousand pots and pans tumble down the stairs to cover him as the kitchen cupboards in every flat empty their contents to the floor.

Shock and pain. Everything moves fast now and Helmut can't keep up. He doesn't run to the cellar, instead his legs carry him out on to the street. The first fires are starting in the neighbouring districts and Helmut runs away from the heat and the light. Not fast enough. He knows he is not fast enough, because now the bombers are here. The roar. Directly overhead. Skimming the tops of the tenements, vast and frighteningly close, they follow Helmut's bare and bobbing head as he runs.

He takes a zig-zag course through the pitch-black streets to escape them, can feel himself screaming, but can hear nothing save the roar of fire and bombs and planes.

The impacts resurface from deep underground, kicking into his hips, his spine. It rains tile and brick and glass, and Helmut cannot see where he runs, the flat pounding of anti-aircraft guns in his ears, noise blackening sight. He is blind but not out of breath. His throat is raw and his face is wet, and he runs in the darkness while the street shudders under him, buildings reeling, each footfall as heavy as a bomb.

A body runs in front of him, black shape towards him. Helmut hears the curses, feels the hands on his coat, and the man's breath in his ear. Torn off course, swung off his feet. A bomb. Two arms. The grip. Helmut twists and screams and is pulled underground. From outside dark to dark inside, but just as loud.

He spends the rest of the raid in a cellar full of strangers. They are silent and still while he lies on the floor and cries. The adrenaline makes him shake, involuntary shudders, uncontrollable, and he is afraid and ashamed, feeling the people stare.

After the noise subsides they are all cold. The man who pulled Helmut down with him says this is good. The fires have not reached this part of Berlin at least. After that they are quiet again. Wet eyes, small movements in the black.

Helmut leaves the cellar without saying goodbye. He has come a long way from home in his flight, at least four or five kilometres. He doesn't know where he is, and everything looks different. Bricks where there shouldn't be, gaps where there should be walls. Helmut feels his way down the first street, to the first corner and on, finds his route blocked by chairs, glass and window frames, an empty, unmade bed. Picks his way round the rubble and on to cobblestones again, towards what he hopes is home. It takes him some time to find his way back. The streets are deserted and deathly silent. His eyes get used to the dark, but the quiet is unsettling, and he feels dizzy and sick. Helmut's footsteps echo loud against the tenement walls and he regrets leaving the wordless company of the cellar.

Slowly people emerge, tiny grey shapes against the black walls. More and more, until the streets are swarming. People fleeing from torn buildings, lost and searching through the dark, new mountains of stone. The sky above the roofs is bright with fire, and the streets have become progressively lighter as Helmut nears home. He hears the clattering of the fire-brigade bells, and walks through streets alive with disoriented people, their clothing ripped and sometimes charred, many of them walking barefoot through the rubble. No matter where he turns, Helmut cannot escape the sound of children crying. He is sweating now in his coat and pyjamas; blinking against the hot air and the soot, thinking, Berlin is full again. Full of children.

His tenement building is still standing, but it is on fire. He watches the firemen working for an hour or so, waiting. No Mutti, no Papi. The skin on his cheeks and on his earlobes prickles, itchy and sore in the heat. No familiar faces at all.

He waits, doesn't know how much time passes, but still his parents don't come home. Afraid to ask, he stands stock still, staring up at his former home, only moving when he is pushed aside. He is not allowed into the back yard to see if his bedroom is on fire, so he walks instead down to Gladigau's.

The windows in all of the shops are broken, and there are people running from the grocer's on the corner, arms full, coat pockets bulging. Gladigau's shop is a mess and the lights are not working, so Helmut finds candles and secures the window as best he can with bits of wood and cardboard. He searches through the contents of the drawers scattered on the floor and finds that not much is missing. Gladigau's display camera is gone from the window, but that hasn't worked in years, and the stock of empty picture frames have almost all been taken, too. The looters did not make it through the heavy darkroom door, although they did throw Gladigau's good chair against it. The chair is in bits on the floor, but the door is hardly dented. Helmut has his keys in his coat pocket, and he lets himself into the darkroom and makes a bed out of Gladigau's magazines and white lab coat. He blows the candles out and lies down on the American women of his adolescent fantasies, their white thighs and small breasts crumpled under his dreamless sleep. The darkroom is pitch black and silent, and he sleeps late into the next day.

—

Helmut is surprised when Gladigau does not come and open the shop as usual. His clothing stinks of smoke and the skin on his face is sore. He drinks some water from the darkroom tap and goes out, still in his pyjamas, coat buttoned against the cold. On the street, people pass with bundles and hand-carts piled high with belongings. The station building has been damaged, but the bombers have missed the tracks. People congregate on the railway platforms waiting for a train to take them out of the city. Helmut looks and listens, but the people are all unfamiliar.

The smoking wet shells of the tenements are still warm when he passes them, those walls left standing now steaming, his old home dripping black water and hollow inside. Helmut cries. People everywhere are crying, but still he feels ashamed. Tears streaming from his eyes, stinging hot on his raw skin, he covers his face with his hands, looking out through blackened fingers. Without his Mutti, without his Papi, Helmut stands alone.

He can't let them find him crying, he must be brave. He tries to stop the tears, but they keep coming, running down his cheeks into his mouth, bitter on his tongue. Helmut waits, watches for his parents, walks through the neighbourhood, returning again and again to the shop, the station, the empty place that used to be home. He searches for his mother's face amongst the drifting people, sees his father's and hides his coward's tears. He wipes his eyes on his sleeve, stands tall, looks back again, but the face is gone. Replaced by another, and another. Grey beards, tired eyes, drawn cheeks. None of them Papi's.

—

In the late afternoon Helmut arrives in Gladigau's neighbourhood. The tenements here are unscathed. The solid, clean lines of blond stonework are imposing, far larger than the houses of his own district. Helmut is shocked by the grand, smooth windowpanes, and the white of the curtains. Where he lives everything is broken and torn, layered in smoke, soot and dust. The stairwell in Gladigau's building is dry and cold, the dark wood of the banister shining, soft day falling in from the skylight above. Helmut knocks at Gladigau's door, breathing hard from the climb. He stays on into the evening in case Gladigau returns, but no one either enters or leaves the building and there are no cooking smells or radios or footsteps crossing hallways or children crying.

Helmut leaves at midnight, afraid of the quiet, afraid of another air raid, spends another night alone on the darkroom floor. Disoriented in the pitch black, unsure if his eyes are open or closed. Helmut lies on the boundary between asleep and awake, walks through shattered walls and finds his parents holding hands. Reaching out, stepping forward, the walls falling, he loses them again.

Helmut dreams of lenses shattering at the shutter's release. Exposures of fragmented glass, shards of picture, prints seen from the corner of an eye. Papi's fingers, Mutti's eyes, her arms; Helmut reaches and the negatives crumble in his hands, black glitter dust on his palms.

Exhausted, he crawls until he finds the darkroom door. It is morning again, and comforted by the light, Helmut sleeps under the counter in the abandoned shop.

———

Days pass, wordless, cold. A soup kitchen is set up at the wrecked tram junction, winter clothes handed out, new boots and coats. Helmut washes the soot and sweat from his pyjamas in the darkroom sink, cleans the shop and secures it against looters, locking everything of value in the darkroom. Ledgers, till, order books, the remaining frames. Helmut closes the business, hanging a handwritten apology to the customers at the door. Charcoal on cardboard, softening, smearing in the autumn rain.

He takes no photos that winter. Camera, films, chemicals, paper, all safe behind the darkroom door. Helmut knows they are there, a small, comforting presence amongst the loss. He mourns. Alone, the coldest weeks go by. Sirens, bombs, fire and hunger. Helmut sees corpses pulled from the rubble and runs away. At night his dreams bring confusion, and he wakes expecting Mutti, routine, Gladigau, warmth, his father's pipe smoke. He starts each winter day crying, covering his face with his hands.

Wet breath, wet cheeks, wet palms, the tears flood on.

In daylight it makes more sense. He sees the change in the city. The blocked streets, the missing buildings. Craters and mountains where once it was flat. Helmut can feel the difference between then and now: the pattern of the city shattered every night and the changes becoming part of each new day. He watches the people; chalking street and shop signs on the remaining walls; walking on and over and under and through. Slow progress across the rubble: ankles twisting, feet slipping, legs disappearing up to their knees. Still they go on.

New paths are beaten, old routines are dropped. After the bakery is bombed, the bread arrives in trucks.

—

Preferring to stay in familiar streets, Helmut finds a cellar to sleep in. It feels safe to him: tucked away in a tiny back yard, the tenements around it all empty, in ruins. He finds a stove in the rubble and installs it on bricks by the cellar steps. Takes the heavy top bolt from the darkroom door, and makes his new home secure.

In the nights when bombs fall, Helmut lies awake in his cellar and listens. If the impacts are close, he shouts into the noise, just like the night he ran from the bombers. Feeling his throat burn with his screams, hearing nothing but the blasts, the air thick with planes and flak. Warm with fear and then cooled by sweat, he makes a fire in the stove at dawn and sleeps in the quiet early light. If the bombs are far away, Helmut finds the distant thump and whine almost comforting, like the goods trains which had accompanied his adolescent sleep.

This far noise is preferable to silence. In the nights where the city lies quiet, Helmut is invaded by the dreams of his darkroom night, sharpened by hunger and cold. The broken windows are thick with frost, and Helmut peers through the glittering pane at his father, hand on Mutti's shoulder, sitting in front of him. The ice melts, the image clears in the warmth of Helmut's breath on the pane, then clouds again. Fogged, smudged by his reaching fingers. Gone.

Without work and without photography, Helmut's days are empty and long, and the hours are drawn out through lack of food. He tries to sleep, but dreams drive him out of his cellar and on to the street, and his cold legs carry him to the station. There is a new guard, and Helmut takes his time, making friends, talking about the trains, just like he did with the old guard when he was a boy. The new man doesn't like Helmut. His persistence, his crooked arm, his dirty coat. But after Helmut points out the tenement shell that used to be his home, the guard takes pity on him, listens to him more closely, lets him into the station to watch the trains. On cold days he sometimes takes a mug of thin soup out to the strange young man by the tracks. He asks after his family, and nods appreciatively at Helmut's descriptions of a hard-working Papi, a devoted Mutti, a dutiful only son. Helmut watches the trains come and go as he speaks, lets his voice drift on and on, drinks his soup, doesn't look the guard in the face. And because the guard suspects that Helmut's parents are not evacuated but dead, he also gives him regular work sweeping the platforms. Helmut doesn't get paid, but is fed a meal in the station canteen, and is also given a coat to wear with the railway insignia on the breast pocket.

The war-torn begin to arrive back from the eastern front, scarred and tattered, with missing limbs. Sometimes they beg on the platform, sitting on raggedy blankets, quietly displaying their injuries, and Helmut always reports them to the guard. It is illegal and shameful: Helmut rages that they should disgrace their uniforms in such a way. The heavy padding of his station coat disguises his lopsided shoulders well, and he tucks his right hand into the deep front pocket, becoming adept at sweeping with his left. He concentrates on his work, making short, thorough jabs with the broom, and the guard praises his spotless platforms. Helmut is proud, conscientious, returns his uniform reluctantly each evening when the guard locks the station gates.

—

In February the British stop bombing Berlin, and the Americans take over. After some raids, the trains stop running for a day or two until the tracks have been repaired. Even on these days, Helmut goes to the station and sits on the platform in his coat. The cold and hunger and the nights spent screaming often leave him drained and disoriented. In the quiet under the shattered glass of the station roof, he slips in and out of sleep, dreaming trains full of silent people, all leaving Berlin in droves, always eastwards. These dreams are not as violent as the ones Helmut suffers at night, but they unsettle him, so he takes to pacing the empty platforms to avoid sleep as long as his hungry legs allow.

—

The summer of 1944 brings a brief respite from the bombing while the Allies concentrate on recapturing France. In the calm, Helmut helps out more at the station, cleaning the offices as well as the platforms. The guard gives him oats or potatoes to take home, and Helmut borrows a pot and bowl from the station canteen, teaches himself to cook. The nights are shorter and milder and the nightmares less acute, stopping altogether for weeks at a time. Now he is not so tired, he can do more, and he starts taking photos again.

The days are warm, and the summer mornings and evenings provide dramatic light to inspire Helmut and his photographer's eye. The low sun is gold on the stone walls and rubble, and casts long, crazy shadows through the ruins, across the pock-marked pavements and squares. He rises early, leaving his cellar before dawn, following the same ritual each morning. He unlocks the darkroom, selects a camera, allocates a ration of film, and then sets out to capture the strong, wide skies and the ruined Berlin. The lonely clock-tower of the Kaiser Wilhelm Church, and the rubble of the Tiergarten nearby. The grand hotels on Unter den Linden reduced to skeleton structures. Their chandeliers glittering in the debris, tapestries hanging loose and torn. Helmut contemplates taking them away to adorn his cellar home, but they are sodden, heavy and stinking from the spring rains.

He trades Gladigau's paper and printing chemicals for food and more film, storing his negatives on the stone shelves of his cellar, neatly marked and arranged in rows. He curtains off a small area behind the sacks and rags of his bed, and spends his evenings processing his films. Helmut numbers and catalogues the negatives in the same leather-bound book he had used to monitor Berlin. Script laid out in columns, as neat and small as possible, saving space, saving paper, keeping his system simple and clear. Everything ready for the victory, for peacetime and printing.

His life is solitary, and his photos devoid of people, but Helmut is not unhappy. Berlin, now empty, ceases to worry him. He walks everywhere, covering vast tracts of the city with his carefully rationed exposures, getting out as far as Potsdam and Brandenburg during the long midsummer days. He sleeps in bombed-out buildings if he's gone too far to walk home before sunset; works out his routes around the soup kitchens; avoids hunger as much as possible. He doesn't appear at the station for days, but the guard learns not to worry about him. Helmut doesn't tell him about the photos, and after a while the guard learns that Helmut will not appear with a bright dawn, but on dull days he will be back. And he always makes up the work.

—

Helmut falls in love with his underground home, enjoying his expeditions into the city beyond, but always glad to return. He devotes one exposure from each roll to his cellar, and builds up a portfolio of glowing stove, cracked and shimmering windowpane, cosy rag-and-blanket bed. In one photo, there is a washing line full of Helmut's clothes, dripping puddles on the broken flagstones of the ruined back yard. Helmut examines his negatives, holding them up against the sun, recognises the pyjamas he was wearing the night the bombers came and his parents went away. He trains his eye. Can tell a good photo from a negative now, judges shape, composition, shade. He learns to invert; white for black, dark grey for pale. Mutti and Papi slip out of focus as Helmut lets the memories slide, the edges soften away. He thinks of Gladigau. Lists his best pictures, looks forward to showing him the prints.

—

When the days grow shorter and the bombing resumes,

Helmut returns to the patterns of the previous winter. Sleepless nights and days dozing on the platform. The darkroom locked and remaining films lying undisturbed, waiting for spring. He hibernates with them until the final, dying days of winter arrive.

The order comes for the last stand of the German people and Helmut is finally given his chance. He runs and tells the guard, who grips his good shoulder, whispers it will soon be over. Helmut agrees, surprised. All he can remember now is war.

He doesn't get a uniform, but a tatty greatcoat, an armband and a shovel are his to use and keep. The few guns are given to the youngest boys, who are sent up what remains of the highest buildings. Juvenile snipers practising on broken bottles, cats and rats in the ruins.

Helmut fetches his camera out of the darkroom and is never without it, photographing as much as he can. He wants to remember it all, this best time of his life. Zhukhov is on his way, with the vast Soviet army and the Mongol hordes from the Steppe behind him. They will surround Berlin, isolating the city, as they have isolated and annihilated German outposts from Stalingrad ever westwards, but Helmut is confident of victory, can see nothing beyond the glorious triumph, which he will take part in, and commit to film.

Occasionally a train comes through the station, invariably crowded and covered with refugees. On the roof, spilling from the doors and windows, and with more people running alongside it on the platform, leaping on, grabbing hold of windowsills, guard-rails, anything, the other passengers too weak, too listless to raise a hand. The trains never stop, grinding slowly, slowly forward, sometimes so slowly they seem to be still, but Helmut focuses in on the wheels and sees that they are always turning.

Helmut's duties are vague, sporadic. His fellow defenders of Berlin meet daily and carry out their uncertain tasks. Making the roads impassable, piling rubble, digging holes. They are trained to fight with whatever they have. The old men in their good hats, holding their improvised weapons in determined hands. They hoard ammunition and pass it on to the snipers, most of it unsuitable for the boys' guns.

When he has no orders, Helmut goes to the station and watches the refugee trains passing through. Half-dreaming in his pile of sacks, the years folding in on themselves, he sometimes wonders if he should try his luck for the price of a bag of liquorice. If the trains come through in the morning when the light in the station is good, Helmut takes photos. If it is evening and too dark, or the afternoon shadows too long, he walks alongside the train, displaying his armband as once he had displayed his arm. He speaks the *Führer*'s rhetoric through the train doors and windows; fate and bravery and the glory of the *Götterdämmerung*, striding alongside the refugees. Some people spit, some curse or cry, others agree, still others join in. Mostly they ignore him, staring beyond the glass of the carriage windows, beyond Helmut, with their dull, bruised eyes.

The refugee masses flood back through Berlin on foot, too. Feet caked with mud, cheeks hollow with walking. Helmut takes their photos and welcomes them home, but like the trains they don't stop. Resting in the hollows of bombed-out buildings for one night, maybe a day or perhaps even two, but rarely longer. Lifeless, but driven forward by the threat from the east. They describe an army the size of a continent, angry and brutal and without mercy. These people speak of punishment, and bring with them a faint sense of deserving. As they pass they tell tales of emaciation and ashes, of stinking smoke and pits full of bodies. Some say they have seen these things, others dispute it. Their voices half-hearted, matter-of-fact. Vague, hungry and weak.

Berlin, April 1945

Helmut assembles his brigade on the rubble they have been piling up all afternoon. Their heroic barricade, backbone of the Reich. The sun is lower now, and the light just right. He takes one photo of them, and then one of the others takes a turn behind the camera, so Helmut is part of the group in the next exposure. With the fat boys and the boys with bad teeth, the old men and amputees. Helmut has a shovel in his left hand, and his right arm hangs loose and twisted, crowding his chest, which has narrowed again with the hunger of late wartime. All of the group look tired, most of them look serious. But the three or four who are looking at Helmut – their photographer having his picture taken – they are all smiling.

Helmut stands between them, relaxed, shoulders crooked, his face upturned and proud. The city behind him is destroyed and soon to be divided. In a matter of days, a suicide will speed the Soviet invasion; the small mound of broken building beneath his feet will mark the line between what is British, what is French; and Helmut will not recognise his childhood home in the Berlin which is to come. But in this photo, Helmut is doing something which he never did in any of the many pictures lovingly printed by Gladigau over the course of his childhood. Helmut is standing high on his rubble mountain, over which Soviet tanks will roll with ease, and he is smiling.

LORE

Bavaria, early 1945

Lore lies on the edge of sleep in the dark bedroom. She heard a noise a while ago, fell asleep, then woke again. Lying still, with the night wrapped quiet around her, frost-flowers blooming across the windowpane. Lore's limbs are warm and heavy. She's not sure now if she only imagined it, watching the walls and window and ceiling unfolding, and beyond them, the room of dreams.

A door slams, and the walls are back again, solid along the edge of her bed. Keeping her eyes closed, Lore listens. Hears her little sister breathing. Whispers.

– Liesel? Anneliese?

No reply: just the long sighs of sleep. Lore drifts. One minute, two minutes, ten. She doesn't know how long before she hears the noise again.

Doors and voices. Lore is sure now, eyes open, waiting for the crack of light from the hall. The house stays dark; the whispers come from downstairs; she slips out of bed to listen.

– What is happening?
– It will be fine. Over soon. You will see.

Vati is here. In uniform at the foot of the stairs. Mutti has her arms around him, a soldier stands to attention in the open doorway, and behind him Lore sees a truck parked in the road. The cold night slips over the threshold and through the banisters, settling around Lore's bare feet. Her father fills the hallway. Her mother's hands grip at his sleeves and he calls her Asta, *meine Astalie*, strokes her hair and she cries without tears. Mouth opening, lips twisting against the small, strained noise.

– Vati!
– Lore. My Hannelore. She's grown again.

Lore's forehead pressed against his shoulder, Vati laughs and Mutti runs a nervous hand across her face.

They work quickly: Vati emptying drawers, Mutti filling bags, the soldier loading the truck. Lore stands at the front door with Liesel. Sleepy and bulky: dress buttoned over her nightshirt, and a coat on top of that. It is dark, difficult to see, but her parents don't turn on the lights. The baby wakes. Vati picks him up and sings to him, Mutti watches for a moment, and then goes upstairs to wake the twins.

Lore's sister holds her hand, stares at her father, her baby brother.

– We called him Peter, like you Vati.
– I know, Lieschen.

Her father smiles. Lore watches him, too. Still Vati but somehow different. From the photos. From the last time. *Not this Christmas, the one before.* He meets Lore's eyes.

– Come on. I'll get some blankets. We'll make it cosy for you in the truck.

They drive for what feels like hours. Out of the village and into the valley. Mutti wordless with Vati in the front, Peter asleep in her lap. No lights. They drive in the darkness and the engine noise.

Lore sits in the back with her sister and brothers, on top of all their bags. Liesel sleeps, mouth open, the twins stare at the back of their father's head. They are silent, sitting shoulder to shoulder, leg to leg. Heads swaying with the motion of the road, eyes glassy with sleep and surprise. Lore whispers.

– It's Vati.

And they nod.

They stop in a yard that glitters with frost. There are people with lanterns, and two beds in a strange room that smells of mud and straw. When Mutti blows out the lanterns it is no longer dark. There is a long window on the far wall, and Lore can see her father; his shoulders; a hunched, black outline against the grey dawn. She is cold in the bed with Liesel. He finds her an extra blanket, tucks it around her, and when he kisses her goodnight she smells his sweat, feels the stubble on his chin.

– Where are we?
– A farm. A safe place.

He whispers, Lore drifts.

– A good place to sit out these last weeks.

When she wakes again it is light in the strange room and he is gone.

—

It is a nothing time between war and peace. Like treading water. Or holding your breath until a bird flies away. Weeks pass, spring arrives, windy and blue, and Lore's days are long and shapeless.

The farm sits on the banks of a slow stream, tucked into the foot of a hill. Deep in the green of the valley. Lore knows there are armies on the march. Russians from one side, Americans from the other. In Hamburg they had the apartment, with the long garden and a maid. Even in the village, after evacuation, they had a whole house. Now they are here, and they are six in one room. Pushing the beds against the wall in the mornings, pulling them out again at night.

Lore watches the cloud shadows drift across the mountainside, remembers her father's midnight visit in snatches, like a dream. *Over soon. You will see.* Months fall by and nothing changes. She does her chores, adjusts herself to the waiting, the war will be won soon. *Only a matter of time.*

The weather is glorious. Liesel and the twins spend their days outside; in the yard at first, but that soon gets boring and they venture out into the fields beyond. Mutti worries when she can't see them: paces the room and then shouts when they finally come home.

Most days, the farmer's wife brings food. Bread, dumplings, sauerkraut, eggs and milk. Sometimes there is bacon, or small, shrivelled apples from last autumn. She stands broad in the doorway and saves her smiles for the baby and the twins.

In the afternoons, Peter sleeps, Mutti and Liesel darn the holes in their stockings, and the twins play under the table. Unable to contain themselves, they fill the room with their whispering games.

On clear days Lore can make out a small town in the far crease of the hills: the pencil-lines of smoke from the chimneys, the darker smudge of a spire. Lore listens for gunfire from the other end of the valley. Sometimes she opens the window a little, in case the battle noise is too faint to make it through the glass. Eyes searching the cloudless sky for the *Luftwaffe*, she imagines bombs in the valley, fire and death. Hears only birdsong.

At night, after Mutti blows out the lamps, Lore pulls an edge of curtain back from the window. In the morning, she opens her eyes to the chink of blue sky above her head. The last and first thought each day is of Vati, strong and clean-shaven, and of the end of the war. In the quiet dark of the curtained dawn, Lore imagines the valley transformed by victory. From high on the mountain she sees the parade through the villages, the fields thick with flowers, the slopes awash with people, sunshine in her eyes, hands holding her hands, voices raised in song.

—

Dusk, and Lore helps Mutti put the children to bed. Through the window she sees the farmer coming, and behind him, his son. Mutti pulls on her coat and Lore goes to the door but Mutti shakes her head.

– Stay in here. I'll be back in a minute.

She goes out and Lore pulls the door to behind her, leaving a gap just big enough to watch the three figures standing in the yard. The farmer has brought bacon, a small sack of oats, but he also wants to talk. Lore can't hear what he says, but she can see his mouth set in the same blunt line as his wife's. He points down the valley, and Mutti's fingers fly to her face. The farmer's son shifts his hard, flat gaze away from Mutti and spits on the ground. When he looks up, Lore feels his eyes on her and she ducks away from the door.

– Where's Mutti gone?

Liesel is up and standing at the door. She leans her bed-warm body into Lore's, shifting her to one side. Reaches for the handle, but Lore catches her arm.

– She said we should stay inside.
– Why?

Liesel twists against Lore's grip, so she digs her nails into her sister's skin.

– Ow!
– If you stay still I won't have to hurt you, stupid.

Liesel starts to cry. The twins sit up in bed and watch their sisters tussle at the door.

– Now you'll get it, Lore.
– No I won't. Be quiet, Liesel, I didn't pinch you that hard.
– Mutti will shout.
– Shut up, Jochen. Go back to sleep.
– We're not tired any more.

Lore tries to comfort Liesel, but she won't look at her, keeps crying and pulling her arm away. Lore knows the twins are right: that Mutti will shout, and that it will be an unbearable night in the tiny room after that.

– Lieschen, please. Anneliese. If you stop crying. I've got something for you.

Lore climbs up on to the chair, takes the sugar pot off the top shelf in the corner, where Mutti keeps it out of sight. Liesel stops crying immediately, licks her finger and dips it inside. She sucks, dips, sucks, and lets Lore dry her cheeks, wipe away the evidence of their fight. The twins have been quiet, watching, but now Jochen gets up and slips across the room to where his sisters stand. Jürgen follows, trailing the blankets behind him off the bed. They both lick their fingers, hold them out ready to dip.

– No. Not you two as well.

– Why not, Lore?

– Just go back to bed, Jochen. You too, Jüri. Please.

– We'll tell Mutti you pinched Liesel.

– We'll tell her you gave her the sugar.

Lore sighs and holds out the pot to them, but Liesel pushes it away from the twins' reaching hands.

– No, Lore. It's just for me.

Jochen shoves her angrily and Jürgen drops his blankets, steps forward to stand next to his brother.

– Shut up, Liesel.

– No, you're not allowed, Jüri.

– You can't tell us what to do.

– I'm older than you.

– Lore said we could and *she's* older than *you*.

Mutti stands behind them in the open door.

Lore's stomach turns to water.

Mutti lays down the food from the farmer, picks up a cup from the table and hurls it to the floor.

They are all quiet now, apart from Peter, who cries. Mutti picks him up and carries him to the chair by the far wall. She sits down with her back to them all.

– Go to bed. You too, Lore. Sleep.

Mutti leaves the lamp on, stays in the chair long after Peter has stopped crying. Lore lies next to Liesel and pretends to sleep. Watching through her eyelashes; her mother's mouth smiling, murmuring to the baby; her mother's eyes darting nervously around the room.

Lore remembers how Mutti cried, dry-eyed, standing with Vati in the hall. Thinks. *It is coming.* The end of the waiting.

———

Morning and the sun falls over the windowsill into the room. Mutti sits in shadow at the table sorting through their things, deciding what to keep and what to burn.

– Why? Is Vati coming? Are we moving again?

Lore doesn't get an answer. She washes the breakfast dishes, standing the bucket in the shaft of sun by the window, turning her back to her mother. She can see the twins playing by the pump in the yard, but she can't hear them through the glass. Liesel is sitting outside by the window, knitting socks and rocking Peter in his pram. The glass is old and thicker at the bottom than the top. Her sister's hands ripple as they work the wool. Behind her, Mutti's fingers fly through pockets and schoolbags. Books and badges and uniforms piled on the table. Green wood cracks in the stove. Outside it is windy and the children play without coats. Inside it is hot.

Lore stocks the stove from the piles on the table and watches Mutti sorting through the photo album. She pulls out the pictures too precious to lose, slipping them gently out of their white corner fastenings, lining them up on the quilt next to her. These are then tied in a clean rag and laid in a drawer, while the album is added to the pile on the table. Lore works through the morning, watching their clothes and papers burn, balancing logs around the chimney to dry for later.

The photo album burns badly at first, too thick and full for the flames to catch hold. The blue linen cover browns and curls and Lore's eyes dry in the heat from the open stove door. Liesel will cry when she finds her uniform gone, the twins will ask for their books. Mutti stares at the now-empty table top, mouth slack, cigarette burning between her fingers. Lore closes the stove door and opens the vents; the pages catch and the job is done.

—

Later, Mutti fishes the badges out of the ashes with the sugar spoon and wraps them in a handkerchief. She keeps the children inside, and sends Lore out instead. Tells her to take Peter with her and walk at least a kilometre, follow the stream, find a wide point where the current is strong.

– Stay by the water. Away from the road, and be quick. I'll watch for you.

Lore walks along the water with Peter on her hip, tells him:

– We are sitting them out here. These last days.

The enemy will be here soon, but she will not be afraid. She will be patient and brave, certain of the *Endsieg*. *Vati said*. *It will be over soon*. Everything will be new again, and she will be ready. The armies will spill over the mountains; the valley will be filled with noise and death; and soon after that will come victory.

She sits Peter down on the bank and throws her handful of metal into the water. The badges sink to the bottom, too near the water's edge for the current to take them. Peter points to the nearest one with his fat, wet fingers. The enamel colours are dulled and the badge has twisted in the heat of the stove, but Lore can still make out the Party sign. She takes her shoes and stockings off and wades out into the cold water to retrieve them.

They walk on a little further, alone in the wet fields, Peter sitting heavy on Lore's hip, humming in time with her steps. She empties the handkerchief into the bramble bushes at the boundary with the neighbouring farm. One or two of the blackened badges spring back against the branches and Lore kicks them into the undergrowth, throwing loose earth and grass after them. She washes her hands in the stream and dips Peter's toes in the shallows to make him laugh. The sun warms their hair and the hills cradle their voices.

Lore thinks about Mutti waiting, watching for them. She cuts across the wide, quiet fields back to the farmhouse, with Peter asleep on her arm. Whispers to him.

– Before the victory there will be pain.

She steels herself for the blood and flames.

—

Lore is scrubbing potatoes at the window when the Americans arrive.

The twins have strayed from the yard again, Liesel has followed them, and Mutti has gone out to shout for them at the gate. Lore knows her mother has seen the jeep, but she knocks on the window anyway, leaving a muddy potato streak on the glass. Mutti doesn't turn round. She was calling for the children, but now she is quiet, watching the jeep make its slow journey along the pasture to the yard.

When the Americans stop to open the top gate, Mutti turns and walks inside. She tells Lore:

– Keep working.

Wipes her hands and runs them through her hair, gets her lipstick from her pocket, and puts on her hat and coat.

Lore watches her mother, but if Mutti is frightened, she doesn't show it. She goes outside and Lore carries on working. Fishing muddy potatoes out of brown water, dropping clean potatoes into clear water. Her hands are pink and the blood sings in her ears. She concentrates on the wet earth smell and her cold fingers. Pulse hammering at her throat.

Her mother meets the soldiers as they pull up in the yard. They leave the jeep running while they talk. Mutti stands straight with her hands by her sides. One soldier has a clipboard with papers, and he flips through these while Mutti speaks. Another leans against the jeep while he asks her questions. The soldier with the clipboard writes something down and then hands a piece of paper to Mutti, which she pulls close to her face to read. Lore stops scrubbing. The group outside is silent, but the jeep is still running. Mutti turns the paper over to read the other side and the American with the clipboard kicks at the ground with his toe. Mutti is speaking now. She passes her hand across her forehead and gestures to the house. The American leaning against the jeep stands up straight and looks over to Lore at the window. The American holding the clipboard holds up four fingers, and Mutti shakes her head and holds up five. This is noted on the clipboard, too. The papers are signed by both Americans and by Mutti, then a copy is torn off and folded and sealed in an envelope which Mutti holds in front of her with both hands as the Americans drive out of the yard without closing the gate behind them.

The children come back late, but Mutti doesn't tell them off. They pull the table out from the wall and eat together as usual. Boisterous with guilt and relief, Liesel giggles and the twins kick at each other under the table. Mutti says nothing about the Americans and Lore knows it is their secret.

She lies in the little bed with Liesel, eyes closed, listening as Mutti slides into the big bed with Peter and the twins and puts out the lamp. Americans are better than Russians. Russians steal and burn and hurt women, shame them. The Americans come with clipboards and don't even look in the house.

Lore opens her eyes, thinks; the fighting could come now, in the night, like the bombs always did.

She remembers the badges in the bushes. She should have thrown them in the deep water; buried them under the stones on the river-bed.

Lore lies still and listens, but there are no guns, just her mother's breathing. Only when she hears it deepen and lengthen does Lore allow herself to fall asleep, too.

—

Mutti says she is sick and sleeps with her face to the wall. The children sit quietly, hungrily, while Lore searches her mother's pockets for coins. She tells the twins to stay inside, takes Liesel and Peter across the yard and up the short track to buy food from the farmer.

His wife takes the money Lore offers and tells them to wait by the door. Liesel sneaks a look inside the house while she is gone, whispers to her sister about the huge stove and the tin bath hung on the wall. Lore watches the farmer's wife making her way back from the barn. Remembers the order of their house in the village; and

further back, the family home in Hamburg before the
bombs. Wallpapered bedrooms and hot water from taps.
Liesel says it's cosy in the farmer's kitchen, with onions
and smoked bacon and five new loaves sitting ready by the
oven door.

– Is your mother still here?
– Yes, of course.
– Well can you tell her my husband wants to speak to her,
please?
– Of course.

– What did she mean, Lore?

Liesel struggles with Peter on her hip, so Lore swaps him
for the egg basket.

– She didn't mean anything. Don't drop them, Lieschen.

– She thought Mutti was gone.

– No she didn't. Be careful with the eggs, hold them
higher or you'll bump the basket on the ground.

Mutti stands at the door in her dressing-gown. Her eyes
are small and her hair flat and dull. She snatches the basket
of eggs from Lore and the children slip out into the yard.

– The boys were hungry.
– They had bread this morning.
– But there's nothing else left.

Mutti gets back into bed and smokes the last of the

cigarettes she has been rationing since they moved. Her remaining photos of Vati are lined up on the quilt in front of her. Peter dozes and Lore sits at the table and cries.

– How much longer do we have to stay here?

She remembers the women in the village: how the queues outside the shops look like funeral groups, and the dye dripped in black puddles from their skirts in the winter rain. The air in the room is hot and dry. Dense with her mother's cigarettes and sickness. In Hamburg, Vati sat out on the step with Lore and wriggled his toes in his thick woollen socks. He wore braces under his uniform. The twins crawled behind him in the garden, laughing, watching their reflections in his high black boots. *Soon the war will be over.* Lore closes her eyes and wills the army to come, the fighting to begin. She holds the valley in her mind's eye. Sees the grasses on the verge along the *landstrasse*, seed-heads unsteady in the breeze. A bird sings close by. She can hear it high and clear through the window-glass.

Mutti's skin is hot to the touch, the hair at her temples damp. She lifts the quilt and pulls Lore into the warm bed. The photos slide to the floor.

Lore feels safer in the bed, wrapped tight and secure. Mutti's tears tickle her scalp, wet cheek pressed against her ear. She moves her lips, whispers, but Lore doesn't understand. She pulls the quilt up higher, over her mother's encircling arms. She is almost as thin again as she was in her engagement pictures, lying scattered on the floor by the bed. Lore looks at them while her mother sleeps. Mutti, Vati and Oma in Hamburg. By the railing on the Jungfernstieg with the lake behind them. *Before I was born*. Their faces are familiar but unfamiliar, too. All three smiling, holding on to their hats, the wind pulling their coats stiffly to the right.

—

Mutti sets off for the town at dawn, promising fresh bread for breakfast, but she doesn't come back until after midday. Lore takes Liesel and Peter down the track from the top gate to meet her. Her bag is empty, and her coat is open, flapping in the wind. Peter shouts for his mother, twisting in Lore's arms, but Mutti doesn't take him. They stand squinting in the sunlight. Mutti's hair blows across her face and Lore can't see her eyes. She tells her daughters. The war is over. Our *Führer* is dead.

Liesel cries, and Mutti strokes her cheek.

– Just think of how he fought for us, Lieschen. He was brave.

Liesel nods and rubs at her tears with both hands. Lore hides her burning cheeks. There will be no battle in the valley now. No suffering or sacrifice. She is shocked and ashamed at her sense of relief. Breathes deep to fight her cowardice, to remember this forever. This field, the way they stand facing each other, how Peter holds his hands out and Mutti lifts him up and holds him against the sky and he smiles.

—

Mutti goes to the town again in the morning, comes back again without food. She gets into bed and stays there. The children are hungry and restless. Lore sends them out, but they play half-heartedly, and soon come back inside. Mid-afternoon, Lore goes through her mother's pockets once more, and takes Peter and Jürgen with her to buy food, from the neighbouring farm this time. They get bread and sauerkraut, and an egg for each of them, which Lore carries in her pockets. She lifts Peter on to her shoulders, which is a bit high for him, and he holds on to her ears to stop himself from swaying. Jürgen walks ahead and they sing in the twilight as they make their way back along the stream. Lore watches her brother marching ahead of her. The back of his head is like a soft version of Vati's in miniature, with the same swirl of hair at the crown. He turns round and walks backwards for a while, skipping to keep up the pace.

– When will the Americans go away?
– I don't know, Jüri. Soon.

She starts a new song and Jüri turns round, faces forward, his legs stamping the tune into the long river grass. Lore watches their reflection in the dark water. She looks like a giant with a lumpy head. Peter has gone to sleep on her shoulders and has slumped forwards so his cheek rests against her ear.

The farmer's son stands at the bottom gate; waiting for them. Lore can't make out his features in the half-light. She sends Jüri ahead with Peter, tells him to wait at the top gate for her. The farmer's son kicks at the fence with the toe of his boot until the boys are out of earshot. Then he leans in close to Lore.

– The Americans are going to put your mother in prison.
– No they're not. They've already been. They didn't even come in the house.
– She's been all round the town, asking people to take you in, but no one wants you.
– Liar. You're just a farm boy. You don't know anything.
– Nobody wants you here any more. We'll have our place back, you'll see. As soon as your Nazi whore mother is locked up.

Lore pushes him, but he doesn't move. He pushes her back, much harder, and she falls on to her side. Two of the eggs crack under her hips. They are both still for a few moments and then the farmer's son steps forward with his hand out to help her up. There is a hard smack and he swears and pulls abruptly away. Something falls into the grass next to Lore. Another something flies past her head and thumps against the boy's leg and he swears again. She looks into the pasture and sees Jochen in the half-light, taking aim with a third stone, Jüri standing next to him.

– Leave our sister alone!

The farmer's son wipes at his bloodied ear with his sleeve. Lore gets up and runs through the gate to the twins. Jochen throws his stone and then they all run up the pasture to Peter who is sitting by the top gate, grizzling and sucking on a bread crust which Jüri has torn off the loaf for him. Lore picks him up and tucks a loaf under her free arm. Jüri has the rest of the bread and Jochen carries the cabbage.

– Why did he push you, Lore?
– How should I know, Jüri, he's just a stupid boy.

They stumble over the rough ground in the dark. The broken eggs have soaked through Lore's dress and are cold against her leg.

– I broke some eggs when I fell over. We'll just tell Mutti I tripped in the dark, yes?
– Why can't we tell her about the farmer's son?
– Because I say so, Jochen.

They are almost at the house now and hiss their argument under their breath. Jüri pulls his brother away and they run ahead of Lore across the yard. She sits Peter down by the water pump and cleans off the worst of the egg mess before she goes inside.

—

– I have to go, Lore.

Mutti has sent the children outside, and now she is

buttoning her coat. She gets the small bag out from under the bed, already packed.

– You must take the children to Hamburg. Here is Oma's address. Rosenstrasse. You will remember it when you see it, I'm sure.

She has drawn a map.

– Line 28 up Mittelweg to the bridge. You know the stop? Left as you get out and then first on the right. The big white house with the tiles in the stairwell? It was only two years ago. You can ask the tram driver if you're not sure.

She marks a cross on the paper where Oma lives.

– Here is some money, and also some jewellery. Use it to get a train. As soon as you can. Yes?

She is taking off her wedding ring.

– Use the money first. You can't write to me, not now. But I will write to you in Hamburg. As soon as I can.

Lore nods, though they make no sense to her, the words her mother says.

– We should all be brave now.

They stand with the scrap of paper on the wide table between them.

– Are you going to prison?

– You mustn't worry.
– I won't.
– It's a camp.
– Yes.
– Not a prison. Prisons are for criminals.
– Yes.
– Everything is changing now.

Mutti kisses Peter who is lying asleep on the big bed; she kisses Lore and her skin smells of soap; she opens the door and the sun smell of outside comes in as she goes out.

Lore is alone for an hour or so while Peter sleeps. She counts the money and looks at the bits of paper on the table in front of her. She thinks; everything is changing, and works out how many eggs the money will buy, how many loaves of bread. She tries to calculate how long it will take to get to Hamburg. Twenty minutes to get to school from the village and that was about four kilometres. And forty minutes to the market in the next town. *Nine kilometres.* But Lore knows the big trains are faster. She thinks back to the journey south from Hamburg. She was younger then, can't remember. *A day, two days. Probably three.* Peter wakes up and she gives him a bread crust and a drink of water. It is time to make dinner for the children: it will be getting dark soon, and they will be home and hungry. When Peter cries, she dips his fingers in the sugar pot and puts them in his mouth.

—

Lore pulls the beds together so they can all be close in the dark. The twins don't remember their grandmother. Lore lights candles, shows them some of the photos which Mutti didn't burn: Oma holding a coffee cup on the veranda; and long ago, a young woman with Opa who died in another war. Lore describes the house; all the separate rooms leading off the long, cool hallways with their wide dark-wood floors. She whispers to them late into the night.

They don't ask about the camp, don't seem worried at all, and only Peter cries. Lore cradles him in the dark, thinks that perhaps it does make sense. *The war is lost. The Americans have camps, not prisons. For people like Mutti who haven't committed crimes.*

She thinks of her father, wonders what he is doing now the fighting is over. Peter dozes against her chest and Lore looks through the photos again, wants to see a picture of Vati before she sleeps. But the pictures she finds are more confusing than comforting. All taken long ago, long before the war. They don't look like her father; more like an older brother; an anonymous young man in civilian clothes. Lore is tired, her eyelids heavy, hungry again.

The children sleep and Lore dreams that the Americans come and search through the bushes by the stream, the ashes in the stove. They take Peter away from her, throw him into the back of the jeep and drive off over the fields.

—

The farmer comes early, and with his wife this time. The children stand behind Lore at the door. The wife speaks first.

– Do you have somewhere to go?
– They can't stay here.
– We are going to Hamburg.
– To Hamburg?
– To our Oma. Mutti told her we are coming.
– They can't stay here.
– She knows you're coming?
– Mutti wrote to her.
– But there's no post, child.
– She is expecting us.
– How will you get there?
– By train.
– They want to go to Hamburg, let them go.
– But there are no trains, Sepp. No post and no trains, child.
– Do you want them to stay here?
– I've started packing already.

Lore leaves the children to look after Peter. She walks to the road, picks up a lift from a farmer into the town. He takes her to the railway station, but tells her: there are no trains.

– How do we get to Hamburg?

The man in the office says she will have to get permission from the Americans; that the last official transport went over two weeks ago. Lore pushes through the turnstile on to the platform. The station is deserted. She crouches down next to the tracks and looks along the line, past the long curve of the station, northwards, away from the town. Lore doesn't know what lies beyond. Another valley, perhaps a city. The weeds have already grown tall between the sleepers.

Through the station window, she can see a tank parked further along the street. There are soldiers who carry their guns slung over their backs, stand and smoke and talk in the sun. Lore's scalp prickles. She doesn't want to ask permission. Mutti said they should go to Hamburg. She didn't say anything about asking Americans.

On the wall is a map of Germany, and Lore traces a line north with her finger from *Ingolstadt*, to *Nürnberg*, and all the way up to *Kassel*, *Göttingen*, then *Hannover* and after that *Hamburg*. She memorises the place names, and some towns in between. Lore steps back from the map, looks up at the ceiling and recites them silently to herself. *Ingolstadt, Nürnberg, past Frankfurt to Kassel, Göttingen*, then *Hannover*. And then *Hamburg*.

She walks on into the town for food, but the shops are closed: already sold out for the day. She finds her way back to the *landstrasse* and starts the long walk back to the farm.

—

Lore goes back to the town in the morning. She leaves early so she can get to the bakery while they still have bread; queues in silence with the women and buys all she can. She goes on to the neighbouring farms; leaving the village by the path behind the mill to avoid the soldiers; hiding her bags of food in the hedgerows before knocking on the doors. There is no meat and no fat, but she manages two more half-loaves of bread, four eggs and a jar of milk, a small sack of meal, and also a bag each of carrots and apples.

Back at the farm, she packs a bag for each child, and puts Peter's things in the pram. A blanket each, plus socks and stockings, shoes, underwear, a change of clothing and three handkerchiefs. They will wear their boots and summer coats and they have the oilskins in case it rains. She divides the twins' chessmen between their two bags, chooses a doll for Liesel and a book for herself. She also packs the bundle of photos from the drawer in her own bag. The money and map and the jewellery which Mutti gave her are wrapped up in more handkerchiefs and sewn into the underside of her apron.

The children come back hungry around midday, and Lore makes them try their bags for weight. They are excited, skipping in the yard with knapsacks and suitcases, dancing on the beds, impatient to leave. Lore knows the bags are heavy. She takes the shoes out and ties them to the sides of Peter's pram. While they eat, Lore realises that they should take knives and plates and cups with them. She slips crockery and cutlery into a clean pillowcase and knots it to the pram handle.

– What will we say if the Americans ask us?
– We are going to Hamburg.
– And who is in Hamburg?
– Mutti and Oma!

The children sit on the big bed and Lore tests them. They chorus their answers happily, munching the apples meant for the journey.

– And will we say anything about camps?
– No.
– Why not?
– Because the Americans will put us in prison.
– Good.

Liesel frowns, twists her plaits together under her chin.

– Won't we be with Mutti then, Lore?
– Mutti is in a camp, silly.

Jochen pokes her and Jüri laughs.

– They have special prisons for children, horrible places.
– I don't want to go to prison, Lore.
– If you're good, you won't have to.

———

They are all too hot in their coats and their bags are too heavy. Their shoes dangle crazily from Peter's pram and the crockery rattles in the pillowcase over every stone. Lore feels sick, hot, unprepared; her hair sticks to her face. She leads the children across the fields on to the track over the hill and out of the valley. It is already getting late, and she knows they won't get far before dark, but she wants to put some distance between themselves and the farm. Get away from the Americans, the stream and the badges in the bushes.

Peter doesn't like the noise and the bumping. He glares angrily at Lore, gripping the sides of his pram with chubby fingers. His face crumples. Lore calls the children to a stop. Peter cries and she takes off their coats, repacks their bags. *Start again.*

Lore and Liesel take turns carrying Peter now, and he chatters with his sisters as they walk. The boys push the pram, piled high with the bags. Lore starts a song and Liesel joins in. The twins march ahead, their voices drifting back through the hot air. They pass another farm, then a series of outbuildings, and a little later a barn, where they rest in the shade for a while. When they walk on, Lore promises the children they will pick up a lift when they get to the road.

Lore watches the twins, giggling and panting their way up the rise in the road. They stop at the top to rest. Lore knows that the slope down is far steeper and longer than the slope up. When she and Liesel are halfway up the rise, the twins start on their descent. They give the pram a shove and break into a run. The pram bounces over stones and the crockery clatters. Lore shouts at the twins to slow down but they don't listen. She hands Peter to Liesel and trots up to the top of the hill. Lore hears the plates smash against each other. She shouts again. Jüri turns round and waves, carries on running with his brother. One of the dangling shoes gets caught in the wheel and the pram veers to the left. Jüri loses his footing. His legs give way and he makes a grab for Jochen to steady himself. Jochen still has hold of the pram. He falls under his brother's weight, the pram tips over and spills its contents over the track and down the slope into the field.

Liesel has got to the top of the hill now, and she laughs at her brothers sprawled in the road. Peter giggles and grabs at her cheeks. Lore runs down the slope to the twins. The pram lies on its side, wheels spinning. Jüri has twisted his ankle and is crying. Jochen is gathering up their things. The bag of meal has burst, its contents strewn in the stones and dust.

Lore rights the pram and pulls her shoe out of the spokes. The leather is torn and the wheel is buckled. She throws her shoe at the twins. It falls short. She picks it up and hits the boys on the arms. The sun is hot and she is sweating. Jüri is crying again now, and Lore slaps Jochen's legs until he screams. She shouts at them to stop crying, and Jüri lies down in the dust and sobs for Mutti. Lore takes off her coat and fights down her tears.

Liesel sings to Peter, her cheeks red and her eyes dark and wet. Lore wipes her own face on her apron and searches through Jüri's bag. She tears one of his vests into strips and gently works his laces open and pulls off his boot. His ankle is swollen, but not too badly. Lore binds it tight and he limps up and down in front of her to try it out. He says he thinks he can walk on, but Lore says it doesn't matter. They will go back to the barn, stay for the night. Jüri sits down next to her. She pulls him close and he hides his face in his hands.

—

Lore carries Jüri along the *landstrasse* on her back. They eat the rest of the apples in the early morning cool, Jüri munching loud in Lore's ears. Her cheeks are raw from the cold night. They all slept badly under their coats and oilskins, too aware of the night-time noises around them. Lore knows they won't get far if they walk today. There is a cart up ahead and she tells the children to wait while she runs and asks for a ride.

The old man refuses payment and motions angrily to his wife.

– She wants to give us her money!

His young wife sits high up on the trunks and crates and laughs at Lore.

– You're from the north, aren't you?

Lore smiles politely. The woman smiles, too, but her eyes are sharp, critical.

– I heard it in your voice. Where are your parents? Your Vati in the army?

Lore nods, avoiding the woman's searching eyes as she waits for the children to catch up. Jochen salutes the old man when he gets to the cart and his wife laughs again. Louder and harsher this time. Lore winces, and the young woman turns to her husband.

– They're Nazi children from the north.

Her husband shrugs. Jochen frowns, confused by the mocking laughter, turns to Lore, but she ignores him. She knows the young woman is watching her as she piles their bags on to the cart.

– Where is your mother then?

Lore tells her Hamburg, but is sure the woman doesn't believe her, busies herself with Peter who is crying in the pram.

– Yes, well, you won't all fit. You'll have to take it in turns like we do.

Lore feels awkward, flustered by the young woman's attentions, heat rising in her cheeks. She makes room for Jüri by shifting a large bundle of clothes and helps him into the cart, careful not to hurt his ankle.

The old man walks with the ox, facing the road ahead, and his young wife sits high on their belongings with her back to them. Liesel rides in the cart with Jüri and Peter. Lore walks with Jochen, pushing the pram in front of her. It rolls unevenly on its buckled wheel, lurching in time with the ox's hooves. Jochen starts flagging after an hour or two, but Lore doesn't want to ask about swapping places with the children in the cart, would rather avoid conversation.

The valley broadens and flattens and farmhouses dot the fields. Lore fills their remaining cup from a well by the roadside. The children share the drink, and Jochen runs back to fill the cup again for later. He walks quickly to catch up, pressing his palm over the top of the cup, handing it up to his brother for safekeeping.

After midday the old man pulls the ox over to the side of the road to graze. The woman unwraps bread and boiled eggs from her pockets. She watches while Lore gives the children their food.

– Did you steal that?

Lore shakes her head, ears burning. She softens bread in the last of the water for Peter. The children rub the earth off the carrots with handfuls of grass, eat a whole loaf between them. Their food is already half gone.

In the late afternoon they pass more small groups of people on the road. Lore sits in the cart, watching as they go by. Some have wooden hand-carts piled high with belongings, most have big bundles tied to their backs. Others join the road from the fields. The people don't greet each other; eyes on the ground ahead as they walk, parting silently to let the ox-cart through. Jochen sleeps against Lore's legs, Peter against her chest. Liesel gives Jüri a piggyback to rest his ankle. Houses grow more frequent along the sides of the road.

The woman pulls the cart up at a stream outside the town to let the ox drink. Lore and Jochen swap places with Liesel and Jüri and they walk on, Jochen's face still blank with sleep. The woman stops the cart at a crossroads.

– Off. They have a soup kitchen here, and places to sleep. We're going further on tonight so you'll need to walk into town.

She watches while Lore pulls the suitcases off the cart, handing them down to the twins.

– Do you have blankets?

Lore nods. The woman opens their suitcases and spreads two blankets on the ground. Next she empties the contents of the suitcases into the blankets and tells Liesel to crouch down. She shows Lore how to tie the blanket around Liesel's shoulders to form a bundle.

– Much easier to carry. And you can use your oilskins if it rains.

The woman smiles while she speaks, but Lore feels she is being mocked. The old man throws the twins' empty cases on to the cart and his young wife climbs up after them with Liesel's bag. The children watch them go while Lore ties the second bundle to her back.

– I think it's better if we don't talk to anybody about Mutti and Vati.
– Not anybody?
– Even people who aren't Americans?
– Yes.
– Why?
– It's just safer that way, Jochen.

There are other people with bundles and hand-carts walking into the town. They cast long shadows on the road behind them in the evening sun. Lore is glad to be away from the young woman and her critical eyes. She searches for a better reason to lie about Mutti and Vati, but the children don't ask her for one. Jüri limps, Peter yawns in Liesel's arms and Jochen skips ahead. Lore relaxes, trusts in their silence.

———

Lore has lost her bearings. She doesn't want to ask directions, worries about inviting questions, but also worries that they are going the wrong way. They run out of food after three days. On the fourth they walk on without breakfast. By early afternoon their silent hunger forces Lore to find doors to knock on.

She asks the woman about the road north while she buys milk and bread. The woman sees the large coins and gives a fist-sized piece of bacon instead of change. Lore doesn't argue.

– How far north do you want to go?
– Not far.
– Well? Nuremberg? Frankfurt? Berlin?
– Near Nuremberg. Not very far.
– Well that's quite far. Do you have a cart?
– No.
– You are walking?
– (nods)
– Well, you are walking in the wrong direction. You are heading for Stuttgart on this road. Over to the French, if you go too far.
– (nods)
– Across that field, the second one, walk along the brook, you'll see the railway tracks. They cross a road going north after a good while. You'll get back on course for Nuremberg there, and be sure to give the milk to the baby.

Lore divides the food and it is gone within minutes. They struggle across the fields with the pram. By evening they have reached the railway tracks and are hungry. There are no houses in sight.

———

Lore doesn't sleep. Lies next to the children, huddled

under their oilskins. The night is dark and endless, cold, and the ground is hard under her hips, against her shoulder-blades. Peter cries. The other children shift, sit up. Jochen stands, wrapped in coats and blankets, teeth clattering. He is crying, too.

They don't wait for morning; walk on before it gets light.

—

They make their way into the town together, but the children are tired and slow, so Lore leaves them by the empty railway station, promises to be back soon with food. Her shoulders ache from pushing the pram and her stomach hurts. Peter has been crying for hours, and she is relieved to get away from the noise. The morning is hot, and by the time she gets to the town centre, her throat is dry.

She drinks from the fountain on the main square, stands under the shade of a tree and looks for a place to buy food. None of the shops are open, but a group has gathered by another tree about twenty metres away. Lore watches them across the glare of the flagstones. They stand quietly for a while and then drift away as other people arrive and take their place. A hush hangs over the group, heavy as the hot air, pulling Lore across the bright square. Two elderly ladies in mourning stand on the left, nearest the tree, and Lore slips into the space between them.

Large, blurry photos have been stuck on to a long plank

and nailed to the trunk. The group stands a pace back in silence, an orderly distance. In front of Lore is a picture of a rubbish heap, or it might be ashes. She leans in closer, thinks it could be shoes. Below each of the photos is a place name. One of them sounds German, but the other two don't. All unfamiliar. The glue under the photos is still wet, the paper is wrinkled, and the images confusing. Lore squints, frustrated, hot in the silent crush. She steps forward out of the group, smoothes out the damp creases with her palms. A whisper sets off behind her and makes its way round the group.

The pictures are of skeletons. Lore can see that now, pulling her hands back, tugging her sleeves down over her glue–damp palms. Hundreds of skeletons; hips and arms and skulls in tangles. Some lying in an open railway carriage, others in a shallow hollow in the ground. Lore holds her breath, looks away, sees the next picture; hair and skin and breasts. She takes a step back, trapped by the wall of the crowd.

People. Lying naked in rows. Skin thin as paper over bone. Dead people in piles with no clothes on.

An old man next to Lore clears his throat. The group shifts, and Lore is pulled back and moved along as the people gather round. Enclosed by hot backs and sleeves and shoulders, the smell of cigarettes on wool.

The two old ladies are back alongside Lore. A gentle pressure under her arms, pushing her further along the line of photos to the edge of the crowd. The last picture is clearer: a man lying against a wire fence. He is wearing pyjamas with the jacket open, and Lore can see his ribs. The trousers are knotted in folds around his narrow waist, and his ankles are huge fists of bone at the ends of his fleshless legs. The man's eyes are black shadows. His mouth is open and his cheeks are hollow because he has no teeth.

The old women are still moving, gently pushing Lore away from the photos, away from the tree. One on either side, they take hold of her arms and propel her forward, off the main square, back to the road. Behind them, the group settles back into silence, closing over the gap they have left. Lore looks round. No one is watching them. The people have turned their wordless attention back to the photos on the board.

The old woman on Lore's right has her handkerchief pressed over her mouth, and she doesn't speak. The other is urging Lore along the road. She is thin, too. Her bony hand lets go of Lore's elbow and pats her softly on the arm.

– Go home, child. Quickly now. There is nothing here for you to see.

Lore walks, doesn't look round. She feels hot, faint, hasn't eaten since yesterday and it is already afternoon. She sits down at the side of the road, thinks she must have some bread, find the children, walk on again. *Something to eat.*

She rests her forehead on her knees, squeezes her eyes closed. Behind her eyelids, she sees the photos on the tree. Perhaps the people had no food, and they starved to death. She can't remember the place names under the pictures, doesn't even know the name of the town she is in now. Lore goes over their route north again, eyes closed, face tilted up to the sky. The sun burns at her cheeks and she tries to remember if the man in the last photo had his eyes open or closed. She wonders if he was dead, and if it is possible to die with your eyes open. She recites to herself, from *Ingolstadt*, to *Nürnberg*, then past *Frankfurt* to *Kassel*, *Göttingen*, and then *Hannover* and up to *Hamburg*. His photo was taken somewhere in Germany.

– Drink this.

There is a young woman standing over her with a small cup of milk.

– When was the last time you ate? Drink it, child.

Lore reaches for the cup and drinks. The woman presses a heel of bread into her hand, takes the empty cup and goes back into her house. Lore eats, swallowing the crust in painful chunks, sitting with her eyes closed until the ache in her stomach subsides. She thinks about the children, doesn't know how long she has been away, knocks at the woman's door.

– I need more food. For my brothers and sisters. One is a baby.

– I have no more.

– Please, we are hungry and we have nowhere to stay.

The woman looks afraid. Lore thinks she might close the door.

– We can pay.

Lore offers a coin, and the woman hesitates, flushing hot red when she finally speaks.

– Do you have anything else? Not money.

Lore tears a hole in the handkerchief pouch in her apron, holds out her handful of Mutti's things. The woman stares, and then picks her way through the jewellery with bitten fingers. Pokes at Mutti's brooch, her pearl earrings, finally selects her ring.

– I can buy you some food with this.

Lore winces.

– Not the earrings?

The woman shakes her head. She squints at Lore.

– If you share the food with me I will let you stay.

—

The woman is waiting for them when Lore arrives back with the children. She stands at the door and smiles at them all, her own young son hiding behind her skirts.

She gives them a bowl of steaming water from the stove and clean rags to wash with, apologising that she hasn't any soap. Lore scrubs the twins' necks and combs out Liesel's hair. The woman cuddles Peter and baths him with her son. When it gets dark, she asks if she can take the pram, says she will be back in about an hour.

– There's a curfew here, you know that? You should all stay inside.

The twins are still angry that Lore left them alone for so long. They stare at her with hard eyes, and Liesel stands close, whispers, tugging at the ends of her plaits.

– Why can't we go and stay with Mutti in the camp?

The woman's little boy watches them, quiet and shy. Lore is furious with Liesel, thinks he might have heard. She pulls her sister away to the window, hisses into her face.

– You don't talk about that. You know that. Do it again and you'll get it from me, understand?

Liesel's face crumples and Peter screams when Lore lifts him.

The woman comes back with food hidden in the pram. It doesn't seem a lot to Lore, fitting easily under the mattress. Her stomach contracts.

– My mother's ring was gold.

The woman shrugs. A little later she says she is sorry. The

woman cooks and eats with them, and her son is quiet, watching Liesel and the twins as he chews. When he has finished, the woman pours him the remaining soup from her own bowl, and when he has eaten that, she pulls him into her lap. She hums quietly to herself, watching him settle his head against her arm.

Lore is tired. She closes her eyes and eats more slowly, holding the food on her tongue before she swallows. She wants to ask about the photos on the tree. If the woman knows where to get food, she might know what happened to those people, too. But when Lore speaks, the woman smiles, puts her finger to her lips, points down at her sleeping son.

Lore clears the table, and the woman lays blankets on the kitchen floor, picks up her son and leaves the room. When she doesn't come back, Lore presumes she has gone to bed, and tells the children to lie down, too.

Lore gathers the food together in a too-small pile on the kitchen table. She leaves half a loaf aside for the morning, and chooses the bag of flour to leave behind. Lore thinks a moment, and then decides to leave a bit of the meat, too. The woman was gentle, asked no questions, gave her the milk she must have been saving for her son. Lore divides the remaining food between their bundles, sits down at the table while the children sleep, works out a ration. If she is strict, the food could last three days.

She blows out the candle and rests her forehead on the

table top. She dreams about the Americans again. The soldiers eat all the bread, throw the rest of the food into the jeep. They leave Peter with her this time, but nothing to feed him with. He is light and thin in her arms. She lays him down gently on the ground, next to the other children. They are all naked. Their bones brittle as bird wings.

———

The children are subdued, tired. Lore has to decide which direction to walk in every morning, which fork to take in the road, where they should stop at night, when they should eat. They stand silently waiting while Lore makes decisions. Move when she tells them, stop when she says so. Only Peter cries and laughs at will.

They sleep in barns, haylofts, outhouses. Sometimes with permission, mostly without. Lore tries to keep the children clean, rubbing earth off their boots with handfuls of grass, scrubbing their clothes in cold streams without soap. She pops their blisters, pads their boots with leaves, walks off the pain with marching songs. Lore repacks the bags every time they stop. Redistributing weight, clothes, belongings. She checks her apron pocket as she walks, feeling for the smooth fold of notes, the hard coins, her mother's brooch, and no ring.

———

Evening, and the twins have been asking all day about the

war. Is it really over? Did we really lose? Why? Lore tries to explain, but her half-answers only lead to more questions, and Lore is exhausted now, and shouts at them to shut up. Liesel cries, Jochen frowns and Jüri yawns, both very tired.

– Is there anything to eat, Lore? We're hungry.
– There's bread, but that's for the morning.
– Please?
– No.

Liesel asks where Vati is now, and Lore tells her he is on his way to Hamburg and will be with Oma by the time they arrive. The lie slips out before she has time to think, and she is shocked at herself. The boys crawl under the blankets to sleep, but Liesel is excited now. Her tears have gone, replaced by smiles, and more things to ask about Vati.

– Lie down, Liesel.
– Lore!
– I'm tired, Liesel. I mean it.

Lore ignores her sister's tears. Liesel sleeps with her head under the blanket; the boys are curled together in their coats; Peter is quiet in his pram.

Lore is woken by dreams of Mutti. The wedding ring is at the bottom of the stream and her mother won't look at her. Crying, buttoning her coat, closing the door over as she leaves. Lore buries herself deep into the stiff oilskin folds, but her eyes won't close, and sleep won't come, and her stomach turns to ice. She can't keep pace with the questions, can't keep track of her lies.

—

Liesel throws up three or four times in the afternoon. They stop for a rest each time, find water for her to drink. Making slow progress, passing above a village, leaving it gradually behind, the church spire still visible over Lore's shoulder. Liesel shivers and complains of the cold despite the afternoon sun. There is a forest up ahead. Lore decides to stop.

The twins find a spot not too far into the trees. They lay out the oilskins, try to light a fire, Lore wraps Liesel in blankets and she sleeps. The twins go to gather more kindling, but they still can't get the wood to burn. Lore divides up the last of the apples from the morning and they rub the potatoes and eat them raw. Liesel wakes up as it gets dark and cries because she doesn't want to spend the night in the forest. Peter cries, too, and refuses the chunks of potato which Lore has bitten off for him. Jochen watches her in the half-dark.

– We could go back to that village.
– And stay in a hotel?
– We could ask. We could knock on doors and ask for a room.
– You have money in your apron, Lore.
– We need to keep that for food.

– But you said Mutti left us money to go on the train. We must have saved money by walking all this way.
– It's an hour down the road, more. It's going backwards. It's silly.
– Please, Lore.

They whisper in the bluish evening light. Peter cries. The trees are thick and silent around them. Lore folds up the oilskins with the twins, and they load up the pram again.

In the village the streets are empty. They are turned away at every house; too many faces, too many mouths. An old man gives them sour milk and swaps their potatoes for eggs. Liesel throws up again in the main square by the church. Jüri fills the cups from the well, and Jochen finds the church door ajar.

Inside it is vast and dim, and smells of damp and dust. The twins scout for places to sleep while Lore unpacks the pram.

– It's all hard benches.
– And they're too narrow.

Lore wheels the pram along the rows of pews until she comes to an alcove. Two or three candles burn low on a shelf covered with dark stubs of wax. Above them stands a robed statue. The twins help Lore spread the oilskins on the floor and gather cushions from the pews for their heads. Liesel sits with Peter at the foot of the statue and yawns. They don't speak, but every movement sets off hissing echoes under the high stone roof. Lore pours half the milk into a cup for Peter and gives Liesel the bottle. She and the twins eat an egg each, raw. The boys giggle, egg white glinting wet on their chins.

Peter won't sleep in the pram, so Lore lays him down on one of the cushions. Liesel sleeps and the twins whisper with each other while Lore sorts through their bundles again. Folding the clothes, tying them away neatly, lining them up next to her, ready for the morning. She blows out the candles and sleeps.

Liesel throws up once more in the night, and helps Lore mop up the mess with her blouse. She says she feels a lot better and Lore strokes her little sister's hair, tells her she is brave. Liesel didn't once ask for Mutti, and Lore is glad, knows that must have been hard. They sleep on into the morning. When they wake up, Peter's pram is gone with their spare shoes still tied to the sides.

—

They walk on a few more days, sometimes with people, but Lore still prefers it alone. They don't ask for lifts and rest frequently, avoiding towns. Lore buys butter to smear on their cracked lips. They dig turnips out of the fields and buy bread in the houses and villages along the way. Lore's bag of coins grows light.

They can carry less now, without the pram. Lore trades Liesel's doll for an empty bottle with a lid. No one wants the twins' chessmen, or her book, so she throws them away. They wear both sets of clothes although it is still very hot. Lore's coat buys them a night in a bed, and Liesel's second skirt a wash in warm water in the morning. She puts what remains of their things in one bag and one bundle, which they share between them.

They reach Nuremberg within a week.

—

The schoolhouse is already filling up when they arrive. The old man at the door gives Lore two straw mattresses, and they make themselves a bed near the middle of the room. Lore would rather be by the wall, or even better in a corner, but all the spaces at the edges of the room have already been filled. Mothers with children, elderly ladies. No men are allowed in, although some come to the door and ask. It is dark outside now and two lamps burn by the long window. Lore spreads their blankets over the thin mattresses, and the children lay their coats on top. She cuts them a slice of bread each, and the twins fill the cup with water from the barrel outside the door. Lore tells them to chew slowly and take small sips. They are all very quiet.

More people come in as they eat, and gradually the floor fills up. There are no more mattresses left, so people make the best of it with their coats and bags on the floor. Lore puts Peter in the middle of their nest with the twins on either side, and she and Liesel take the two outer edges. Lore takes off the twins' boots, but leaves their socks on.

They shift and fidget under the blankets and coats while Lore packs their shoes away. She lies down with them, though she is not sleepy, with the bag by her head where she can keep an eye on it.

Even after the lamps are put out, more people arrive, black shapes shuffling in the dark. Lore keeps her eyes closed most of the time and hopes the children are asleep. The straw smells of cats, but she doesn't feel the floor through it, and she is warm.

She is woken by Peter grizzling. Jüri passes him over to her and shifts closer to Jochen, into the warm centre of the bed. Peter is hungry, so is Lore. She feels the people around them shifting, irritated at the noise. She searches through Liesel's pockets for the last of a loaf, and tears a piece off for Peter to chew. He stops whimpering almost immediately, and Lore sits up with him while he eats his extra meal. The entire floor of the school hall is covered with sleeping shapes. Lore is thirsty, but she can't see a path through the bodies in the dark, so she decides to wait until morning.

Peter has finished his bread and is whimpering again. He tugs at his raw cheeks and lips with balled fists. Lore lays him down on the mattress and rubs his feet and his tummy to distract him. The woman lying next to them has her eyes open. Lore can see them, wet and blinking in the dark bundle of coats. She lies down and pulls Peter close under the blankets. He is sleeping again. The woman is still watching Lore. She whispers in the dark.

– My house is gone. Stones on the ground. I sleep every night next to strangers.

Lore nods and closes her eyes.

– He betrayed us. Like a coward. He sent our men to die and then abandoned us.

The people around them hiss in shocked whispers. Lore keeps her eyes shut tight, doesn't respond. She hopes the woman won't think she is rude: that she goes to sleep soon and stops looking at her. They lie still for a while. Lore can hear the woman breathing in sighs. It is warm under the coats and blankets and Lore pulls them up to cover her ears. She is tired, doesn't want to think now. The woman wakes her again a bit later, muttering, but Lore is too drowsy to make out what she says. Another voice, from somewhere near Lore's feet, threatens the woman into silence.

—

They queue in shifts. Standing in the slow-moving, murmuring line. Sitting on the wall across the road from the shop, watching the bags. Swapping when the church bell sounds the quarter hour. When the twins aren't queuing, they throw stones from the road into the river below, dare each other to run along the top of the wall. The woman behind Lore gives Peter a couple of raisins from her ration and he holds out his hand for more. Lore pulls Peter's hand away and thanks her, embarrassed, but the woman smiles.

At midday they are inside the shop.

– Nuremberg coupons?

Lore takes a coin from her apron pocket.

– No money. Only coupons here.
– But we've been queuing all morning.

Liesel can't help herself, Lore jabs her in the back. The woman with the raisins steps forward.

– Give the children something to eat. There's five of them. A baby, too.
– They don't have coupons, Frau Holz.
– Look how thin they are.

The twins push their way into the shop and up to the counter next to Lore. An old man at the door grumbles loudly to himself.

– Why don't you share your rations with them?
– You know I have children of my own.

The shopkeeper raises his voice.

– I am not running a black market here. Nuremberg coupons only.
– Why don't you let them wait? Maybe you can give them what's left at the end?
– And what do you think the Americans would say to

that, Frau Holz?
– I suggest you don't tell them, Herr Roeding.

Frau Holz gives them a slice of her bread before she leaves. The grumbling old man gives Liesel an egg. Lore isn't sure if the shopkeeper will give them anything or not. They stand in silence by the counter and the people avoid eye-contact as they collect their rations. Lore shares out the bread: one bite each. The street outside slides into shadow as the sun moves overhead. Peter cries and Liesel walks him up and down on the pavement until he falls asleep. The twins whisper with each other for a while and then lapse into restless silence: standing at the window, sitting on the bundles.

The queue dwindles, ends. Lore fixes her eyes on the shopkeeper as he wipes down the counter, sweeps the floor. She wonders if she should call Liesel in with Peter. There's still at least one loaf, some butter, too. Also some sugar. She steps up to the counter.

– I'll pack you what's left, but not a word to anyone. Understand?

Lore nods. She sends the twins outside to sit on the wall with Liesel, unties the bundle, ready for the food. Behind the counter, with his back to the door, the shopkeeper wraps two loaves, butter, an egg. The door opens. The shopkeeper turns round, shields the parcel from view.

– Can I help you?

The young man doesn't speak until he is at the counter. He touches his fingertips against the wooden surface.

– If you have any rations left, I would be very grateful.
– Coupons?
– I'm not from Nuremberg. I only thought, if you have any left.

The shopkeeper turns back to his work, gestures to Lore.

– This young lady is my last customer today.

The young man looks at Lore. He smells sour. His wrists hang long and thin from his black sleeves.

– My brothers and my sister.

Lore points out of the window. The children are lined up against the wall, watching, waiting for the food. The man nods, smiles, and leaves the shop.

—

Lore asks for some water, and the old woman offers them a room for the night. There is a cot and a quilt which Lore gives to Liesel and Peter. She and the twins build a nest on the floor with the bags and blankets. Lore pools their food with the old woman and helps her cook a thin stew. They eat in her tiny kitchen, crowded around the crooked table, standing because there are no chairs. It is cold and damp in the house. They go to sleep with their clothes on.

The old woman wakes Lore in the night. She carries a

candle, her sleeve pulled down over her hand to protect it from the wax.

– I'll need something for this. You can pay me now, please.

Lore stares at the pale eyes, the yellow hooded lids.

– You have something to pay me with? The Russians killed my sons. I have nothing.

The old woman pulls at Lore's collar, wax splatters on the floorboards. Her mouth is flat; lips pulled taut over her teeth. Angry tears well up against her sparse lashes. Lore fumbles under the blankets for her apron pocket and hands her two coins. The old woman sniffs at the money.

– Nothing else? A spoon perhaps? Silver?

She waits, Lore looks past her into the black room. Apron corner tucked into her fist, Mutti's jewellery sewn inside. She will give no more. The old woman blows out the candle and leaves.

Peter screams in the morning, pulls at his clothes. He doesn't want to be lifted or touched. Liesel sits next to him on the cot and scratches at her sides, her legs. Her ankles are raw under her socks. She lifts her blouse to show Lore the red, itchy skin over her ribs. It is still cold in the house. Lore takes Peter out into the sun, pulls off his clothes. He screams, choking. The old woman is in the garden.

– Lice. You'll have to burn his clothes. Wash him with

paraffin, too. That will kill them. I think. You need to kill them.

She points at Peter's neck, pulls at her chin, can't keep her fingers still.

– I have some paraffin. Wash the baby in it, and the girl. I'll burn their clothes.

She brings out the paraffin and a tub, goes through their hair with her bony fingers. Lore flinches as she scratches at Peter's scalp with her broken nails.

– You and the boys are clean. But you should soak your clothes. And all of you should wash, all of you.
– Yes. Thank-you.
– I will need something for the paraffin.

She holds the bottles against herself. Lore wants to cry. Peter screams and twists in Liesel's arms.

– I am sorry but I can't give it to you. Do you have something?

Lore turns her back and lifts her apron. She tears the hole in the handkerchief pouch a little wider, pulls out Mutti's silver chain.

– But it's worth more than the paraffin.

The woman says she has nothing more to give, they can stay an extra night instead.

They undress at the side of the house, hidden from the

road by the trees. The old woman pokes at Liesel and Peter's clothes with a stick, takes them inside and stuffs them in the stove. Lore soaks the rest of their things in the tub of paraffin, biting her lips to stop the tears. Liesel holds Peter, crouching on the ground. The boys are quiet. Lore rubs paraffin into the children's limbs and chests and hair. Peter screams again, his body red. The oil smarts in the torn skin around Lore's fingernails, the cracks around her nose and mouth.

The twins rinse the clothes, but there is no soap, so the paraffin won't wash out. The woman boils water for them, carries it out of the kitchen in buckets. She brings scissors, too. Drops them in the grass next to Lore and looks away while she speaks.

– You should cut the girl's hair, and the baby's. Take it all off.
– But you said it would kill them. The paraffin.

The old woman shrugs, Mutti's chain around her neck. Lore looks away too now, and the old woman goes back into the house. Liesel picks up the scissors and cuts off her plaits. She sits down in front of Lore and promises not to cry. The twins stand by the wall and watch while Lore works her way closer and closer into Liesel's scalp with the blunt scissors.

Peter's curls are long and soft. The blades look huge against his face and he won't keep his head still. Lore wishes she could save his hair. Send it to Mutti, but she doesn't know where her mother is. She cries and sweeps Peter's hair into a pile with Liesel's, takes it inside to the stove and fills the old woman's house with its bitter smell. Outside, she rubs the last of the paraffin into the stubble on her sister's head.

The twins lay their shorts and shirts and vests out in the sun to dry. Lore pulls on wet clothes and walks into the village to get food and something for Liesel and Peter to wear. If no one wants Mutti's money now, Lore doesn't know how she can make Mutti's jewellery last. She is furious, frightened.

A cart comes towards her on the road, the farmer raises his hat. Behind him sit people with bundles. The young man in the black suit is among them, legs dangling from the back of the cart. Boots bound in rags, twisted knots of cloth, huge at the end of his thin legs. He catches Lore's eye, shrinks back in recognition, hands moving up to cover his face. Lore looks away, too, shock like a clamp around her guts.

She looks round again after the cart passes. The young man is watching her. He raises one hand slightly in greeting. Lore waves back, hurries on. Blushing in her wet, paraffin-stinking clothes.

—

Jüri points out the young man again the following evening, behind them in a soup queue.

– He wanted the food in that shop, didn't he?
– Yes. Not so loud.
– Why did the shopkeeper give it to us?
– Because we were there first.

The man has seen them, too. Lore can feel his eyes on her as she asks for an extra portion to give to Peter. They crouch down to eat at the edge of the square. The soup is watery, but it has small chunks of meat at the bottom. Lore fishes two or three out of the steaming liquid and blows on them for Peter to chew. The hot food is painful against her gums. They smear dripping on to the bread with their fingers. The man sits down in the middle of the square, leaning back against the sandbags around the statue, facing the children while he drinks his soup from the bowl. He eats quickly, ravenously. Lore feels him watching them. She rubs dripping into the raw corners of Peter's mouth, but he licks it away again.

Jüri helps himself to more bread, and Lore doesn't stop him, takes another slice for herself. Jüri stands up and walks across the square with the fistful of bread and dripping held out in front of him. He stops in front of the man, offers him the food. Lore sees the man take it and push it straight into his mouth. Jüri pauses for a second, watching, then runs back across the square to Lore. He crouches down quickly, as if to duck out of sight, whispers:

– He took it.

Jüri looks at Lore, holding out his empty, greasy hands. His eyes are red and wet, surprised.

– He didn't say anything to me.

He wipes at his eyes with his sleeve.

– It doesn't matter.

Lore divides the rest of the bread between them. Jüri passes his share to Jochen. Lore looks over to the fountain, but the young man is walking away from them across to the other side of the square and out of sight.

—

They are on a long straight road. Pale yellow-brown sticky clay, with heavy wet fields on either side. It runs along a low ridge and Lore can see for miles: the long walk ahead, and the young man behind. He has been there since dawn; head down, keeping pace with them. Lore has Peter and the bundle, and keeps the children ahead of her, the twins at the front and Liesel in the middle with the bag. The boys have spent most of the morning whispering to each other, but they are quiet now. The rain started about an hour ago, a fine mist that wets their hands and faces and works its way through their stockings. Lore wraps Peter in the oilskin and hopes he isn't cold. She wipes his face every few minutes with her hand-kerchief and he smiles up at her each time. She is thirsty, but the children haven't said anything. Lore guesses they have been walking for around three hours. They will stop in an hour or two. She notes a tree on the horizon and decides to pass it before lunch. They have no more food.

Lore hears a humming noise. Coming from the left or the right. She's not sure. Her feet are warm and wet in her boots, and Peter smiles when she wipes his face. How long has the noise been there? She looks back along the road, but there is nothing to see apart from the man. In front of her is the tree, their target, and the bulk of the bag strapped on to Liesel's narrow back. The morning is mapped out. They can easily keep walking like this for an hour or two: tree, twins, Liesel, smiling Peter, and then Lore, and behind them the man. The hum is still there.

She can see something now, a flat black shape moving parallel with the horizon, seemingly through the middle of the field to the left of the road. A jeep, maybe. The wheels are hidden behind a ridge. It is still a long way off. Half a kilometre. Perhaps not so far. Lore wipes Peter's face, but he is asleep now, and she gets no smile. She looks back at the man and he is still there, no closer, no further away. She looks ahead at the tree and that, too, is still on the horizon: their no-food-lunch-marker. The jeep is a fast thing in a slow landscape, gaining ground. Peter sleeps.

Perhaps we should run. Lore doesn't know where they are. Who the fields belong to. Maybe they aren't in Germany any more. *We should run.*

– We have to go over the field.

She tears at the bundle, struggling to pull it off her shoulders, shifting Peter from arm to arm, jolting him. He stays asleep. Blankets trail from his legs, getting wet. Lore grabs handfuls, stuffing them up under the oilskin.

– Over the field. This one.

Still Peter sleeps. The children watch their sister grappling with the baby's blankets, shocked at standing still after the long hours spent walking.

Lore glances behind her to look for the man. He has seen the jeep, too, and is walking faster now, head up, white smudge of face under a black hat. He has one arm raised, as if pointing to something in the sky, but he looks straight ahead, at them, coming forwards, half walk, half trot.

Peter hangs around Lore's neck, a sleeping dead-weight. No warmth comes through the oilskin. Like a sandbag in her arms.

– Take the bundle, Jochen, we have to run.
– Now?

Lore can see the jeep out of the corner of her eye, so she knows it is too late. She doesn't want to look for the man. She's got it wrong, everything is too close now.

– Yes, come on.

She pushes Liesel forwards into the ditch dividing the road from the field. Jochen picks up the bundle but doesn't move. Jüri slides down the grassy bank on his bottom.

Liesel holds out her arms to take Peter and the jeep pulls up next to them. Sharp exhaust in the damp air.

Lore turns her head away, facing down the road towards the man. He is gaining on them, only one hundred metres away now, still walking, trotting.

The soldier speaks, in German. Maybe. She can't understand him. There are two of them. The soldier speaking at the window, and another pair of eyes in the driver's seat. Lore looks down the road to the man. He has almost caught up with them, still holding one arm in the air. He is speaking, but she can't hear what he's saying. *He should be shouting if he wants us to hear.*

The soldier speaks again. American, but speaking German, his accent difficult.

– Where are you going?

The other soldier whispers to him. The man is still there, coming closer. Lore can see the mud on his trouser cuffs. Yellow on black wool. His face is wet, like hers, like Peter's.

– Where are your parents?
– I don't know who he is.

Lore points at the man as he comes alongside the jeep.

– What?
– She's talking about this other one.
– I don't know him.

Lore knows they don't understand her, but at least they both turn and look at the man now.

His neck is long and thin, and his head is bony. Full of teeth and gaps where teeth used to be. The jawbone works on and on. He is speaking quietly, persistently, and his Adam's apple jumps between tight cords in his neck. He slows down now, and carefully lowers his arm to his side as he reaches the group.

– Do you have papers?

The other soldier is speaking to Lore, now. His accent clearer. The man is almost at the jeep, slowing down, walking, breathing, talking.

– We lost them.
– We're going to Oma.

Jochen puts the bundle down as he speaks. Lore watches the soldier for his reaction.

– Not far away. We're nearly home. She's waiting for us.

The man comes to a stop next to Lore. Too close. She steps aside and Peter shifts in her arms. The man reaches out and touches the door of the jeep. His nails are wide and pale, his fingers wet.

– I have papers, here, I have the papers, look. We need a lift, if you have the room. We're nearly home. We have people waiting.

He shuffles on the yellow clay, keeps up his slow insistent monologue, hands going through the pockets of his dark suit. Lore can't look at the soldier, has to keep her eyes on the man. She stands between him and the children, holding Peter hard to her chest, making herself wide.

– I have my papers. Where are you driving? If we could go as far as Fulda with you, maybe, that would be very helpful. Let me find them. We lost the others, you know how it is, but I still have mine. Here they are.

The man has an identity card folded into a damp square of thick grey paper. He pushes up his sleeves and holds out the paper to the soldiers; resting his pale, bare arms against the jeep; keeping up his slow chatter as they consult with each other.

– Anywhere further ahead would be good. We've been walking for a long time you understand. So if you have the room, the children are tired, you can see that, of course, not strong.

He looks at Lore, smiles and nods. His eyes are friendly. Pale. Lore feels the children edge closer to her.

– Where have you all come from?

The soldier speaks to the man now, and the man stretches out his long, bare arm and points at his sodden papers.

– Buchenwald. You understand? We were moved to Buchenwald and we were there until the liberation, you understand?

– Yes, but where from today, yesterday, the day before?
– We've been travelling from Nuremberg this last week now.
– Movement is strictly forbidden. You did know that?
– No, no we didn't know. We're very sorry.
– You have a Grandmother where?
– In Hamburg.

Jochen again.

– Yes in Hamburg, but also in Hemmen. We're going to Fulda and then it's not far to Hemmen, as my sister says.
– You are all brothers and sisters?
– Yes.
– Where are your parents?
– They are dead.

The man points at his card in the soldier's hand.

– You understand? Yes? This is why we have to go to Oma.

Lies pour out of his mouth. Lore's heart races; the children are quiet, watching her. The soldiers confer. The man doesn't look at Lore again. He has stopped talking now, but is still restless, breathing through his mouth. The rain grows heavier, rattling against the canvas of the jeep roof. Jochen warms his hands on the hot, wet metal of the bonnet.

The soldiers hand back the grey square of paper. One of them gets out and folds back the canvas. He motions for them to get in, and the man starts his monologue again.

– Thank-you, it's very kind of you. We are tired, you see. Come on children.

The soldier helps Liesel out of the ditch and beckons Jüri over from the field. Lore knows the children want to get into the jeep. The man from Nuremberg is standing on tip-toe, eager that they should all climb in. He tries to catch Lore's eye. Her arms ache with Peter's weight. *He knows where we are.* And Fulda leads to Kassel and Göttingen, after which comes Hannover, which is on the way to Hamburg. She doesn't trust the man. Doesn't want to pretend he is her brother. Lies piled on lies. Hard to keep track. The rain is heavy now. She is tired. *He can't do anything to us while the Americans are there.*

Lore pushes Liesel up into the jeep and hands Peter over to her. Then she lifts Jüri under the canvas and climbs up after Jochen. The man hands her the bag and the bundle, pulls himself into the jeep and sits on the floor. The soldier ties down the canvas, and they are out of the rain, in the dark and on the move again.

—

The man walks ahead in the dark and the children follow. Lore carries Peter and her arms ache. Their footsteps sing on the wide metalled road. They walk for an hour, a little longer; turn off the main road on to narrower, rougher surfaces. Lore's boots have dried tight around her feet. They ate American chocolate in the afternoon and she has stomach pains now, can't straighten her knees. *Perhaps if we stop, he will keep walking away.* She pictures the man disappearing into the dark up ahead, but feels anxious, not relieved. *He looked at the American map. He knows where we are.* Lore needs to lie down.

– We have to stop.

The man turns round sharply. As if he'd forgotten they were behind him. He stands and squints at Lore briefly, then he climbs off the road into the field. The children follow and stand dumb and still as the man wraps his jacket tightly around himself and lies down to sleep in the bushes. Lore sways with Peter asleep in her arms. Liesel sits down and starts to cry. She is hungry. Lore tells her to be quiet. The twins ask how soon they will get to Hamburg; will this be the last night outside? Lore tells them to be quiet, too, feels the sweat on her upper lip, in her scalp, the ache in her shoulder-blades. She needs to lie down.

She whispers to the twins about Oma's house again as they spread out the oilskins. The walnut trees in the garden, the curly black ironwork of the gate. Lore feels the blood rush in her head, clouding black and hot in her eyes. She can't remember the names of Oma's maids, only the cakes they baked. She asks Liesel to continue, but Liesel is silent, running her fingers over the patchy stubble on her head. The man lies quiet in the bushes, but Lore feels him listening, not sleeping.

Peter cries when she puts him down, and won't stop. Her arms are lead, her wrists and fingers burn; she leaves him to cry. Later, she wakes and sees Liesel cradling him next to her. She sleeps again, feels the ground beneath her: cold and uneven, a sharp pressure against her ribs.

—

Dawn. Lore closes her eyes against the low white sun. The man crouches over her; black hat rim and shadowed face. He says he will walk on and get food for them. Lore's head hurts. She keeps her lids low, says they haven't any money. She feels Liesel turn to look at her, but her sister says nothing. The man says it will help if he takes Peter. Lore stands up, trailing blankets, takes Peter away from Liesel and lies down again. Peter cries and kicks next to her, furious and hungry. Lore watches the man leave and sleeps, heart knocking hard and sore against the walls of her chest.

When she wakes again, Peter is gone, and so are the twins. Liesel sits a few metres away watching the road.

– It was Jochen's idea. They took him and went to catch up with the man.

Lore stands, unsteady. The road is empty and the sun is high in the sky. The wind chills the sweat in her hair, on her back; a sharp pulse beats in her skull. She hits Liesel and Liesel pushes her away. Lore falls back and Liesel kicks at her legs, boot heels hard against her shins.

– People always give food for Peter.
– He will steal him.
– Why didn't you give him some of Mutti's things?
– He wouldn't come back. He would steal them. He will take Peter, now.
– The twins won't let him.
– What can they do?

Lore screams at her sister. Liesel cries, too. Lore watches the road for a while, but has to lie down. Grass against her ears, the landscape swims.

She wakes again. And again. And they are not back. Liesel watches the road; Lore sweats and shivers under the blankets.

———

In the late afternoon Jochen gives her porridge wrapped in a clean rag and she eats. They have got tins of American meat, bread and jars of creamy milk. Peter has eaten and sits next to Lore and smiles. The skin on his cheeks is still red and dry. The man hammers open a tin with a stone. The twins call him Thomas. Thomas says they have found a place to stay not far away.

———

They close over the shutters in the hayloft and it is dark enough to sleep. Peter whimpers in the straw and Liesel squashes bread into a ball for him to suck. Narrow tears of light glow between the planks in the roof and fade as the pale sky darkens.

The twins share a blanket, Lore lies under another with Peter and Liesel next to her, an ache gathered hot behind her eyes. Thomas sits apart from the group near the wall. He rests his head against the beam but Lore knows he isn't asleep. She keeps her eyes open as long as she can, to watch him. The barn jumps and flickers and she sleeps.

In the night, Thomas lights matches in his corner by the wall. Light flares briefly and Lore wakes. He is a shadow against the beams. Hands cupped round the flame, neck and shoulders rigid. He does not look round. The third time, Jüri sits up and calls for Mutti. Thomas puts out the match and lies down. They are all silent. Lore sleeps again, and a little later Thomas lights another match. The pattern continues until the sky shows light through the gaps in the planks. Lore sits up and Thomas lies down to sleep.

—

The sun is warm in Lore's hair and on her arms. The headache is still there, but not so bad, and she is outside, back in charge.

Liesel doesn't want to take off her stockings. The blisters have burst and the blood has hardened. Lore peels the black wool away from the broken skin, tearing open the sores. Liesel cries and Lore makes her soak her feet in the stream. The water softens the blood and the stockings come away more easily. Liesel's feet are raw and her toes swollen, but Lore washes them gently in the cool water. Liesel lies on her back and holds her clean feet up to the sun. She says it will help them to heal quicker and Lore laughs.

Peter sleeps in the grass on the bank and Lore wades out into the stream. She crouches down into the shallow flow; enjoys the cold water against her dry skin; takes her clothes off underwater, rinsing the sweat and sickness out of her dress. She feels light-headed, still a little weak. Hungry. Lore looks over to the barn, the clump of trees next to it. She can see the twins, chasing each other around the barn. Thomas is in the trees, collecting firewood. He has his back to them. Lore stands up out of the water, naked, and pulls on her wet dress, buttoning it quickly over herself, facing away from the barn. She wades back up on to the bank, hangs her underwear in the bushes and starts on the rest of the washing. Liesel crouches down next to her in the shallows.

– Thomas says it's dangerous to talk about Hamburg.
– When did he say that?
– He told me yesterday when you were sleeping.
– What does he know about Hamburg?
– I said Mutti and Vati are in Hamburg and he said we shouldn't tell people about Hamburg because we're not

really allowed over the border.

– What border?

– To the British zone. That's where Hamburg is. We're in the American zone now. And there's a Russian zone and a French zone, too.

– I know that, stupid. You didn't say anything about the camp, did you?

– No! I said Mutti was in Hamburg. I'm not stupid, Lore.

– Scrub a bit harder. Look, Liesel. See, it's still dirty.

– It's a lie, anyway. Mutti always says we shouldn't tell lies.

– Things are different now, Liesel, that's all. Everything's changed.

The pain is back behind Lore's eyes.

– But Thomas is German. Why do we have to lie to German people, too?

– We don't know him. We just shouldn't talk to people we don't know.

– I know him. I think he's nice. He's been helping us. He got us that food when you were sick, and the barn. He says he can help us over the border, too. He said it is dangerous for us to go by ourselves.

– What does he know? Mutti wouldn't have told us to go to Hamburg if it was dangerous, would she? It's a silly thing to say. Get your stockings. We need to wash them, too.

Liesel walks awkwardly on the sides of her feet to protect

her blisters.

– Thomas says the Russians hate us. All of the enemies hate us, and we can't be trusted any more, so that's why there won't be any Germany now and only zones. Is that true, Lore?

– I'm not listening to you any more, Liesel, so you can be quiet now.

The glare off the water stings at Lore's eyes.

– And he said that everyone will be punished. The men especially. Will Vati be punished?

– What did you tell him about Vati?

– Nothing.

– Anneliese?

– I said he was in Hamburg, with Oma. That's what you told me.

– You didn't say anything else?

Lore pinches the flesh on the back of her sister's hand, and twists it hard until the skin shows blue.

– Ow! Lore! I didn't do anything wrong. He asked me where Mutti and Vati were and so I told him about Hamburg. I said we were going to stay at Oma's, just like you told us. I didn't say anything else.

Lore drops Liesel's hand, wipes the sweat out of her eyes.

– They won't hurt Vati, will they?

– No. Of course not. Vati is safe. That's enough now. We

won't talk about it any more.

They wash the blood out of one stocking each and lay them out to dry.

———

Thomas insists that they don't move on again until Lore is well. The children enjoy their two days of rest and swimming in the stream, but Lore is uneasy, watching Thomas all the time. Wondering what he knows about punishment. Waiting for the questions about Mutti, Oma, Hamburg, and Vati, but the questions never come. Thomas sees her watching him, nods, half smiles, and Lore can't make out the expression in his eyes.

Shortly after dawn on the third day, when Lore is sure that Thomas is sleeping, she pulls the photos of Vati from her bag and slips out into the trees behind the barn. She digs a hole with her fingers and buries them as deeply as she can, pressing the heavy soil down firmly with her heels, and covering the spot carefully with twigs and leaves. After that, she runs around under the trees to confuse her tracks, and before she goes back to the barn, she takes care to wash her hands clean again in the stream.

Thomas is still sleeping in the corner with his back to the wall. Lore lies down again next to her brothers and her sister and pulls the blanket over her arms. She is sure that no one could find the pictures now, but still she can't close her eyes.

—

They shifted direction half an hour ago; as soon as the river came into sight. They are still walking towards it, but not directly any more. Approaching the wide water flow at an angle. Walking along, as well as towards; delaying the need to cross it. The grass is long and the ground uneven; they walk as if they are wading already.

About five hundred metres up ahead there is a bridge. The stone pillars are still upright in the slow current, but nothing connects them: dynamited and the remains washed away. On the other side of the river is a water-filled crater, and the road is cracked and pock-marked, too. Caterpillar tracks have ground deep gouges into the muddy banks, dried hard as rock in the hot summer weather.

They walk along the river in silence, below the line of the flood barrier, level with the water. The river defences have been damaged in the fighting, and the ground here is marshy. Water seeps in through the holes in their boots. Thomas carries the bag, Liesel carries Peter, and Lore has the bundle tied to her back. The twins walk behind her. She can hear their boots squelch, marching in step with one another, in step with her.

They walk over the road which rises steeply to the bridge. The twins run up to the top and stand at the edge where the road stops. Twisted fingers of metal poke out of the blasted stone. The boys lie on their stomachs, heads dangling over the edge, and call down to the water. Their laughter echoes against the stone pillars. Thomas stops. He walks back towards Lore, taking Peter from Liesel as he passes. Liesel trots to keep up with him.

– If they blew this one, they'll have blown the lot. All the bridges within a day or two would be my guess.

Lore takes Peter from Thomas, the twins run down off the road.

– Shall we swim it, Thomas? We can see the bottom.
– It's not very deep.
– You can see the bottom?

Thomas walks down to the water's edge. Lore crouches down to ease her back, sits Peter in front of her. The river is wide. About forty metres.

– I don't want to swim across, Lore.
– I know, Liesel.
– It's not deep. Tell her, Lore. We saw the bottom when we were up on the road.
– I still don't want to.

Thomas calls them down. Lore can see the bottom, but it is at least chest-deep. Over head-height for the twins. Each of the pillars has a wide base which forms a shelf about a meter below the surface. Thomas beckons Lore closer to the water.

– We can swim between the pillars, and rest on the shelves.
– It's too deep.
– But we'll take it in stages.
– I don't want to, Lore.
– It's only four metres between each pillar.
– Only four metres, easy.
– Be quiet, Jochen.

Thomas steps closer to Lore. She squares herself.

– We'll get all our things wet.
– But it's hot. We can dry them on the other side, build a fire, camp here for the night.
– The bags are too heavy.

Lore crouches down again, shifts the weight of the bundle across her shoulders. Thomas runs along the bank, picking up driftwood. The boys join in.

– Only the big bits, Jüri, bigger than that, twice the size. We will have to walk miles along the river before we find another bridge. If we do find one, it will probably be like this. We could lose a day, two days, more.
– What about a boat?
– What boat? We could lose more days waiting for a boat.

Liesel kicks the ground next to Lore, unhappily.

– How will we get Peter across, then?
– I'll take him. We'll tie him to me, and I'll swim with him. Easy.

– No.

Thomas ties the wood together into a frame. A handkerchief at one corner, his shirt at another, Jochen's vest at the third. He pulls one of Liesel's stockings out of the bag and ties off the last corner. He sits the bag in the middle and carries it down to the water. It floats. The bag sags through the middle, and it is heavier on one side than the other, but it stays on the surface. Thomas ties the end of Liesel's other stocking to one corner.

– I can pull it like that, you see? We'll take this bag over first, then I'll come back and take the bundle.

Lore doesn't look at him. She can see the road snaking off into the distance on the other side of the river.

– It will take us half an hour. We can dry our things and walk on a bit in the evening.

Lore picks at the knot holding the bundle to her back.

– Or we can stay the night.
– I'll take Peter, not you.
– Very good.

Thomas takes off his boots and ties the laces together. He drapes them round his neck, buttons his jacket, and wades out into the water with his raft. When he is waist-deep he starts swimming, holding the stocking between his teeth, pulling the bag after him to the first pillar. When he gets there, he stands up out of the water and pulls the raft over.

He turns to them and waves. Water streams out of his sleeve in an arc, and the twins both laugh and wave back. They run to the water's edge, but Lore calls them back.

– Yes, wait. I'll go across and then I'll come and help you.

Thomas steps off the shelf into the water again and swims to the next pillar. The boys crouch at the water's edge, watching, tying their boot laces together as Thomas had done. Lore squeezes Liesel's hand and tells her to take her boots off, too.

Thomas is past the middle of the river, now. Still swimming. He hasn't looked back again, and Lore wonders absently if he will come back and help them. She calculates what is in the bag. Food and clothes. The last tin of meat. But no money, no valuables. No great loss. Thomas wades out on to the far shore, pulling the bag behind him. He doesn't look round or wave. He walks up on to the road, out of sight. The twins both stand up and turn to look at Lore. She shrugs, makes a mental list. The tin of meat, the half loaf, three blankets and Liesel's coat. She still has the oilskins, two blankets, the twins' coats, Peter's jacket, Mutti's brooch, the money. No food.

Thomas walks back from the road into the river. He is carrying the raft, but doesn't have the bag with him, or his jacket. His chest is bright white against the brown river bank. He waves and starts swimming again, stopping only at the middle pillar on the way back. He pushes the raft ahead of him through the water and speaks to them as he swims, even before he is in earshot. Skin glowing through the murky water, shoulder-blades working like sharp wings.

– There's a good spot for a fire not far off. I've spread the blankets and things on bushes to dry, anyway. It won't take long in the sun. They didn't get too wet. And there's plenty of firewood, too.

He is out of breath, greenish. He crouches down on the bank, breathing hard, while Lore and Liesel tie the bundle tight with oilskins. The twins take off their shirts and stuff them into their shorts, boots dangling ready around their necks. Lore takes the thinnest blanket and tears it in two. She holds Peter's back against her chest and Liesel ties the blanket round both of them. Thomas stands up.

– You should tie him to your back, then he'll be out of the water when you swim.
– I'll swim on my back.

Lore ties the other half of the blanket around herself, knotting it firmly around Peter's waist. His arms are tied under the blanket and he kicks his legs out and complains as they walk down to the bank. The twins set the bundle in the middle of the frame. Thomas checks the knots and tells the boys to pull it between them. He says he will help Lore with Peter, but Lore tells him to help Liesel.

The twins go first, wading into the water, holding the bundle at waist height, then swimming steady and serious to the first pillar. When they get there, Jüri climbs up on to the shelf and waves. Jochen treads water and laughs. Lore waves back and Thomas applauds. They set off for the next pillar.

Liesel allows Thomas to take her hand, and he leads her into the water. She looks round at Lore, but carries on walking until she is waist deep.

– It's cold, Lore!
– You'll be fine.

She slides into the water and swims, shouting and splashing. Thomas swims beside her and her strokes calm down. She waves when she gets to the pillar; Lore can see she is smiling.

The twins are still swimming on, over halfway there, stopping at each pillar. Their shoulders are hunched round their ears with the cold, but they keep going, jumping back into the water, pulling the bundle between them. Lore ties her boots around her waist and wades into the water. Thomas helps Liesel up on to the shelf by the second pillar and treads water.

– Go back! Wait. I'll come for you when I've got the others across.

Lore ignores him and carries on wading. Peter shifts against her stomach, uncomfortable in his blanket binding. He tries to look up at her face, his soft head pressing against her chin. He is breathing very fast. Lore has her arms around him, scared to let go, although he is bound tightly to her by the blankets. The river bed changes from sharp pebbles to soft mud, silky against her feet and warm compared to the water. Lore sinks up to her ankles in the slime. The water is heavy around her thighs and she steps out further and faster.

It is much colder now she is out of the shallows. Her ankle bones ache and her stomach contracts, shrinking back from the water. The slow pull of current bends her knees. Peter's feet skim the water and he shouts and kicks. Bright splashes of cold in the sun. Lore can see Thomas swimming towards them. He has left Liesel at the pillar and is shouting at Lore to go back to the shore. She turns her back to him and lies down into the water, keeping her arms wrapped around Peter, kicking her legs.

The cold knocks the air out of her lungs. Her boots, heavy with water, drag down at her waist. She flings her arms out to keep her torso afloat, but too late, and she pulls Peter down into the river with her.

When they surface, he is screaming rigid against her chest, arms straining to get free of the blankets. Lore has the grit river taste in her mouth. She can't reach the bottom. Peter's head is under the water again. She kicks, pushes her arms out to steady herself, coughing, and lies back into the river. She hears Peter's screams through a wall of water, like ice around her neck. Her boots kick heavy and lazy at her thighs as she pushes against the current with her legs. Peter's head is out of the water, but his body is in the cold river with hers. Water floods into her mouth. She sinks again.

Thomas swims underneath them; his arms under Lore's shoulders; pulling her chest up out of the water and Peter with it. Lore retches, wants to cry. Thomas pushes her up on to the ledge, jarring her cold bones against the stones. She stands up out of the water and Thomas unties the blankets. He is not angry as Lore expected. Peter still screams, but with tears now, and not so stiff. Once his arms are free he pulls himself up against Lore and presses his face into her neck. Liesel is standing and watching at the next pillar, arms wrapped round the stone, and the boys are watching from the opposite shore. Thomas shouts to them to build a fire, and tells Liesel to wait until they get to her. She nods, silent and shivering.

Thomas pulls Peter away from Lore's chest and he screams again, fists and feet attacking the air in fury. But Thomas puts him back down against Lore's shoulders; high up, so he can wrap his arms round her neck again. Thomas wrings the dripping blankets out into the river, and ties them back around Peter and around Lore's chest. He pulls them tight and Peter screams, but Lore makes no protest. After he has checked the knots, Thomas hangs Lore's boots around his own neck and slides back down into the water. He holds out his hands.

– Ready?

Lore hesitates; eyes fixed on the reaching arm; on the blue smudge below the greenish skin; the tattoo half-way between wrist and elbow. Numbers. Blurred. As if the river water has seeped under the skin and smeared the ink. Thomas takes her hand and Lore sits obediently down on the ledge into the water. Peter grips her neck, but he is quiet now. Thomas lets go as Lore slides down into the river, swimming with her to the next pillar. Peter breathes in gasps in her ear. Thomas smiles encouragement. Liesel pulls her up on to the ledge and they rest in silence for a few minutes, Thomas treading water in the river next to them. They swim on together. When they get to the last pillar, they wave to Jüri who is waiting for them on the shore.

— We've built a fire!

He gestures over the rise. Peter starts to cry again before they reach the river bank, but he is not angry any more, just cold. They wade out of the water. Liesel's lips are ringed blue and Lore can't feel the stones under her feet. None of them can undo the knots in Peter's blankets, even Jüri's hands are still weak with the cold. They walk over the rise of the road together. In a dip on the other side, their clothes and blankets are spread out over the bushes to dry, and Jochen is stoking the fire in the middle. He has hammered open the last of the tins with a sharp stone and has cut the loaf into slices, toasting on the flat rocks around the fire.

– The bread got wet in the bag.

———

Lore is woken by the twins murmuring on the other side of the fire. Liesel and Peter are asleep next to her and the embers glow warm against her cheeks. She lies still and listens to her brothers, separating out their voices. Jüri's whispers are squeaky, small; Jochen's are bolder; and the third voice, low and even, belongs to Thomas.

– I was in the east before. While they were still fighting.
– Who? The Amis, or the Russians?
– The Russians. I was in a forest east of here that was full of Russian soldiers.

Thomas points to the dark horizon, his arm a jagged shadow against the blue night.

– Did you shoot at them?
– No, I didn't have a gun.
– I will have a gun when I'm a soldier.
– Did you fight with them?
– They had guns, so I had to hide from them.
– Did they find you?
– No. They stole lots of things, the Russians. From the villages. And then they threw most of the things away again. I got this suit in that forest.
– And after that?
– At night, when they stopped shooting I ran away, back into the American zone.

– Why did you run away? I would have stolen a gun from them while they were asleep.

– Best to keep away from the Russians. Anyway, when I got to the American zone again people told me the war was over. I already knew it would be. Weeks before. When the Russians arrived, that was it.

Lore tells the twins to go to sleep. They lie still and Thomas pulls the blanket over himself, shifting. Lore closes her eyes and listens for Thomas's movements. After a few minutes he sits up and puts more wood on the embers, blowing to encourage flames. He shifts away from the twins and leans back against the tree trunk a metre or two from where Lore lies.

Lore wakes up when the birds start to sing. The sky is still dark but the fire has gone out. Thomas is awake by the tree.

When Lore wakes again her hair is soaked in dew and Peter is shivering. There is light on the far horizon. She looks over to the tree and finds Thomas sleeping. Slumped, one arm lying in the wet grass next to him, stretching pale and thin from his sleeve. Lore can see the tattoo again, and the prominent veins leading from elbow to wrist. She rolls quietly off her oilskin on to the cool soil, towards the outstretched arm. She doesn't get too close; she doesn't want to wake him. Just close enough to examine the dark numbers scratched into the pale skin. Green-blue lines, some of them edged in tender pink.

Tiny flakes of dead skin peeling off the new-healed scars. Lore watches Thomas, holding her breath, afraid that any small movement now might wake him. But he sleeps on, eyes dancing under his lids as the dawn creeps up.

Lore rolls on to her oilskin again, on to her back, holds Peter close. The sky is gold at the edges and blue above. Mist lies like milk on the fields.

—

In the village, people tell them. No one gets over without papers. They have jeeps going along the border, British and American. If you don't have papers, you will be sent back. If you have the wrong papers, they will take you away, take you back to where you started, put you in prison. Thomas asks what they mean by wrong papers, but no one can tell him: they only say what they see.

Lore begs potatoes. Thomas builds a fire at the edge of the road and buries them in the embers. They wait in silence, staring into the flames. It is still early, grey dawn; the long day of walking ahead. Lore scoops out hot potato with her fingers for Peter, burning herself, blowing on the food. Thomas eats the blackened skins of his share and the twins copy him, their faces smeared with hot ash. Liesel's mouth is bleeding again and she doesn't want any food. She rubs at her gums, holds her wet, red fingers out to Lore and cries. Lore throws a charred potato at her, tells her to eat, promises salt from the next village to rub into the sores. She has an ulcer in her lower lip, worries at it with her tongue, irritated by Liesel's complaints.

—

Inside the barge it is dark and the beating engine is smothered by the coals, thudding against their legs. The boat man gives them raggedy sacks to hide under in case he is searched at the border. He is nervous about taking Peter in case he cries. Lore can see he is changing his mind. Thomas talks to him, quietly, persistently, presses Mutti's brooch into his hand. The boatman nods, avoids eye-contact, squints upstream. He pushes them down into the hold, rough hands leaving black coal dust smudges on their shoulders.

The hold is full, the load sloping down at the sides and at the front. They crawl forwards along the barge walls, to where they can no longer be seen from the hatch. Lore leads, coals sharp against her knees, Liesel holding on to her sleeve, afraid of the dark, noisy interior.

The twins crouch down at the bottom of the pile, Liesel squatting next to them. Lore lies next to Thomas, with Peter on her stomach. It is pitch black with the hatch closed. No light leaks in at all. Lore stares into the darkness, widens her eyes, but no sight comes. She concentrates instead on listening for the others in the din. The twins shifting their small boots on the coals, Liesel's wheezing cough. Peter cries for a while and then lies still, a reassuring weight on Lore's chest. She can feel Thomas's arm against her own, the rough wool of his jacket sleeve brushing her skin with each breath. She turns her face to him, but can see only black. His breath is warm on her chin. Damp with a sour edge. Lore shifts her head gently closer. Thomas stops breathing. She lies still. He starts again.

The boatman insists he can't take the risk, asks them to leave. He apologises over and over, unwrapping Mutti's brooch from his handkerchief. He says at least they are closer now, only half an hour from the border. He can't stop talking, moving; gives them slices of his wife's home-baked bread, coals to build a fire.

The children blink in the evening sun, sleepy from the hours spent in the dark, brushing the black dust from their hands and knees. Peter cries and coughs and they say their goodbyes. Lore carries him ahead of the group, furious, kicking the ground as she walks. The day has been wasted, the dark hours unsettling. Thomas is hunched and unwashed in the evening light: she avoids looking at him, doesn't like to think she was lying so close to him before. They will camp soon, but first she wants to get closer to home. She walks on along the river, following the boatman's instructions, pressing on to the north.

—

– Our mother is with the Americans.

Thomas nods. The children lag behind. Lore can feel the stones in the road through her boots.

– It's a camp. Run by the Americans.

– The Americans.

– It's not a prison for criminals.

– No.

– Please don't tell anyone, just in case.

Thomas nods again. They pass through two villages. Beg for food, are given milk for Peter, hot water to wash with. Lore finds a bright rag to wrap around Liesel's head, and Thomas shaves. He and Lore walk ahead again.

– I was in a prison.

– When?

– For a long time.

– Will they keep Mutti for a long time?

– I don't know. I don't know about American prisons.

– It's a camp.

They rest briefly in the third village, drinking water from the well. One of Jochen's soles has worn loose, flapping as he walks. Lore tears a nappy into strips and binds his boot together again. They walk on.

– Were you in a Russian prison?

– No I was in a German prison. I was moved around. Different prisons. Places they took us to work.

– One of our prisons?

– Yes, until the Americans came.

It is hot again. They are silent for a while, each absorbing what has been said. The sweat runs down Lore's back under the bundle. Thomas keeps his jacket on. His face is damp under his hat.

– Are you a criminal?

Thomas puts his head to one side, doesn't answer.

– What did you do?

His jaws work into what looks like a smile.

– Before I went to prison?

Lore shrugs. She doesn't want to know now. She turns round to look at the children, straggling far behind, knows she has said too much.

– I stole from people. Money. Names, too.

Lore keeps pace with Thomas. She doesn't speak, hopes he won't say any more.

– What about your father?

Lore drops back. Thomas keeps walking, doesn't look round, but he slows down, too. The children's footsteps are louder now, closer, and Lore can hear Peter's chatter. She falls into step behind Thomas, watching his heels, keeping a gap between him and the family as they walk.

—

– If I call you over, don't say anything, let me talk. I am your brother. Your mother and father are dead. Our mother and father. Just agree with me. We can say we are going to Hamburg this time, but it's better if I speak. Pretend you don't understand if they ask you something, I will answer. I am your brother, remember.

Thomas walks ahead to the border control. They stand and wait, watch him talk, gesture, shift, talk. He gets papers out of his pockets, rolls up his sleeves. The soldiers look at them while he speaks, points, shrugs. They give him back his papers. He walks back to the children. He looks at Lore, shakes his head, apologises. He leads them back down the road the way they came. Once they are out of sight of the checkpoint, they cut across country, parallel with the border.

They keep moving through the evening, along the edges of a forest. When the moon rises, Thomas leads them into the trees. He shows no sign of wanting to stop. Lore loses sight of him, his black suit melting into the thick dark ahead. She calls for him, hurries forward. The children are too tired to hurry with her. Lore strains her eyes for movement in the undergrowth, stops, shouts Thomas's name again. She stands still, hears twigs cracking, leaves shifting underfoot.

Lore calls, Thomas calls back. They meet in the trees.

They walk back together to find the children and decide to stop for the night. Peter cries himself quietly to sleep, and Lore leaves him in peace.

—

On the other side of the forest they find railway tracks and follow them. They see no trains all day, but towards evening they find a small railway station. It has been bombed. Rabbits run through the craters; the buildings are shells; but the tracks have been repaired.

There are men gathered on the platform. They are thin, like Thomas. Lore watches as he speaks with them. They have teeth missing and hollow cheeks: heavy wrists and ankles on long, slow limbs. Some of them say they will wait for a train. Others want to try walking over the border. A few have already tried it. They say most of the time you get sent back, but you can be lucky. They say as long as you stick to the roads, you won't get shot. Peter wakes up and starts crying, Lore stops listening. She goes to sit with the children, helps Jochen retie the rags around his boots.

Thomas hurries over, agitated.

– We've come into the Russian zone, over the border. We must have crossed it in the forest. Maybe in the night.

He holds Lore's arm tight.

– We should go back to the forest. We should go now, keep walking. We can sleep when it gets light, walk on again tomorrow night.
– We can't walk now, we've been walking all day. We can sleep here, Thomas. Please. I don't want to sleep outside again.

Thomas pulls Lore away from the children, whispers. He is close to her, the brim of his hat pressed against her scalp, but his eyes look away. At the men on the platform, into the trees.

– It's safer at night, much safer.
– Why can't we wait for a train?
– We can get over to the British zone through the forest. Stay away from the soldiers.
– But the people said they shoot at you if you go off the road.
– They only meant if you run off the road when you're crossing. We should just keep away from the soldiers, from the Russians.
– But won't there be Russians everywhere?
– Not everywhere. We just have to be careful.
– I think we should maybe wait for the train, Thomas.
– You don't have any papers. Only I have papers and that's not enough. You can hide in a forest, you can't hide on a road.

Thomas watches the men on the platform. Lore can see his lashes, a flickering pulse under his skin.

– Are they Russians?
– No, they are Germans, most of them.
– Why do they look like that?
– They were in a prison.

The skin around his eyes is fine, almost blue.

– The same prison as you?
– No. They were soldiers.

His eyes skim her face, look back into the forest.

– Not a word about that, understand?

Lore nods.

– It's nearly dark.

He lets go of her arm. Lore calls the children, pulls the bundle higher on to her shoulders. They walk on along the tracks, passing the station on their way to the forest. The men lie side by side on the platform, sleeping under the remains of the roof. They make thin, wheezing noises as they breathe, mouths open to the night air. Lore watches them over the dark shape of Thomas's shoulder. She stares hard at the man nearest her on the platform, his large head all hollows and loose skin. The station roof shields him from the moonlight, and Lore can't see if his eyes are open or closed.

They are deep in the forest before Thomas lets them lie down. Half in dreams, Lore sees skeleton people crowded in the trees. Roots are limbs, half buried in the ground; twigs are fingers in her hair. She sees the moon above her through the black leaves, feels the tears wet in her ears. She lays Peter against her chest, presses her cold hands against his warm back. He stirs but doesn't wake and Lore sleeps.

A train comes to take them across the border. The tickets are in their schoolbags, folded and refolded so they are soft and brittle. Lore hands them over to the guard, who makes them lie down in the carriage. The people behind them in the queue lie down on top of them. Lore feels their bones against her skin.

—

Thomas moves them on before dawn, stopping again when it gets too light. The British zone is somewhere up ahead beyond the trees. Thomas is certain of it, keeps reassuring them as he spreads the oilskins, sits them down. He has found a small gully, thick with bushes: a place to hide until dark. Thomas makes them sit apart from one another, covered by the undergrowth. He walks around the top of the gully, checking they can't be seen; unties the rag from Liesel's head, because the red shows bright through the leaves.

Thomas says, we must be very quiet, all day. And we have to rest, ready for the night. Lore listens to his whispers, watches for the small dark movements in the bushes as he speaks. She can't see Liesel or the twins, hidden by the dense growth between them. The birches are in full leaf, pale green fluttering in the light breeze. The forest floor is mossy, soft and moist. Peter sleeps on and on against Lore's shoulder. His eyelids are puffy, grey-yellow, veins showing blue through the skin on his temples. Lore traces the fine line of his cheekbone, strokes his head, feels his scalp tight and dry under her fingers. She tries to remember how long ago she fed him, closing her eyes against the day. Birds sing, crowded high in the trees. She is sleepy. Cool and still. Her skirt soaks up the damp earth. A smell of cooking reaches them through the trees.

Liesel and the twins guess in whispers what it might be. They all agree on meat. Lore tells them be quiet, go to sleep, stomach lurching, saliva flooding painfully in her cheeks. Jochen crawls to her through the bushes, pulls at her clothes with hungry fingers.

Thomas has smelled it, too. He leans forward, head emerging out of the leaves. He turns his face towards the smell, locating the source: withdraws slightly when the wind blows away the trail, waits for it to return. He moves, climbing past Lore out of the gully. He whispers to her to stay put, stay silent. Wait. She thinks, hopes: food must be more important than the border now. Lore listens for his footfalls, snapping twigs. Lifts Peter on to her shoulder, follows Thomas up the gully towards the food. Liesel and the twins are close behind her. She can't see Thomas. Stops, looks around.

Across a clearing there is a house, set back into the trees. Lore can see no people, but smoke rises from the chimney. The clearing is maybe a hundred metres wide. The grass grows in long clumps and the berry bushes are covered in tiny, green fruit. Thomas is a dark shape, deep in the forest, making his way slowly towards the house.

– There he is!

Jochen points, his voice carries far into the quiet morning. Lore hisses at him to be quiet, makes a grab for his finger. But he is already gone, running through the forest. His shirt flashes grey-white as the sun reaches between the leaves.

Lore sits down on the mossy ground with Liesel and Jüri, pulse thumping in her ears. Thomas will be angry. Minutes pass in the cool leaves. Birds sing overhead. Peter is still asleep in her lap. Liesel shifts next to her, lies down. Lore dozes.

Jochen shouts from across the clearing, then Thomas. Jüri stands up. Lore hears metal and boots; running and branches snapping. Liesel lifts her head, eyelids heavy with sleep. Lore looks through the bushes and sees Jochen running at them across the clearing. She hears the breath pushed out of his lungs like hiccups. A gun is fired, three, four times.

Lore sees the birds lift out of the trees into the air, but hears nothing. She ducks down, hits her chin on a tree-root, teeth snapping in her ears. Her eyes water, the ground is cold, the leaves are wet, and noise returns. Jüri shouts for his brother. More bullets. Lore pulls him down on top of her, on to the ground.

– He fell over, Lore.

Jüri tries to stand up again. She holds on to him, fingers in his hair, looks for Liesel. Twigs scratch at her eyes, Jüri twists against her grip.

– Where is he?

Lore can see Jochen's shirt in the long grass; a small flap of grey. Liesel is behind her on the ground. Lore can hear her breathing, short and high. A gun is fired again. Two Russian soldiers crawl out of the trees. They are fast on their bellies through the grass, making their way towards Jochen's shirt.

– Jochen!

Jüri screams shrill in Lore's ear. The soldiers flatten themselves against the grass; two short clicks and then gunfire in the trees. The leaves tremble, Liesel gasps on the ground next to Lore. Peter cries, briefly. Everything is still.

Lore watches the Russians crawl forwards again. When the first one gets to Jochen's shirt he shouts. The second one crawls on through the grass. The first one pulls Jochen's shirt towards him. The grey flap disappears into the long grass. Both soldiers are shouting now: harsh voices cracking. Lore pulls her arms around Jüri and Peter and waits for the guns.

In the middle of the shouting come footsteps and snapping twigs, and then the food smell is back. Thomas pulls them up.

– Quickly. We have to go *now*. *Quickly*.

His hand grips Lore's wrist, twisting the skin. She makes herself heavy. He lets go, pulls Jüri to his feet, pushing him back into the trees, away from the clearing.

– Now. *Now.* Quick.

He is angry, eyes wide. Neck pulled tight like rope. They run through the trees.

The food is still hot. Thomas eats first, stuffing the bread into his mouth, ladling handfuls of the stew after it. He orders them to keep watch and food falls out of his mouth on to his chin. He pushes it back again, chewing loudly, swallowing quickly, painfully. He passes the pot to Lore, stands up to keep watch. Lore takes a handful of the hot meat out of the pot and eats, Liesel eats and cries. Jüri tears chunks off the loaf and stuffs them into his cheeks. Lore pinches together soft pieces of bread and hot stew, presses them into Peter's mouth. He wakes, chews slowly. Lore presses more against his lips to encourage him to swallow. Jüri and Liesel wipe out the sides of the pot with the last of the bread. Thomas throws the pot into the bushes and they run on.

—

Animal tracks lead them through the long ferns. They keep low to the ground, bending forwards, crawling. Peter throws up the food but doesn't cry. Lore holds him tight against her side, tries not to jar him too much as she pushes further through the undergrowth.

Lore follows Thomas's back, looks behind her for Jüri and Liesel. For Jochen, too. The ferns smear the tears across her face and neck into her hair.

There is a sandy ditch, barbed wire, a little beyond that a metal post. Thomas tells them he thinks they are in the British zone. He breathes hard through his mouth, neck shining wet with sweat above his collar. Lore is still crying. Her throat is cold and her lungs are tight and raw. She can't pull in enough air to fill them.

Thomas says they need to walk further, that it isn't safe yet. Jüri asks if they can wait for Jochen to catch up with them. Thomas stares at him. Jüri steps closer to Lore, but she wants Thomas to say it. Tears drip from her chin, but her arms are full of Peter and she cannot wipe them away. His head hangs heavy over her elbow, and his mouth is slack. She sits down, shifts his sleeping weight against her chest, and waits for Thomas to speak. Liesel crouches, rubs her gums. Thomas keeps looking at Jüri.

– They shot him.

Lore lies down with Peter among the stones and cries. Jüri stands still and small.

Thomas shouts now.

– He ran the wrong way. He should have stayed in the trees. He should have stayed in the gully. All of you, like I told you.

Liesel holds her knees to her chest. Lore can feel Jüri watching her, but she can't stop crying. Birds sing in the ferns, fly high above her head. Peter sleeps while she cries under the pale sky.

Thomas says if they don't come now he will go without them. He walks away and Jüri follows him along the dusty track.

———

The hay smells sweet. Lore lies hot, awake, listening for the others in the dark, counting them. *One too few.* She doesn't cry now, but she doesn't sleep either. Her bed is soft, her throat is dry and her brother is dead, far away.

Thomas shifts slowly, quietly, inching towards the ladder. Lore asks him where he is going. Liesel and Jüri sit up. Thomas lies down again in the hay.

———

Thomas walks with Lore to the village to beg for food. They leave Liesel and Jüri in the barn, tell them to stay quiet in the hayloft, not to move. Thomas doesn't want to go to Hamburg. Lore keeps pace with him, pleads.

– You have to come with us. I don't know what to do.
– There are no more borders to cross. You can get to Hamburg by yourselves now.
– Please don't leave us.

Thomas shakes his head, breath whistles through his lips,

drawn tight across his teeth. He walks fast. Lore jogs to keep up with him, Peter cries, uncomfortable on her hip. She shouts above his wailing, into Thomas's impassive face.

– But Mutti and Vati aren't there.
– I know, you told me. Your mother is in a camp.
– I don't know what to do.
– Go to Hamburg. Find your Oma.
– But I told the children that Vati will be there, Thomas.
– I know.
– Thomas!

Jüri calls to them, up ahead on the *landstrasse*, waiting for them. He waves, and Thomas and Lore drop their voices to whispers.

– What do I say when we find Oma, and Vati isn't with her?
– I can't help you now.

Thomas stops walking, divides off his share of the food, stuffs it in his pockets. Lore panics.

– You can live with us. With Oma. She has a big house.

Thomas laughs, but Lore knows he doesn't find it funny.

– Oma can help you find a place to live, and a job.

He shakes his head. Peter wails, hands gripping at his stomach. Thomas pulls the bread out of his pocket, tears off a chunk for him.

– Let's just take the food back now. I'll carry it for you.

Thomas stands up. Jüri races towards them. He runs hard at Thomas, head thumping into his stomach, fingers clasping tight to his shirt. Thomas throws his arms up, neck and shoulders rigid in shock. He pulls away and starts walking again. Jüri clings to his arm, walking alongside, taking hold of Thomas's hand. Lore watches her brother squeezing the long white fingers together. Thomas shakes his hand gradually free as they walk.

—

Crowds mill around the railway station. The old people sit on their bundles and the children cry. The air is heavy and hot. Women carry bags and babies, follow the soldiers, asking questions. Thomas joins the long queue at the ticket window. Lore is afraid to let him out of her sight. She sits in the square with the children and watches him. Liesel sleeps, Peter dozes and coughs, clouds settle overhead. Thomas crouches on the ground, wipes at the sweat on his face. When the queue moves, Jüri gets up and goes to stand with Thomas. He crouches down next to him, fingers tracing the cracks between the flagstones. Lore watches their heads lean gently together, as though they are whispering. But she is too far away to see if their lips are moving.

The ticket window closes long before Thomas and Jüri get to the head of the queue. The soldiers try to disperse the crowds, intoning the same phrases, over and again;

movement is prohibited without permission; no more transports until further notice. Thomas pulls the children aside, against the wall of the station building, herding them along and down the road. Liesel asks if they will get tickets for the next train, but Thomas doesn't answer.

The train pulls in to the station behind them. Thomas hurries them on, down the road, along the wall. Around the corner, the wall dips and levels out. Thomas pushes the children up and over. Other people climb the wall, too, a little further along, and more are following from the square. Thomas throws the bundles over and scrambles up after them, landing awkwardly on the other side. Jüri is already through the fence and on the tracks.

They run along the sleepers, back towards the station. The platform is overflowing with bodies, straining forward. The people call to each other in shrill voices, pushing in close against the train. Children slip off the edge of the platform, landing between the wheels, mothers lift them up again into the crush. They grip their tickets and papers in tight fists, holding them up above their heads. The soldiers order the people into columns at the doors, but nobody moves.

Thomas leads them around the other side of the train, walking alongside, pulling at the windows until he finds one that gives.

– Same as before. Brothers and sisters, same as before.

He grabs Jüri under the armpits, pushes him up into the carriage. Jüri's legs flail, his boot catches Thomas on the jaw. The people inside the compartment shout, shoving at Jüri and then Liesel as Thomas lifts them into the train. More people crawl through the bushes on the far side of the tracks and sprint across to the carriages. Lore sees a man carrying a brick, his hand wrapped in a rag. He smashes a window, reaches through and opens the door. The people inside kick at him, and a fight breaks out.

Liesel reaches her arms out of the carriage to take Peter. The people behind them in the compartment push them against the glass and shout at them to get out. Lore can see Jüri through the window. He shouts back, face crumpling, covers his ears with his hands. The man with the brick is walking towards them, behind him is a soldier with a gun.

Thomas takes Peter from Lore.

– Stay calm, same as before.

He passes Peter up to Liesel and turns to the soldier; walking to him with his palms open; talking already. He takes off his hat and holds it against his chest. His hair is flattened in a damp ring above his ears. The soldier listens, squinting concentration, while Thomas repeats himself. The rhythm of his voice drifts back to Lore through the moist air, but not his words. The man with the brick stares at Thomas, turns to look at Lore. His arm is bleeding, cut above the line of the rag around his fist. Lore looks away.

Thomas opens a wallet and pulls out papers, soft and worn. He holds them out to the soldier, who takes them and reads them. They lie limp on his palm. The man with the brick says something, kicks at the ground by Thomas's feet. Thomas ignores him, steps closer to the soldier. Still talking, he points at the paper in the soldier's hand; pushes up his sleeves, shows the soldier his pale arms. The soldier asks a question. Thomas nods. The man with the brick spits at him. It lands white on Thomas's dark collar.

The soldier shouts, points his gun. The man with the brick steps away, puts up his hands. The soldier shouts again. He gives Thomas back his papers, pulls a handkerchief out of his pocket and presses it into Thomas's palm.

Thomas hurries back to Lore, wiping the spit away, stuffing the wallet back in his pocket. He smiles, lifts Lore up to the window. The people inside the carriage are still angry, still shouting. Thomas whispers.

– It's good, it's good. It's fine, you can go.

Lore twists away from the window, but Thomas pushes her higher.

– No, please Thomas, no. You as well, you as well.

She pleads, kicks. He lifts her further into the carriage. Jüri screams, pushes his arms through the window, reaches past Lore to Thomas.

– You must come. Brothers and sisters. You must come, too.

He curls his fingers into Thomas's jacket; Thomas raises his arms. His face contracts, shrinking away from the little boy's fury. Jüri keeps screaming until Thomas pulls himself into the carriage.

———

They sit for hours on the carriage floor. They have found a place in the passageway, by the door. Above the wheels, screaming slowly along the rails. When the train stops, no one gets out. Soldiers jump down from the roof and stand ready along the rails. They are quieter than American soldiers. Their uniforms are darker and their movements smaller, but they still keep their hands on their guns, ready to stop anyone who tries to run. Lore is glad they are there. Thomas sits opposite her and avoids her eyes.

When it gets dark, Jüri crawls into Thomas's lap and sleeps with his head against his chest. Thomas has his eyes closed and doesn't push Jüri away, but Lore knows he isn't asleep. She dozes. Liesel leans against her shoulder and Peter sleeps on the bundle between their legs.

She wakes with numb feet and shooting pains in her thighs. Thomas has shifted a little, but Jüri still lies sleeping in his lap. Lore takes off her boots and pinches at her feet, avoiding the sores and blisters. The train rocks and rattles. Her toes prickle with blood, now, but she can't ease the pains in her legs. She stands until the pins and needles subside, and then walks along the train. Over the sleeping bodies, her arms outstretched, palms on the walls to steady herself, Lore lurches along the swaying corridor, through the adjoining door into the next carriage. The window is open. Lore stops, lets her hair blow in the wind. She leans out and looks for the shrill wheels below in the dark, the rim of the window pressing against her hips. They pass flat, open fields and the cool, dark shapes of trees. The night is humid, and the air smells full and green.

There are people talking in the compartment behind her. She leans away from the window, keeping her back to them, but listening.

– If you've seen enough of those pictures, you can tell they are all in the same place.

– But the newspaper said there were lots of camps, hundreds maybe.

– I'm not saying these camps didn't exist. Every country has its own prison system, after all. I'm just saying they didn't kill people.

– And the pictures of the bodies?

– It's all a set-up. The pictures are always out of focus, aren't they? Or dark, or grainy. Anything to make them unclear. And the people in those photos are actors. The Americans have staged it all, maybe the Russians helped them, who knows.

– Who told you this?

– Fahning, for one, and Mohn. Torsten and his brother

heard it, too.

– Did they see it in the newspapers?

– Listen, I've seen the photos. The same ones keep getting shown everywhere. Different angles on the same scene. Any fool can see that.

Lore watches the young men out of the corner of her eye. They are not much older than she. Their faces are smooth and thin and their eyes gleam. They sit on their bundles by the compartment door, smoking. A stub of candle is fixed to the floor between them, flickering in the draught from the open window. One is missing an arm. His sleeve is pinned to his shoulder and flaps as he speaks. He catches Lore's eye, lifts the empty fold of cloth.

– Grenade.

He is smiling at her. Lore feels her cheeks burn, is glad of the dark.

– I've seen those pictures, too.

– There you see, everyone has seen them. And the people were all thin and lying on the ground, yes?

– I thought they were dead.

– They're actors, Americans. Or some of them are dummies, models. The ones that look the most dead.

His friend blows out the candle.

– I'm going to sleep now.

He ignores Lore. The young man with one arm winks at

her in the dark. The end of his cigarette glows between his lips and Lore's cheeks burn hot in the gloom. She closes the window and makes her way back down the corridor. She opens the carriage door and the screaming wheels fill her ears.

—

They awake when the train stops. The soldiers open the doors, knock on the windows, tell everyone to get out and wait on the platform. Thomas pulls the bundles together, lifts Jüri down off the train. It is dark in the station, a few lamps casting a dim glow around the huge building. It is filled with noise. Crying children, shouting voices, slamming carriage doors. Men stand by the walls in angry groups. They smell of unfamiliar food, murmur unfamiliar words.

The next train will leave at dawn. Jüri holds on to the hem of Thomas's jacket. Liesel lies on the bundles, one arm covering her eyes, the other her hair. Peter screams in Lore's arms. She asks the people around them if they can spare any food, but they say nothing, turn their faces away.

Peter's fists are reddish-blue. Lore rubs them, blows on his fingers. She looks up and finds no roof above them, just a jagged hole and dark sky.

—

They wait for trains, continue on foot when they don't

come. Walk on to the next town and the next, until their luck changes and they find a station with a train and a soup kitchen. Thomas holds a long discussion with a soldier while the children eat their watery meal. The soldier knocks at the window before their train moves off, hands in an egg. Thomas thanks him, shaking his hands through the open window as the train pulls away. He holds the egg out to Lore.

– For Peter. He's too thin.

—

A lift from a farmer brings them to the Elbe. They stand at the water, a day away from home. The river banks are lined with orchards, but none of the fruit is ripe. Thomas says he will get them to Hamburg. He lifts Jüri up on to his shoulders, promises to be quick, that they won't have to walk. Lore takes Liesel and Peter and queues for food at the Red Cross building. They wait for Thomas and Jüri under the broken clock. Children stand pressed into doorways, sell sour apples and tiny hard pears from sacks tied to their waists with string. They take flight at the first sight of uniform.

Lore feeds Peter the powdery bread, and then hands him to Liesel. She is nervous, can't sit still until Thomas comes back with a hungry Jüri and news of a boat.

—

Hamburg sits on the horizon, a black shape torn out of the

evening sky. It is a damp, cool dusk: misty after the heat of the day. Water slaps against the side of the boat and inside the passengers are silent, watching the city approach. Lore gathers their bundles together, uneasy at the vast harbour and jagged city rising ahead on the far banks. There are no lights in the windows, no other boats on the water, no sounds of work or play. Lore shuts her eyes, concentrates on the tasks ahead.

She pictures the tram journey to Oma's. The leafy weekend streets and white buildings; sitting still in her good shoes in the sunny-outside, cold-inside house. Can't fit the images into the dark city that crowds the shore. Thomas crouches down next to her. He looks at Lore, and in the half-dark she feels the smile, sees the crease in his cheek.

– Ready?

The sun dips below the horizon and they stand by the town hall with their bundles. No one waits with them for the trams.

– There will be a curfew here. We shouldn't be out so late.

Thomas's footsteps ring out across the empty market place.

– How far is it to walk?

Lore can't remember, says they should wait another few

minutes. Thomas frowns and Jüri takes his hand.

– I don't like the buildings.

The streets between the river and the main square were dark and hollow. Lore keeps her eyes on Peter, away from the charred walls.

– How long did it take by tram?
– Half an hour, I think.
– That's too far to walk, Lore. Not tonight.
– Where can we go?
– We'll find somewhere. An empty building.
– Not one of those, Thomas.
– No, we'll walk out of the centre, Jüri. I'll find us something.

They walk north along the edge of the lake. Fog drifts in across the water, bringing with it the smell of salt and rust. It hides the outlines of the remaining buildings, fills in the empty spaces, a dirty grey blanket over the rubble.

They lie down in the shell of a house. What was once a floor is now a roof, blocking off the night. Roosting birds shuffle in the beams above them, water seeps through the bricks. They make themselves small in the corner, hiding away from the broken walls. Thomas whispers with Lore after the children go to sleep.

– Do you know if your Oma was bombed?
– I don't think so. Maybe. I don't know.

Lore lies next to him, not touching, but close enough to know when he moves. She closes her eyes and sees stones where the house used to be. No Oma, and no Vati either.

Jüri cries in his sleep, and Lore takes his hand, holds it to her cheek. The quiet of the ruins settles around her on the cold floor. The rubble is bone and skin, and Jochen's shirt is lost among the limbs.

———

The sun shines again in the morning and burns off the mist while they pack their things together and hide them among the broken stones. Thomas fetches them soup with chunks of sausage. The meal tastes of meat and tears in the forest. Jüri cries again and Lore hides her face against her baby brother's chest. *If Jochen can die, then so can Oma.* Peter screams, and pushes at her cheeks. Thomas whispers to Jüri, Liesel sits quietly and eats, and Lore is glad they don't watch her.

– Lore will find your Oma.
– And Vati.
– It might take a little while, Liesel, so we all have to be patient.
– How long for?
– Well, a few days. Maybe. I don't know. The roads will be blocked and they may have moved house, so we'll just have to see.

Thomas looks awkward, his thin neck flushed red. Lore

smiles but he doesn't look at her. They arrange to meet at
the black church spire before sundown, and he clambers
off over the rubble to the street with Liesel and Jüri
behind him.

The city is full again and lively. People walk and talk and
don't look at the shattered, blackened buildings around
them. They wear hats and raise them in greeting. Cars
drive down the broken streets, slowing down for piles of
rubble, driving round them if they can. Smoke rises from
chimney pots on top of ruined apartment blocks. Cooking
smells drift out from the shells of buildings, though Lore
can't imagine there are kitchens inside.

She walks, shocked at the torn walls, the sudden open
spaces. Peter cries all morning, a low and terrible noise.
People look past her, avoiding eye contact. Lore searches
the faces in the queues, recognises hunger and looks away,
too.

She makes her way to the Alster and then walks along the
lake shore as far as she can, but the blocked roads force her
further and further away from the water. She loses her
bearings once she can't see the water any more, walks on
for a while, but can't tell what is street and what is not.
She asks directions and is pointed back the way she came,
but the woman isn't certain either. She asks again, and
after that the buildings become more familiar. The streets
are wide, and the trees are mostly still standing, bright new
green sprouting from the splintered limbs. *Oma must be*

alive. Lore walks up and down the same street for a while, convinced she has found the right place.

The photos are all burnt or buried now, so Lore works from memory. The garden filled with walnut trees; the drawing room with vases and heavy padded chairs. She stands in the driveways and stares. Some of the houses are damaged, others are whole, none of them match with her mind's-eye images. She walks on, finds herself back at the water again.

There are potatoes piled in the street. The man ties some into Lore's apron and shoos her away. Further on, she begs powdered milk, mixes up thick mouthfuls in her palm with water from a standpipe. Peter stares up at her face while she feeds him. The white mess dribbles over his cheeks and chin, but some of it finds his tongue. Peter stops crying and sleeps, and Lore sits with him in the late afternoon sun. She stares across the wide lake, whispers to him.

– In summer, we took the ferry home, and Vati was always there on the other side.

She remembers the boat, the jetty and the car, but her father's face is unclear. Lore tells Peter the houses are still there, assures him that Oma has to be close by. She feels certain, light-headed, and uneasy, too, watching her brother doze pale and small in her lap. The sun will set soon, and she knows she should go and find the others, but thoughts of finding her grandmother crowd her head. *If Oma is alive, she will ask after Jochen*. The children will want to know where Vati is. *Oma will want to know who Thomas is, too.*

Everything has changed. She will have to lie again. Too much has happened to explain.

It gets cool by the water, and Peter wakes. Lore gets up, holding him tight in her arms. She finds the black church spire on the skyline, and walks away from the lake. Peter blinks silently up at his sister, his eyes dark in his narrow face.

—

Lore is woken by noises in the dark. English male voice, whispering. German female, coaxing. Shifting rubble, no more talking, only breathing.

Lore knows Thomas is awake, too. She is uncomfortable under the blankets, shifts back against the cold grit of the bricks behind her. She doesn't want to hear what they are doing under the ruined walls. She counts the beams in the floor above her to block it out but her mind keeps forming pictures. Liesel turns over next to her. Lore fights the urge to cover her sister's ears.

Then there is whispering, and after that, walking.

Lore wakes again later to more noise: stifled breath and sobs. She battles her straining ears, wills herself to sleep again. The sounds are closer, muffled by blankets not rubble walls. Lore allows herself to listen to the dark around her. Thomas cries with his jacket over his face, arms wrapped over the top to keep the sound inside. He pulls in gasps of air; body a heaving shadow against the opposite wall. Lore doesn't want to see it or hear it. She would cry, only his tears have taken over. She lies awake and furious until daylight seeps through the cracks in the brickwork over her face.

In the morning Thomas builds a barrier of broken chairs and stolen wire across the open section of their shelter. He takes charcoal from the fire and makes a sign which Jüri hangs against the barricade: PRIVATE. Thomas whispers to Lore.

– I will send people away if they come again.

Lore decides to forgive him his tears.

—

– Hannelore! Hannelore Dressler!

A young woman calls from across the road. Lore holds her breath, eyes on the tramlines under her feet. The young woman waves again. She wears a large black coat and heavy boots.

– Don't you remember me? It's Wiebke. Wiebke Nadel. Oma's maid. It's not so long ago, you must remember!

Wiebke Nadel crosses the road, takes Lore's hand.

– You are so thin. Have you come back from the south

with your mother? Where is your lovely mother?

The young woman holds tight to her hand and she cries and laughs while she speaks. Lore remembers Oma's kitchen and Wiebke. Shelling peas with her on the back step. Long ago when the twins were babies and there was no Peter yet. *Does she really look like that?* Lore gazes into the smiling freckled face. *The house is dusty but Wiebke has a loyal heart.* That's what Oma always said.

– She will be so happy to see you.
– Oma?
– Yes, yes. We were in the shelter, with the neighbours.

Wiebke pulls her across the road, almost running.

– The bombs got the house, but not the firestorm. Come on. Your Oma is at home. She will be so happy.

The black iron gates are the same, the dark evergreen hedges, too, but the house is utterly changed. The upper stories are missing, and most of the ground floor. A single chimney stack juts up at the back, tiles still clinging to the fireplace at its base. The remaining windows are shattered and the walls blackened, but Lore recognises the hallway. The sun comes in where it couldn't reach before, lighting the patterns in the cracked tiling, the wide, dark wood floor.

Wiebke makes Lore stand outside the door that was once inside and is now weather-worn. She sings as she goes in, calls to Oma. An old woman's voice answers, quiet at first and then shrill. Lore pulls the wrinkles out of her stockings and Oma stands in the doorway, fingers outstretched. She touches Lore's hair.

– Hannelore, child. Where have you come from?
– From Bavaria, Oma.
– Where is my Asta? Hannelore? Where is your Mutti?

There is only one chair in the room but they insist that Lore sits down. Clothes are hung from nails in the wall. There is a stove, some bedding and an empty cupboard. Their voices are crammed into the small interior. Lore can't work out which room this used to be before the bombs. Wiebke closes the door and pulls the curtain away from the window for some air. She gives Lore bread, with slices of apple laid on top.

– I got fruit today. You must have some.

All their food sits in a small crate on the floor. They are silent while Lore eats. The apple is sweet and sharp, stinging at her gums, the raw edges of her tongue. Oma says she has grown into a young woman. Wiebke takes a brush from the cupboard and loosens out Lore's plaits. Her hair crackles with static and stands out around her head. Lore feels its light touch against her cheeks, the lazy warmth of being cared for. Wiebke's fingers stroke her scalp, dividing the hair into sections. Oma stands by the open window.

– Mutti is with the Americans, isn't she, child?

Lore nods.

– I knew it. As soon as I saw you, I knew it.

Wiebke's fingers feel strong and sure in Lore's hair.

– And Vati? Do they have him as well?
– I don't know.
– Do you have Mutti's address?
– No, Omi.
– So she doesn't know you are here now?
– No, but she told us to come.

They are quiet for a while. Wiebke's fingers brush against Lore's neck as she plaits. Lore hears her Grandmother's breathing, soft and hoarse, smells the late summer sun on the stones outside, the musty damp of the cool walls inside. Her throat is too thick to speak. *There is too much to tell.*

Oma steps across the room, pulls Lore to her feet and puts her arms around her. Lore shuffles to steady herself, catches the seat with her knees, chair-legs scraping loud against the bare floor. She puts her hands on the old woman's back, feels the spine beneath her blouse.

– You mustn't feel ashamed. You mustn't feel ashamed of them.

Her grip is angry. Lore breathes hard against the tight circle of her arms. Oma pushes her away, holds her at arm's length. The old woman's hair is dusty, the same colour as her skin. Her eyes are grey and watery, fixed on Lore's face. Lore feels her neck flush, itchy and hot. Wiebke sits down on the chair next to them with her brushes.

– We can find them. The Red Cross will have their addresses. They will come back, Mutti and Vati. They are only away for a while.

Lore can't look into Oma's face. She looks at her cheeks instead, the soft folds of skin on her neck. The old voice crackles as she speaks.

– It is all over now. Finished.

Sweat prickles in Lore's armpits. Oma's fingers hold her fast, pressing into her shoulders.

– Some of them went too far, child, but don't believe it was all bad.

—

Lore scrubs at Jüri's face and fingers, ties the red rag neatly around Liesel's head.

– Oma is coming to fetch us, so we have to get ready.
– Is Vati coming?
– Vati isn't there.

Lore tries to make it sound as normal as possible, as if it was what they were expecting all along. She looks round to see if Thomas is watching, but he has his back to them, packing away their things. Jüri's eyes are blank. Liesel cries, and then she screams. Thumping Lore's arms with her fists.

– You lied!

Her sister's punches numb Lore's arms, but she doesn't defend herself. Lets Liesel cry. Says nothing: can think of nothing to say. She ties her plaits into place with neat strips of rag. She rubs her boots clean and tears new laces off the edge of Peter's nappy. She inspects the silent Jüri and raging Liesel, decides to wash their shirts, at least rinse out the worst of the dirt before Oma arrives.

Thomas fetches water for Lore, sits with her while she works at the children's clothes.

– I didn't tell Oma about you.
– No. Yes, that's good.
– I don't mean about the prison. I mean I didn't say anything. She doesn't know you are with us.
– Yes, I know.
– I didn't know what she would say. I couldn't do it. Not yet.
– No, it's good. I have told the children I'm a secret brother. For now.
– Yes.
– You will tell her about Jochen, and that will be enough.

Thomas's fingertips rest against the sides of the bucket. Lore waits, but he doesn't touch her.

—

Wiebke climbs across the rubble to fetch them for Oma. Lore watches her count the children.

– Jochen isn't here.

Jüri stands between the broken walls. He doesn't remember Wiebke.

– Where is Jochen?
– He is dead, in Russia.

Wiebke looks at Lore.

– The Russian zone. They shot him at the border.

No other words will come.

Wiebke clambers back ahead of them. She whispers to Oma out on the street while Lore tidies the children, stands them in line, straightening their still-damp clothes. Oma stares at them, lays a hand on each head in turn. Lore waits for the questions, wonders if Thomas is hiding nearby. Watching from the ruins, seeing the thoughts swarm in her head. The things to tell and not tell, the struggle to explain. Lore wonders if Thomas is surprised, too, when Oma asks nothing about Jochen. She thinks he might see Oma nod at her from where he is hiding. But knows he will be too far away to see the old woman's clouded eyes. The high spots of colour in the cheek which Oma presents for a kiss.

—

Liesel cries again when they get to Oma's, says that Lore had promised her Vati would be there. Oma is surprised, irritable at first, frowning as she unpacks their tatty belongings. After she has folded the blankets and closed the cupboard door, she explains gently to Liesel and Jüri that Vati is probably with the Americans. Liesel stops crying, wipes her pale cheeks, whispers:

– Is he being punished now?

Oma blinks at her granddaughter and they all stand in silence while Wiebke slices a loaf for them to eat.

—

The first night they sleep with Oma and Wiebke in one room. Curtains are hung from hooks in the ceiling, dividing the small space into even smaller sections. Oma and Wiebke have a bed each, with a fabric wall between. Wiebke insists that Lore and Liesel take her bed, and she makes up a mattress for Jüri next to it on the floor. Wiebke lies on their blankets and makes a bed for Peter in an old drawer. Oma says goodnight to them all, and then draws the heavy curtain around her bed.

Lore stares at the dark folds, tries to hear if her Oma is crying. About Jochen, Mutti, Vati. No noise penetrates the divide. *We are home.* Lore tries to whisper to Liesel, but her sister lies with her back to her, refuses to respond.

With Oma. Lore repeats the words to herself. The bed is soft and hot, the room is quiet. Mutti is with the Americans, and maybe Vati too. Thomas is hidden in the ruins and Jochen is dead. Lore cries, can't stop herself, stuffs the sheet into her mouth. Jüri slips over to her in the dark. He strokes her hair clumsily and dries her eyes with his sleeve.

– I knew Vati wouldn't be here, Lore.
– How?
– Thomas told me.
– Oh. Why didn't you say anything?

Jüri shrugs.

– He told me that men get put in prison after wars. There are lots of fathers in prison now, Lore. I think it's really not so bad.

Lore puts her arms around her little brother and he climbs into the bed next to her.

– Is Thomas alone now?
– I think so, Jüri. Probably.
– Will he be sad?
– I don't know. Maybe. When did he tell you about the fathers?
– Ages ago. Can't remember. Thomas said we should come and find him by the church spire again. Will we do that?
– Yes, of course.

– Tomorrow?

Lore can't remember what she told Thomas about Vati, if she told him anything at all. She thinks of all the fathers in prison, repeats to herself *it's really not so bad*, can't make herself believe it.

Still, she is glad to have Jüri warm in the bed with her. Glad that he and Liesel said nothing to Oma about Thomas, too. One lie left intact, one secret brother kept. She kisses his head.

– You were very good today.

———

Wiebke sits in the hospital corridor with Lore while Peter is weighed and measured.

– Your Oma is a proud woman. It's all very different for her now. She has nothing left. Only me.

She laughs. Wiebke has freckles and fine lines around her eyes. Her hand rests cool and soft on top of Lore's.

– She will get extra ration cards for you, now. You will have food every day, more for Peter, and some clothes, too. She will take care of it.

Lore leans gently against Wiebke's shoulder, feels the light hum of her voice through her skin.

– And she will get used to having you all back. Your Mutti stopped writing, even before the end. Oma was very worried. I know she was.

Lore fills her head with the touch of Wiebke's hand and her calm lasts into the evening.

—

Jüri is excited and leads the way. They clamber across the mountains of rubble. Lore lifts Peter on to her back and he holds tight around her neck while her boots slide over wallpapered chunks of house. They climb down into a small courtyard. The paving is cracked and sunken in places, but it's sunny and colourful. Weeds flower yellow and purple through the broken slabs and along the tops of the walls.

A door hangs loose on its hinges at the far edge of the courtyard. Jüri pulls it open and leads Lore down into the cool dark. Thomas is inside. He lights a candle and smiles. His thin face creases and his tongue shows pink through the gaps in his teeth. Jüri jumps on the cellar steps.

– He says he will stay here. Didn't you? You said that?

Thomas is looking at Lore, still smiling. Her fingers tingle.

– I cleared it out. I can build a stove and then it will be warm and I can cook.
– He'll be here and we can visit him.

Jüri races round the courtyard shouting while Thomas collects floorboards and window frames in the rubble. He builds a fire outside and Lore cooks potatoes, warming bricks in the embers for Thomas. Something to ward off the chill of the cellar night when she and Jüri and Peter have gone back to Liesel and Oma and Wiebke, and Thomas is alone.

—

What remains of Oma's house is even smaller than the room at the farm. The houses across the street are not so badly damaged, and Oma finds a room for her grand-children to sleep in at her neighbours, the Meyers, who remember Lore and Liesel as small children, and who have apple trees in their garden which leads down almost to the lake.

Oma establishes their daily routine. Each evening, they sit down and eat with her and Wiebke, and then she walks them across the road to sleep. In the morning she fetches them again for breakfast, exchanging pleasantries with the Meyers as Lore hurries her brother and sister down the stairs. Wiebke spreads out the tablecloth and lays cutlery for every meal. She divides the food out carefully under Oma's direction and they eat together three times a day. Oma cuts up her bread with knife and fork, tells the children to chew slowly, but the food is always gone too soon, and they always leave the table hungry.

Summer is fading, but the weather is still fine. Liesel stays angry with Lore. She spends her days helping Wiebke, hanging out the washing in the overgrown garden, cleaning, going out with her for the long hours spent queuing at the shops. Oma sits at the table by the window and writes letters. Spends whole mornings away at the Red Cross, and afternoons resting behind the curtain around her bed.

Lore takes care of Peter, and Jüri tags along behind. He whispers to himself, kicking at stones in the road, and Lore blocks her ears. Thinks he is talking to Jochen, doesn't want to hear. Whenever they can, they go to the cellar. Quick visits to their secret brother, in the quiet time while Oma sleeps and Wiebke sits with Liesel, knitting and mending the holes in their clothes.

Thomas is always pleased to see them, smiling quietly. Lore thinks he waits for them. Listening out for their sliding footfalls on the rubble around his cellar home, lonely on the days they don't come. She is shocked each time at how thin he is. The gaps in his teeth, the rags bound around his feet. Between visits she remembers him differently, and it always takes her time to adjust to his grubby reality, his prominent bones. She stares at him; his clothes, his skin, and even his eyelashes powdered with dust from the crumbling cellar walls.

—

Herr Meyer fiddles with the camera. Old fingers uneasy with the settings, old eyes mistrustful of the light. He shuffles the children into place by the gate, in front of the hedge, to where the broken house is hidden from view.

– We should have started earlier. Before lunch. I can't

promise you anything now. It could really be a waste of film and Herr Paulsen will charge us too much for the printing anyway. We should wait until tomorrow.

The photo is for Mutti. Oma knows which camp she is in now, can send it to her. It will help her, she says. Oma has borrowed clothes for them to wear in the picture. Peter keeps pulling the sailor's cap from his head, but Liesel is pleased with the blue silk scarf covering her spiky hair.

Oma has written a letter to Mutti, from all of them. They have signed their names at the bottom, without reading it. Lore doesn't want to know what it says. She is glad Oma didn't make her write it. She helps Wiebke get the children ready. It is cold. Jüri rubs his hands and knees, Liesel lets her teeth chatter.

Herr Meyer brings the photo back towards evening. A serious large-eyed group standing on cracked paving stones. Lore tall, Liesel next, then Jüri, and last of all Peter, standing right at the front holding on to Jüri's leg. The shoes on Liesel's feet are too big, and Jüri's ears jut out from his narrow head. Lore's parting is crooked despite Wiebke's best efforts, and her eyes are half-closed. All of them thin. Cheek and wrist bones prominent, knees large and borrowed clothes limp against their frames. Lore feels she is looking at strangers, or people she knew long ago.

The picture is stuffed into the envelope with the letter. Lore feels her stomach shrink while Oma writes the address. Mutti will see that Jochen is gone.

—

They wait for news and the days grow cooler. Peter cries less, has started to smile again, and his face fills out a little. He talks to Lore in half-words, standing next to her, determined to walk. Instead of carrying him, Lore reaches for his hand, but it doesn't replace the reassuring weight in her arms. She agrees with Thomas, the time is not yet right: Jüri and Liesel stick to the bargain, their secret brother remains a secret. Still Lore risks going to the cellar more often.

She watches Jüri with Thomas while she plays with Peter in the autumn sun. He follows Thomas around the courtyard, gathering up the driftwood that Thomas pulls from the lake and lays out to dry. Thomas is quiet and Jüri whispers incessantly, laughs loud and long in the still afternoon air. Lore sees Thomas take Jüri's hand, and sees Jüri's palm form a fist, gripped tight to Thomas's index finger.

Wiebke's boyfriend sneaks a radio out of his barracks. She brings it round in the evening to show Lore and they listen to the jazz together. Wiebke teaches Lore to dance the way they do in the American films her Scottish soldier takes her to see. When Lore cries, Wiebke puts her arms around her and sways her gently to the music. She tells her that Mutti will come home and everything will change. Lore enjoys the soft embrace, the arms shielding her face. Doesn't tell Wiebke that it's Thomas she misses.

—

A letter arrives at Oma's, addressed to Lore. An envelope with her name in Mutti's hand. She stands at the window and reads the brief words.

Mutti says that Vati is safe, she will send an address as soon as she has can. She has sent word to him, through the Americans, and he knows they are at home in Hamburg. Lore and the children should send letters too, because he may be away for a long time. The schools will start again soon. They should work hard and think of tomorrow and all that it will bring. Mutti asks Lore to kiss Jüri and Liesel from her and to make sure Peter has enough to eat. Lore reads the letter aloud to Oma, looks again at the inky loops which form her name. The letter says nothing about the camp, the bed Mutti sleeps in, the food she eats, and what she sees from the window. And it doesn't say anything about Jochen.

She reads the letter to the children. They ask to hear it again, and Jüri demands his kisses from her, laughing, Liesel wants to know about Vati. Again and again she asks Oma when they will have an address. They get into bed together and chatter in their rented room. Lore doesn't speak about Jochen, or Thomas, and neither do Liesel or Jüri.

—

It is a bright autumn morning and the broken shadows fall

across the pavement and touch the street. Oma has taken Liesel to queue for shoes; Wiebke has taken Jüri to fetch coals. Lore has the whole morning free to visit Thomas. She has saved a few spoons of sugar to take to him, feeds Peter in pinches as they go. Licking her fingers clean of the grains he misses, tiny bursts of sweet on her tongue. Peter refuses to be carried. He sways solemnly as he walks, steadying himself against Lore's legs, skirt gripped tight in one fist. They make their way along the tram lines in the sun. In the middle of the road, far from the leaning walls of bombed-out buildings.

Lore hears a jangling behind her, a metallic whirr. She turns to see a tram on its way up the rise of the road towards her. It is crowded with people, cheerily waving her off the track. She bends down and takes Peter in her arms, starts trotting at the side of the road, picking up speed as the tram draws alongside. The passengers laugh and wave and Peter waves back. They hold out their arms to Lore and lift her off the road. Her legs dangle in mid-air and she grips Peter tight, and then she is smiling and breathless among the happy faces on board. Pushed into their backs and chests and arms, rocking with the motion of the tram.

A young man makes room for her at the back, and she sits down with Peter next to two young women. One is blonde, the other has dark hair. Their coats are patched and their shoes are cracked and old, but they wear lipstick, and sit sideways with their legs neatly crossed. Lore pushes her hair behind her ears, pulls the loose threads from her skirt.

The young women share a newspaper. They murmur and point, shake their heads as they read. The dark-haired woman sees Lore watching, holds the paper so she can see, smiling encouragement. The tram jolts and bumps and Peter stands on her lap, chattering in her ear. Lore's eyes scan the text, find the same words over and over in the columns of newsprint: prison camps and work camps, crimes and trials. The woman turns the page and there are pictures. Dark and blotchy on the thin paper, and familiar, too. Skeleton people. Wire fences and gaunt faces and piles of bones and shoes and spectacles.

– Those are the American actors, aren't they?

Lore points at the photos. The dark-haired woman laughs. The blonde-haired woman says it's not funny.

– No, I know it isn't. They're Jews.

Lore flushes. The dark-haired woman is angry.

– Look at them. They're not acting, they're dead.

She turns the page. Lore sees familiar black collars with bright lightning flashes. Pictures of men in uniform. Clear-eyed portraits: SS, SA, Gestapo. The dark-haired woman points.

– They killed them. With gas and guns.
– Heide! She's just a child.

– Well, she can read it for herself, then.

Lore watches their perfect red lips. Her heart lurching, the tram jolting, rolling and coming finally to a stop. The dark-haired woman stands up, holds the paper out for Lore. Her blonde friend stands up, too.

– Please don't show her any more. It's too much.
– The Americans say they should learn about it in school. And the British want to teach democracy.
– Oh please, enough political talk.

The blonde woman turns to Lore.

– Listen, they were bad men and they are in prison now, where bad men belong. And that's all.

The young women get off. Lore looks round at the other passengers, still crowded together and chattering. No one looks at her and the tram rolls on. She shifts to the end of the bench with the newspaper, sits Peter down next to her by the window. Lore turns the pages quickly past the skeleton people to the portraits. She looks closely at the clothes, the eyes, noses and jawlines. Some wear Vati's uniform, none have Vati's face.

—

– Have you seen the pictures, Thomas?
– What pictures?

Thomas blinks in the sunlight outside his cellar door.

– The skeleton people. The dead ones.
– Oh.

Lore's stomach feels twisted out of shape. She stands in the cellar doorway, holding Peter who strains against her arms, reaching down to her apron pocket and the small knotted handkerchief of sugar. Thomas says nothing, bony hand shielding his eyes from the sun.

– They have started punishing them. The ones who killed them.

Lore's chest pulls tight around her heart. Thomas nods, rubs at his forehead, the pale skin stretched over the bone.

– You told Liesel they would.
– I know. It's started now?
– Yes. I saw it in the newspaper.

His eyes are paler than usual. Thomas turns away. He walks down the steps into the cellar gloom, one arm reaching forward as if to steady himself, fingertips brushing against the crumbling wall. Mortar dust rattles to the floor.

– Thomas?

Lore follows him cautiously down into the cool dark, blind after the blue sky and midday glare outside.

– The woman on the tram said they were real people.
– Yes.
– They were Jews. That's what she told me.

Lore's eyes are adjusting, and she can see Thomas now. He has his back to her, and his shoulders are set square like a wall, but she has to ask.

– Thomas? You remember you told Jüri about all the fathers who are in prison now?
– What?

Thomas turns slightly to face her, and Lore sees his lips drawn back from his remaining teeth.

– What do you want from me?

Her stomach folds in on itself. His breath fills the room.

———

Lore doesn't go to the cellar for a week, waves Jüri off down the road alone in the afternoons. He stares at her reproachfully at mealtimes, whispers to her in the dark of the bedroom. Says that Thomas asks after her, wants to know why she doesn't come.

Lore lies awake while the children sleep, keeps the lamp lit by her bed. She fights against her closing lids, afraid of the pictures which sit behind her eyes, the threads which knot themselves together in the dark.

She dozes in the daylight. On trams with Peter, in the queues with Liesel and Wiebke, sitting at the table by the window with her Oma.

Mutti and Vati and Thomas circle her thoughts, are

pushed away, and then return.

—

It is late afternoon and Jüri has not come home. Oma is awake and has asked after him twice already, worried that he may be playing in the ruins.

– They are dangerous, Hannelore. I have told him to keep away from them.

Lore goes to the end of the road to look out for her brother. Waits twenty minutes, half an hour, but still there is no sign. She looks back to the house, sees Oma standing in her coat, watching by the iron gate at the end of the drive. Lore waves, uneasy. Shouts to her that she shouldn't worry; that she will go and look for him; that she is sure she won't be long.

Lore watches from the tram, walks fast along the streets. She doesn't want to see Thomas, wants only to find Jüri and then go quickly home. She calls for her brother, but there is no reply, and she draws ever closer to the cellar. She waits at the corner, but it is already so late. She clambers across the rubble, heart full of misgiving, head full of the hate in Thomas's face. But when she slides down into the courtyard, Jüri is crouching in the cellar doorway alone.

The stove is overturned, loose bricks have been torn from the walls, and the door hangs off its hinges. Jüri is pale and breathless, his eyes ringed dark like bruises. Lore sits down next to him and he presses his fingers into her skin.

– What happened?
– Thomas has gone.
– Where has he gone?
– I don't know.
– What happened?
– We went out to get wood. He told me to wait at the corner by the station and said he would get some soup, and I waited but he didn't come back.
– How long did you wait?
– Two hours.
– Maybe he had to queue?
– But he broke the door, Lore. He did this. I know he did.
– Did you have a fight, Jüri? Did he hit you?
– No. He's gone away. He was looking for his things. But I hid them.
– What things?
– He said you knew, Lore. He told me you knew. I said you would never tell, but he didn't believe me because you didn't come any more and now he's gone away.

Jüri wails, holding on to Lore's arm. His face is wet with mucus and tears. He speaks and she can't understand him.

– You must never tell. Not even Liesel. Or even Peter. Not ever.
– Jüri.
– Promise? Please, promise you won't tell.
– What did you hide?

Lore helps him lift the paving slab. Woodlice curl up and run for cover in the rubble and Thomas's wallet sits snug in a hole at the base of the wall. Small and brown, the leather cracked and worn.

– I only did it so he wouldn't go. I didn't want him to be angry. Will he be angry with me, Lore?

Jüri is still crying. Lore pulls the wallet out of its hiding place and opens it with stiff, clumsy fingers, the contents dropping to the floor. At her feet lies a scrap of cloth with a yellow star sewn to one side. Underneath that is another piece of the same cloth, also torn, also fraying, and with a familiar set of numbers running across its grubby stripes. Still inside the wallet is a thin piece of grey card, folded over, and inside that is a piece of paper, with a photo, and a large black stamp. Jüri watches as Lore holds the picture up to the light.

– You didn't know?
– What?
– It's not him.

The photo on the card is of a man with dark hair and sunken eyes. Smudged and worn and crumpled. Lore thinks it could be Thomas, at a glance. Even when she looks closer she sees his blunt cheek, the run of his jaw. She spreads the papers and the cloth out carefully on the broken ground. Her wrists feel weak; the paper is brittle. The face on the photo has a soft mouth. Perhaps it isn't Thomas, perhaps Jüri is right.

– He took it. He had to have it. For when the Americans came to let everyone out.

– Thomas stole these things?

– You mustn't tell, Lore. He said it didn't matter. The man was a Jew, you see. He was dead already.

Lore hasn't stopped looking into the face. The gaunt features, the fine lips parted, eyes cast downwards, lids almost closed. *Dead already*. Lore studies the paper, but the name has disappeared in a crease, lost in the nervous folding and refolding.

– Thomas said the Americans like Jews, so he used these things to pretend.

– He told you this?

– He said you knew.

Jüri crouches, with his bony knees pulled up against his chest, watching for Lore's reaction. *What do you want from me?* Her stomach coils itself tight again, the saliva turns sour on her tongue. She spits, sits with her head between her knees, and Jüri shivers next to her.

– Thomas said that people are angry now, so it is safer to be a different person. I said he could be in our family and then no one would know it was him.

Jüri's eyes are red and his jaw pulled taut. Lore can't listen to him any more.

– We will burn it.

– He said he is my brother, Lore.

– I know that. I know. We will burn it and then we will go home.

Lore builds a fire in the rubble with bits of wood from the broken stove. She lays the dead man's belongings on top, the wallet and the photo, the crease where his name was and the last scraps of his clothes. The flames lick around the edges of the cloth and the striped weave blackens first, then glows. The paper sits untouched on top for a long time, but at last begins to curl. The charred edges fold over the thin face in the photo, and when they fall away again the dead man is gone.

The courtyard grows dark around the small fire. Jüri is still shivering, but Lore sweats in its warmth, sits away from it, pressed into a gap in the wall. *What do you want from me?* She tries to unravel Thomas and prisons and skeleton people; lies and photographs; Jews and graves; tattoos and newspapers and things not being as bad as people say. In the middle of it all are Mutti and Vati and the badges in the bushes and the ashes in the stove and the sick feeling that Thomas was both right and wrong, good and bad; both at the same time.

Lore pulls on her boots as soon as the sun shows over the trees in the Meyers' garden. Jüri has been asleep for an hour or two, eyes swollen shut with tears. Liesel sits up, but Lore tells her it is still too early for breakfast, she will come back and wake them when it is time. Her breath shows in the Meyers' hallway, and she leaves footprints behind in the frost on Oma's drive. Wiebke answers the door with sleep in her eyes and makes some bitter acorn coffee, which Lore drinks while Oma dresses. It is still not yet light when Grandmother and Granddaughter walk down to the lake.

They stand at the pier, crunching the frozen sand under their shoes.

– Why are Mutti and Vati in prison, Oma?
– They did nothing wrong.

The answer comes neither quickly nor slowly, betraying nothing. Lore searches Oma's eyes, grey and calm. No anger, no question about last night. Back long after dark, covered in rubble dust and stinking of smoke. Lore's secret presses against her lips, but Oma lets the moment pass in silence.

– I told you before. Hannelore? I said it, and you must remember it.

Oma takes Lore's hand and her glove is smooth to the touch, slipping across her skin. The secret belongs to Jüri, too. And Thomas.

– Everything has changed, Lore. But your father is still a good man.

———

The days get cold.

Liesel learns English words from the soldiers: *butterscotch*, *chocolate*, and best of all *humbug*, which makes her laugh because it sounds just like Hamburg.

Jüri finds friends after a while. Boys his own age, and though Oma forbids it, he plays shouting war games with them in the wreckage. Lore watches him run out from the cover of the ruins, across the open street. He falls and lies still. Counting off the seconds on the fingers of one hand.

Lore goes back to the cellar once. Looks for traces in the ashes and upturned boxes. She finds nothing, only the blankets in the corner where Thomas lay at night. Lore walks down the road, fills the bucket from the standpipe, and washes out his bedclothes in the courtyard. She cries, head full of badges and photos, feeling sick and alone.

A tram passes, the noise recedes and the ruins are quiet again. Lore closes her eyes, arms plunged deep into the bucket, forehead pressed against the cool metal rim. She empties the cold water across the flagstones, takes rubble from the mountain around her and buries the wet blankets under the stones.

Mutti sends an address for Vati, and a photo of herself, smiling, sitting outside somewhere on a bench. Her hands are puffy, folded in her lap. Her face round, her hair cut short and her clothes unfamiliar. Lore props the picture up against the wall in their small bedroom, and Jüri and Liesel crowd round to look at their mother, quietly taking her in.

– She will come to the British camp next year.
– Can we visit her then?
– Maybe. I think so.
– Will she look like that?
– Of course she will.
– What does Vati look like, Lore?
– You don't remember?

Jüri shakes his head and yawns. Lore doesn't allow herself to think for long.

– He is about this tall and his hair is the same colour as yours.
– But my hair changes colour. Blond in the summer.
– And Vati's does, too. Dark in the winter, just like you.

Jüri asks questions at first, but soon falls asleep. Liesel listens to Lore and smiles at her for the first time in weeks. Lore holds her breathing steady, heart beating on and on. She describes a man as she undresses: one to fit with the new plump happy Mutti, to replace the one who has been burnt and buried and bombed.

The face watching her from the fire is Thomas. It folds away into black ash curtains and is gone.

———

It is winter now and more than half a year since the end of the war. Lore's birthday arrives; five weeks since Thomas left; two months since Mutti's first letter; over four months since Jochen died.

Jüri and Peter give her a hair ribbon each, which Lore knows Frau Meyer has cut from her curtains. Liesel is to bake a cake with Wiebke's help, has been saving up her sugar ration for weeks. Oma promises Lore a pair of shoes, as soon as some are available, and has bought her tickets for the ferry as a treat.

– One for you and one for Jüri, schatz. Peter can go for free.

Oma walks with them to the tram stop and waves them off into town. They go past the stop for the cellar, and Lore watches Jüri but he does not look round. They take the tram all the way to the Hauptbahnhof, and then weave their way down through the city on foot. The sky is ash grey, flat and low. The cold reaches in through their clothes. Lore leads her brothers along the still canals in the centre, and then they turn and head for the lake. Doubling back where the bridges are down, taking shortcuts made possible by bombs.

– There were buildings here before, Jüri. Between the canal and the lake, it was all buildings. See? You can still see how all the rubble is in squares.
– When?
– Before the bombs.
– How old were you then?
– The same age as you.
– How old was I then?
– The same age as Peter.

The wind blows bitter across the lake and Lore wraps Peter into her coat. They turn their backs on the dark water and wait at the Jungfernstieg for the ferry to take them home. The centre lies flat before them. Blackened and broken and crawling with life. Everything changing, the old being buried by the new again. Lore sits Peter down on the bench and points across the debris for Jüri.

– They are going to build houses there. On top of where the rubble is now.
– Why?
– So people can live in them, silly. People can't live in ruins for the rest of their lives.
– Will we live in a new house?
– Yes. We will.
– With Mutti.
– Yes, and Vati.
– Vati's in a prison.
– Yes, but we will live together again when he comes home.

They board the ferry and sit towards the back, out of the wind which tugs at the tarpaulin below the rail.

– Where is Thomas now, Lore?
– I don't know.

Lore watches the tarpaulin, and the ropes snapping against the taut cloth.

– Does he think about us?

– I don't know.

– How old will I be when we live in our new house?

Lore shrugs, her brother's questions grate. She can see other passengers in front of them, sheltering from the wind, but beyond them is the empty foredeck.

– As old as you are today?

– I don't know how long it will take, Jüri.

Lore shifts forward and the wind bites at her face. The air is cold on her teeth as she speaks, tugs at her hair.

– Will you be as old as Thomas then?

– No, because he will always be older than me, silly.

Jüri laughs and Lore stands up. Jüri gets up too, but she tells him to sit with Peter. She steps out into the wind. The air rushes across the deck and hurls itself at her legs, and Lore's skin shrinks back from her clothes. She takes hold of the rail to steady herself. The water is far below her and dark, churning slowly under the ferry. Lore lifts her head up away from it, keeps her face high in the icy blast of the wind, feels the air currents pull and twist around her limbs.

She moves along the rail beyond the cabin, away from Jüri's questions and from Peter and away from the other passengers, until she is out at the front of the ferry and hidden from view.

Alone now, she takes the full force of the wind. Lifting

first one hand and then the other from the railing, standing firm, facing out to the shore.

Lore looks forward to the silence at Oma's, to Wiebke's smiles, and Liesel's cake. She looks forward to when there will be no more ruins, only new houses, and she won't remember any more how it was before.

She stands on her own and the wind claws her skin, tears through her clothes. Lore doesn't look down at the water, faces the far shore ahead. She unbuttons her coat and lets the wind rip it open, pounding in her ears. She stretches her mouth wide, lets the winter rush down past her lungs and fill her with its bitter chill.

Lore hears and tastes and feels only air. Her eyes are closed, seeing nothing, streaming brittle tears.

MICHA

Home, Autumn 1997

It's a long walk across the car park to his grandmother's place and the young man's feet get wet. The high-rise stands white in the green of landscaped lawns. When the sun shines, residents walk slowly in pairs along the yellow gravel paths, and his Oma sits out on her balcony, twelve storeys high. On days like those, the young man will stop on the grass and, after counting eight windows down and three across, he will wave and wait for the tiny speck of movement in reply. Today it rains and the young man walks alone.

This is Michael. His Oma's name is Kaethe, and she was married to Askan.

Oma Kaethe. Opa Askan.

The nurse at reception smiles in recognition as he signs himself in. His glasses mist over in the warmth of the lobby and water slips from his hair down his neck as he waits for the lift to arrive.

Just lately, Michael has taken to mapping his family. In queues, on trains, in idle moments, he will lay them out in his head; layers of time and geography; a more-or-less neat web of dates and connections to work over, to fill out the corners of the day.

Oma Kaethe and Opa Askan. Married, Kiel, 1938. Two children. Mutti, Karin, Kiel. 1941. And later Onkel Bernd. In

Hannover, after the war. After Opa came home.

Oma is at her door when Michael steps out of the lift. She waves at him from the far end of the corridor. I saw you coming, she calls. Walking in the rain. He takes his glasses off and Oma polishes them on her apron. She finds a towel for his hair and another for his feet. His shoes are left by the door, and his socks are hung on the heater.

Michael is tall and Oma Kaethe gets smaller all the time: the top of her head is well below his shoulder now. Filling the cream jug, arranging the cakes on to plates, Michael absorbs the regular Sunday shock of his Oma getting older. *Born 1917; fifty years before me; twenty-four before Mutti, her daughter. Five years after Opa.* Today Oma's long fingers shake as she talks. Michael squeezes them tight in his rain-cooled hands, and his grandmother smiles.

Through the week, Michael cuts articles out of the paper for his Oma; saves them up for his visits. He lays them out on the table covered by the red wax cloth that still smells of Oma's old house. His grandmother follows the printed lines with her quivering fingers while Michael eats; pastries with glazed fruits and marzipan stollen although Christmas is still weeks away. In front of Michael, all along the wall, are Oma's uncles who died when she was a girl. Dark oil paintings of boys in uniform. *Mutti's great uncles. My great-great uncles. Im Krieg gefallen; fallen in war. Not Opa's war; the one before.*

Rain streaks the windows, and Michael walks through the

small flat, turning on the lamps. If it were a clear day, Oma would take him out on the balcony now, to enjoy the city view. *Stadtwald, Wolkenkratzer und Main.* I can see forever from my bird's nest, she would tell him. And Michael would look out over the forest and the river to the skyscrapers and agree.

Instead they play a long game of cards, which Oma wins, and then the afternoon is over. Oma pockets her keys and keeps Michael company down in the lift. They smile at each other as their ears pop. We weren't designed to live so high, Oma tells him. But think of all the things we wouldn't see, Michael replies, and then she laughs.

Tonstraße; Wiener Straße; Steinweg; Kirchenweg; Kastanienalle. Michael lists his Oma's addresses as he walks away. *Kiel, Kiel, Hannover, here, here. The middle three with Opa; the first and the last without.*

He turns when he is halfway across the car park, and his grandmother waves from the door. She is still watching as he climbs into his mother's car. He winds down the window and waves as he drives away.

When Michael gets home, Mina is standing in the open doorway, waiting for him as he climbs the stairs. He walks slowly up the last flight, taking her in. They smile at each other.

– I saw you coming.

Her breath smells of alcohol. Michael knows that his

smells of cigarettes.

– We've opened some wine.
– *We?*
– Luise. Me and Luise.

My sister; a doctor, three years older, only granddaughter. Luise shouts from the kitchen while he takes off his coat.

– Mina tells me you took Mutti and Vati out to lunch last week, Micha, which I think sounds very nice. But you know, I am just wondering how it is you forgot to invite me?

She is laughing, but Michael knows she is hurt. And not really expecting an answer, either; just wanting to let him know. He shrugs at her, smiles. *Shit.* Mina pours him some wine, walks back over to Luise. They are sitting on the windowsill by the heater, the glass steamed up against the evening sky. It is almost dark, but they haven't turned on the lights. Michael stands by the fridge, on the other side of the room.

– *How are you, anyway, Luise?*
– I'm fine, thank-you, Michael. And you?
– *Not bad. Good.*
– How's school? Any staff-room gossip?
– *Oh, no, God. Just the usual little power struggles in the mid-morning break.*
– Well, Herr Lehner, I'm starving and Mina said it's your turn to cook.

Luise laughs again, and Mina smiles at Michael across the room.

– I did not. I only said we should wait until you come home.

She raises her glass to him in a toast. Luise, too, with a smile that Micha finds impossible to read. *Luise, Luise, Luise. Jesus.*

– *You want to stay for dinner, then?*
– Ouch! Mina? Is he as nasty with you?
– Enough now, let's cook.

Mina walks across the kitchen, opens the fridge and the light spills out over the kitchen floor. The label is sticking out from her collar, and Micha reaches out and tucks it away.

– *I think I'll go up to Mutti and Vati's, take the car back. I'll not be long.*

Luise stands up and pours herself more wine.

– You've got Mutti's car? Have you been smoking in Mutti's car again? I can smell it on your clothes from here, Micha. She never tells you off for it, but she hates it, you know that.

Michael doesn't answer his sister, he just smiles and nods. Mina winks at him, squats down on the floor next to him, rests a hand on his calf.

– Could you buy bread? We need some bread.

Michael empties the ashtray and drives for the first few minutes with the windows open. *Mutti and Vati, Karin and Paul. Two children, no grandchildren, married thirty-three years, at home in the suburbs. Twelve kilometres; half an hour if I take the train; no more than twenty minutes by car.* It is early evening, the traffic in town is light and the autobahn clear. *Fifteen.* His mother has a place laid at the table for him.

– A little bite, Micha? Just a bite before you go.

Michael's mother took early retirement. Only six months and she still can't get used to it. I'm a young woman, she says. I should be busy. Every week she has a new hobby. Michael calls Mina, stays for dinner, and then his father drives him home.

– Your mother is crazy since she retired, driving me crazy.
– *It'll be your turn soon.*
– *She* should be working, *I* should be gardening, learning Spanish, yoga, astronomy.
– *You're jealous, Vati, that's all.*
– Jealous? No, it's much worse than that, son. She makes me feel *boring*.

Michael laughs; the windscreen wipers smear the city lights across the glass. *Vati. Born in '34, Mutti '41: one at the start, the other in the middle of it all.* Michael's father is quieter now. He asks about school, about Mina, but Michael can see the focus shift in his eyes: Sunday to

Monday; home to office; son to work. Michael tells him to come over in the week; bring Mutti, bring some wine. His father smiles, the electric window hums shut, and he is away; sights set on the day ahead.

Mina wakes Michael in the morning before she leaves for work. It is still dark. Her breath smells of coffee; his mouth tastes of cigarettes; *again*. He keeps his lips closed when she kisses him.

– Cem's birthday tonight, remember? I'll be going straight from work.

He watches her cycle up the road before he gets dressed.

Yasemin Devrim; Mina; physiotherapist; love of my life.

Micha makes coffee; he eats a roll and honey. *Me and Luise, Vati and Mutti, Oma and Opa. Opa and Opa and Opa.* Half-asleep at the window, Micha weaves over and under his threads of family; reciting, listing, working on and on.

Opa Askan. Opa Askan. Opa Askan Boell.

Though it is automatic, internal, it is also only partly subconscious. Michael is all too aware of his mind's-eye maps. All too aware of where they are leading him.

It is the first day of the autumn break. Micha should be marking, preparing, buying Mina's brother a birthday gift. Instead he cycles to the university in the rain. He joins the library. He goes to the computers and calls up the catalogue. He types in *Holocaust*, lists the class numbers and finds the shelves. Micha only reads the spines today. Black and gold and red lettering. Green and brown and blue bindings. Metres and metres and metres of shelving.

———

Why now?

Michael asks himself this question all the time.

We learnt about the Holocaust at school. We were taken to see the camp nearest the city, we watched documentaries, wrote essays. I remember our teacher crying. That was at the camp. He went outside while we were eating lunch in the canteen. We thought he was having a cigarette, but when he came back his eyes were red.

Micha doesn't remember crying. *I don't think I did cry*.

It was his uncle's birthday recently, Mutti's baby brother. The family went out together for a meal. They didn't talk about the war, the Holocaust; they didn't really talk about the past at all. Only in family milestones; births, marriages, deaths. It was the age difference that caught Micha: Mutti and Bernd and the fourteen years between. *A daughter before and a son after the war*. Micha had never really given it much thought before: Bernd was always just Bernd, uncle and cousin rolled into one.

Mother and uncle. They read each other's moods, finish each other's sentences. *Brother and sister*. Micha knows the contrast to him and Luise is stark. *The war got in the way. That's what Oma says: the war got in the way, but they found each other all the same.* It is her customary toast to her children. How happy they make her.

– *But the war was only six years.*

Micha said to Oma, up in her bird's nest the following Sunday.

– *Not fourteen.*

He stood outside with her, on the balcony. So she could smell the autumn leaves on the air.

– Opa came back New Year 1954. He was *Waffen SS*, you see.

She said it as if Michael knew already.

– He went away in '41, the Russians got him, and I didn't see him again for thirteen years.

SS. No one had told Michael before. He stood with Oma in the sun and looked out over the green and gold of the park below. *Why did the Russians hold on to Opa so long?*

He'd never thought to ask.

—

A week after Cem's birthday, Michael goes back to the library. He finishes at school around mid-afternoon and heads for the centre. The university precinct is empty, the paved streets swept clean. It is getting dark already and the air is dry and cold, smells of snow.

In the library, people work quietly at the computer clusters. Michael knows where the books are, but he searches the catalogue again. Nazi: entries 1–12 of 1547 are displayed. He has a coffee and a pretzel in the café. He doesn't know where to start.

Michael walks up and down the rows of shelves. He is the only one reading in the section. On the far side of the room, a librarian is shelving returns. Michael works his way along the spines. Top row, middle, then bottom, pulling out anything general, anything overview. His arms start to ache. He puts the pile of books on the floor next to his feet and continues along the shelves. He reads the back covers, now, about authors. Academics, historians, survivors, survivors' children. Israelis, Americans. Some Germans. Many of the books are in English. Michael teaches English; he can read English. The pile next to him gets taller.

He opens the books and reads the dedications now. Brief names, lonely in the blank page. Often they are parents, grandparents. Michael is aware that they are dead. That they were killed.

Another shelf holds diaries. American servicemen; journalists; a German woman. *From the same city as Oma. Born in the same year, too.*

Michael carries the books to a desk by the window. Three journeys back and forth from the shelves. The librarian has made her way round the room. Her trolley is almost empty. Outside the dark is streaked with yellow-white lights. Michael goes downstairs to phone Mina, but gets the answerphone. He says *I'll be back later; eat, don't wait.* He smokes a quick cigarette out by the lobby.

The librarian is hovering over Michael's books, surprised to see him.

– You're back.

She smiles briefly, not friendly, moves off along the shelves. Michael feels uncomfortable, wonders if she noticed the titles. He shakes himself: *what else would people be reading here?* Still, he turns the spines to the wall.

He has three hours. Michael reads from the top of the pile, taking notes as he goes. A diary, mixed with newspaper clippings. An American journalist: in Berlin before the war, and back again after. He talks about indoctrination, obedience, street violence: anti-Semitism in school classes, on posters, and on the crowded city trams. Michael reads, dismayed; reads again, makes notes.

Seats all taken, old woman got on. Heavy bags, no one helps. Journalist angry, stood up for her, but old woman wouldn't sit down. Tried to ignore him. Another man told the journalist don't bother. Points with umbrella, draws a J on the floor at the old woman's feet. She stays by the door and says nothing. Angry?

The tram stopped, she got off and walked. Man with umbrella laughed. Spat at her out of window.

Reaching for the next book on the pile, Micha glances over what he has written. He stops short, alarmed. His notes are impassive; words on a page. He writes again; *more visible, more vulnerable,* pressing hard with his pen. He underlines it; *spat and laughed*; but even with emphasis it still feels feeble; all wrong. Micha thinks his notes should say more, not less, than the books. Should reveal something about himself. But beyond discomfort he has nothing to show; no ready response.

Micha thinks; *she was Jewish*, but when he writes the words down, they look so cold and indifferent, he quickly turns the page.

Michael is frightened. By the quiet of the library; the cool distance of his notes. He decides to go home.

Mina is on the phone when he gets in, laughing with a friend. Michael is hungry, and he searches through the fridge for food. He brings his plate into the hallway, watches Mina talk while he eats. She doodles; black ink on her fingertips, the backs of her hands. Speaks in Turkish, then German, then Turkish again. Later, she climbs into Micha's bath with him. He thinks at first he will tell her about his notes and how they scared him, but Mina has gossip from friends, plans for the weekend. Micha listens and washes the biro from her skin. *I might find nothing.* He tells himself. *There might be nothing to tell.*

Tomorrow is Saturday, and he lies in the warm water with his arms around Mina, and feels relieved at the time they can spend together.

—

When Micha remembers his Opa, he thinks first of all the good things.

I was his only grandson. Opa drew pictures for me when I was born; birds and horses and a squirrel. He drew them in blue biro on hospital stationery, talking to me in my crib.

Michael has heard this story so often, it's like a memory. He keeps the drawings in a box in a cupboard on the shelf above his shoes. They are beautiful; precise and fine. The squirrel has a nut between his paws, and tiny splots of blue ink in his tail which have smudged over the years.

—

Michael also keeps two photos of himself with Opa.

The first one is black and white, taken when Michael was a baby. Opa is wearing a black suit and Michael is in his christening robe. Opa is standing, holding Michael, who is looking up at his Opa, surprised. He has one baby hand held up to his grandfather's face, and Opa smiles back at him, eyebrows raised. It is supposed to be a formal portrait, but Opa has forgotten about the photographer.

– *That's what I like about this picture.*

Michael told Mina, the first time he showed it to her.

— *He's not looking ahead, like he should be, you know. He only has eyes for me.*

Michael blushed when he said this, and Mina laughed, but she could see it was true. And Michael smiled, through his blushes, because he could see it, too.

The second photo was taken just before Michael started school. *Just before Opa died.* This one is colour, taken at a family dinner, with Opa in shirtsleeves and Michael in pyjamas: orange and blue.

— *It was time for bed. I was sent down to say goodnight, and Opa let me stay.*

In this photo, Michael sits on his Opa's lap, legs dangling, smiling into the lens. Behind them, his Uncle Bernd is laughing, facing the camera, wine glass raised. Opa has his hands folded across Michael's tummy and is smiling, too, but not at the lens. He is looking only at the boy on his lap; his food and wine abandoned on the table, the photographer forgotten again.

—

Why not earlier?

Another question which circles Michael's brain.

It should have been important all along.

—

On Saturday afternoon Micha and Mina go to her parents. It's not far, but it's cold, so they get the bus. Mina bought cakes in the morning and the paper bag smells heavy and sweet on Micha's lap. Mina's mother loves German cakes; her father says she loves them a little too much.

He came here thirty years ago, worked hard, saved money, so his wife and children could follow. He has family, a whole history far away, but a business, a community, grandchildren, all in Germany; all within five minutes' drive of his home.

Mina's father says, I am Turkish: that doesn't change. Germany is racist: that doesn't change. He isn't confrontational. *He's not saying this to make me uncomfortable.* Michael reassures himself, but he still doesn't know where to put himself. Between Mina's father and the fridge and the wall, in the kitchen, apple juice in one hand, biscuit in the other. Mina's father looks up at Michael and smiles.

– Micha, my son, this is a good and a bad country we live in.

They like me, Mina's parents. They like my family. They would like us to get married. Her mother told me. She told me to ask Mina, but Mina said no.

Michael asks her again this evening, walking home across the park.

– No.

She smiles and holds his hand.

– I don't want to be married. You know that.

Michael asks her all the time and she always says no. It doesn't worry him as much as it used to.

– *Are you Turkish or German, Mina?*
– Oh God, my Dad. Is that what he was saying in the kitchen? I thought so.
– *I'm interested, though. Would you say you were German or Turkish?*
– According to the government or according to me?
– *You, of course. Forget the government.*
– Both. Turkish and German. Both.

She laughs.

– *Which one first? German or Turkish?*

Mina looks at him. It is dark under the trees but Micha can see she is smiling.

– Promise not to tell my dad? Or my brothers?
– *Promise.*
– German. German-Turkish.

Mina laughs again.

– Can you imagine my dad's face if he heard that? First plane back to the village, and married to the nearest available cousin.
– *Oh come on.*

– Yes, I know, but he wouldn't like it.
– *No.*
– What do you think I am?
– *German-Turkish.*

She nods, satisfied. Micha nods, too. But he thinks: *Turkish-German,* and that bothers him. Even the next morning on the train it bothers him.

———

Michael reads in the library every day after school for the next two weeks. He tells Mina that he's planning new lessons for next term. He is afraid to tell her what he's really doing. In case he finds Opa Askan in one of the books, in case he stops before he finds him. Either. Both.

Waffen SS. Soldier elite. Heroes of the front line. Michael has a list now of their triumphs, *Demyansk, Kharkov, Kursk.* More names, more dates and connections running across the pages of the maps in his head. But with them also comes the list of their crimes. *Oradour, Le Paradis, and there when they destroyed the Warsaw Ghetto, too.*

His reading is not so random now; more deliberate. He works on the books like he works on his imaginary maps: reading footnotes, finding references to other books, articles. He looks them up in the catalogue. If they are there, he reads them. If not, he adds them to his list for other libraries, other times. He has a pile of notebooks by now.

Photos are difficult, painful, but Micha seeks them out. The dark line of evidence in the middle of the book, bound firm into the centre of the spine; description, interpretation feeble next to what they disclose.

cheekbones
nose
forehead
the way he held his cigarettes (he turned them in to his palm)

Micha can't find his Opa's face. *Young Askan Boell*. They all look like him and none of them do, the young Germans with the guns and the Jews.

—

Luise is older. She remembers Opa better than me.

– He was a drunk. He screamed, smashed windows, shit the bed.
– *Do you remember that?*
– No. Tante Inge. Bernd told her and Inge told me. He was lovely with us. He drew pictures. He danced with me, taught me to waltz. I thought he was wonderful, I loved him.
– *Me too.*
– Oma still loves him.

—

On his way home from work, a day or two after he spoke with Luise, Michael remembers a morning over two decades past.

Opa stood in the hall with his waistcoat buttons undone. I must have been about five or six. A family breakfast. Everyone at the table, chatting, waiting for Opa to come downstairs.

He was in the hallway. Standing still, but nodding his head. I stood in the kitchen doorway. I thought he might be nodding at me, but he wasn't. He saw me after a while. I remember I was holding a hot roll. Opa held out his hand, and it was unsteady, like his head. He said:

– Sit down, child. Eat.

Opa followed me through to the dining room and he sat down opposite me. The family was chatting, and their voices got louder when he lifted his glass. I lifted my glass of juice, too, and I saw that my hand didn't shake, and my head didn't nod; not like Opa's. His glass was twice the size of mine, but gone before I had tasted my juice.

Mutti cut open my breakfast roll and I pulled out the insides. It was warm, the bread, and I squashed it into balls. Opa sat still, and after a while, he stopped nodding. He lifted his hands, held them steady above his plate, and then Oma buttered his bread for him while he buttoned his waistcoat.

—

Micha takes Mina with him to Oma's.

– She enjoys seeing us together, you know.
– It's fine, Micha, really. I like your Oma.

Mina works with old people all the time at the clinic. Micha likes the tone of voice she has with them; con-spiratorial, as if she's known them for years. Friends chatting while she coaxes old limbs into action. He enjoys watching Oma respond; gentle and easy; having fun.

Micha follows while Oma pulls Mina along the wall, showing her Opa's drawings. The pictures are framed and arranged exactly as they were in the old house. Exactly as they were the last time Mina came to visit, too. But Mina talks as though they are all new to her, and as though she knew Micha's Opa, too.

– Askan drew very well, didn't he?
– Yes he loved to sketch. Trees and water. He was good at light, I think, very good. Light on water, light through trees. Look.
– This is my favourite.
– The birches? That's your favourite too, schatz? Micha?
– *Yes.*

Oma takes Mina's hand, and Micha's, too.

– That was on our honeymoon, a beautiful place. I swam, and Askan sketched and took photos—
– *Can we see them?*

Micha's question feels loud, too fast, too obvious, but Mina and Oma just smile and agree. Oma gets the album from her bedside table, props it open on the table for them, on the honeymoon page. Birch woods and streams, watery landscapes. Oma with plump, smooth skin in a swimsuit, hair still wet from the lake.

– Oh look, I wore lipstick, then. Can you see?
– You were beautiful, Kaethe.
– Yes, I wasn't bad.

Oma and Mina laugh and Micha stares at his Opa as a young man. *Younger than me.* On his honeymoon; standing in shirtsleeves; holding a bicycle; smoking a cigarette; in front of a lake. *He looks the same. Thinner. But really just the same.*

Micha takes the photo out of his pocket on the train home. Mina looks up from her book.

– Did Oma Kaethe give you that?
– *No, I took it.*
– What? Micha. Just now?
– *Yes.*

Mina frowns at him.

– You should have asked. I mean, she'd have given it to you, I'm sure she would.
– *I don't want her to know I've got it.*
– But she'll see that it's gone.
– *I'll copy it, put it back. She'll never know.*
– It's so rude, though, Micha. That's her husband, her memories, you know.

She's angry now, and so is Michael. He thinks she has no

right to be angry.

– *She'll never notice.*
– That's not the point, and you know it, Michael.
– *My grandparents were Nazis.*
– God, and whose weren't?
– *No, Opa Askan was in the Waffen SS. Not just in the Party.*

Micha looks at her. He said it to shock her, and she is shocked.

– *I want to find out if he did anything. Killed anyone.*
– Any Jews, you mean?
– *Anyone. Jews. Yes.*

Mina blinks.

– *That's why I need the photo.*
– Right.

Micha sees her jaws clench, feels the ache in his own clamped teeth.

– Have you found anything?
– *No. Not yet.*
– Right.

The train stops, and people get on. They sit in silence for one stop, two. Then Mina takes Micha's hand, and he feels his stomach unwind.

Oma was a Nazi. Opa was, too.

It's not real to him yet, still held at arm's length, but he sees it all the same.

Micha closes his eyes. Holds Mina's hand. Feels how strange it is. That he can be glad she knows.

—

The university has a video collection, too. Micha works his way through two shelves of documentaries over the Christmas vacation. The library is almost empty these days. He is alone in the video booths, but he still watches with headphones on.

It is cold. Outside the snow is frozen hard on the paving stones, and old people take small, deliberate steps to avoid a fall. Inside the heating is on low, and Micha wears his coat.

After lunch in the canteen, he drops off. He is rewinding tapes, making notes, and the room is cool. He slides further down in his chair, rests cheek against palm for a while. The video hums on in front of him, quieter as he slips away. When he wakes again, the tape is playing in the machine. Heinrich Himmler inspects his ranks of saluting SS. Chin receding into skinny neck, coat belted high over his chest. The headphones have slipped out of their socket, silent pads over Micha's ears. He hears his breath loud and long; still in the pattern of sleep. Memory rattling out Himmler facts. *A schoolteacher. Had copies of* Mein Kampf *bound in human skin. Said the SS were righteous killers; right to kill the Jews. Great nations must march over thousands of corpses. Something like that.*

Himmler killed himself. A cameraman filmed what they found. Micha watches it now. Dead Himmler lies on bare wooden boards, blanket clutched in small fists under his chin. Glasses on; wire-rimmed and round over closed eyes. His lips are tight, mouth twisted with poison, dark flecks of blood in his narrow moustache. The room he has chosen is full of chairs. *Like a classroom.* The window, and the wooden floor. The judgement avoided. A mean death at the end of a corridor.

Micha ejects the tape and goes home, furious, on the bus. Footsteps loud cracks in the brittle snow.

– *Perhaps Opa admired him, you know.*

He lies in bed with Mina, talking in the dark.

– *He could have met him, maybe he touched him. Maybe Himmler inspired him.*
– Mmm.
– *Can you imagine admiring Himmler?*
– No, but I know what he did. He looks ugly to me because he was a Nazi.
– *Yes, but Opa doesn't look ugly to me.*
– That's completely different.
– *How?*
– It just is. He was your Opa. If Himmler was your Opa, he wouldn't be ugly. It would have made you sad to see him dead, not angry.
– *Do you think my Opa is ugly?*
– I didn't know Opa Askan.

– *But now, if you see the photos at Oma's?*
– The ones you steal?
– *Just photos, any photos. If I talk about him?*
– He's not a Nazi in my head.
– *What is he?*
– Your Opa, Kaethe's husband, Karin's father. I don't know. All of those things.

Micha looks at Mina, but her eyes are closed. She speaks without opening them.

– What is he in your head?
– *My Opa. Mostly. But sometimes he's a Nazi, now.*
– And he doesn't look ugly?
– *No.*
– When he's a Nazi?
– *No.*
– Do you think he should?
– *Yes.*

Mina sighs. Her eyes are still closed. She pulls the blanket up over her chest, holding it in fists under her chin. Micha winces.

– So how do you tell the difference? When he's Opa, and when he's a Nazi?
– *I don't know, it feels different. Cold.*
– Cold?

Micha reaches over and pulls the blanket out of Mina's fists. She opens her eyes and frowns.

— Sorry. It just looked weird. The way you had the blanket.

—

Mina brings a video home from work.

— I thought it might be interesting for you. Sabine brought it in. She says it's very good. One of her friends made it. He went to Israel last year and filmed it.
— *Did you tell Sabine about Opa?*

Michael is defensive, smoking at the kitchen table. Mina sits down.

— No, Micha, of course not. We were just talking, you know. It just came up. Shall we watch it? It does sound very good.

An old man stands under a desert sun and remembers school in a cold place. His family was German then, he says. Germans who were Jews. Jews who were Germans. There was no internal hyphen, no line drawn between; no start of one, end of the other place inside.

An old woman sits on a wide sofa with the film-maker. He has found a photo of the house where she was born; has brought it with him to give to her; from Berlin to Tel Aviv. She holds it and stares at it, and they are quiet for a while. The film-maker asks: what do you feel when you see this picture? The old woman says: Nothing. In German: *Gar nichts*. Nothing. When the interview is over, she holds on to the photo. Can I keep this? Can I keep it?

Yes, of course. It's for you.

Mina cries about the old woman and her old home, and Michael leans across the sofa and puts his arms around her.

– It's amazing. She still loves the place, that bit of Germany. After everything that was done, after all that.

Micha is surprised; that's why she's crying. To him, the old woman was angry. *Gar nichts.* This is what makes him want to cry. That she is angry; that he thinks she is right to be angry; that he doesn't know who she is angry with. Hitler, Eichmann, the guards at Bergen-Belsen, the neighbours who drew their curtains when the police came. Opa. Him.

– *Didn't you think she was angry?*
– Yes, but she was so happy to see the house again. You could see that.

Mina kisses him, stops the tape and turns the light on. Michael stays where he is, even after she leaves the room.

Stupid to feel guilty about things that were done before I was born.

—

The notice in the library is tattered. Someone has scrawled a swastika on it, with *Jew* underneath, in red. Someone else has scribbled it out again, in black. A plain, word-processed announcement. Database of survivors and their testimonies; published and unpublished. Database of criminals; convictions from Nuremberg to the present day. Micha notes the number, but it is almost a week before he phones.

He waits until Mina is downstairs at the washing machines. She has taken a book. A man answers after five rings. He sounds out of breath. Micha says he has called about the database.

– Survivors?
– *No, criminals.*
– Aha.

He asks Micha to hang on. At the other end of the line, Micha hears his breathing and the click and bleep of a computer starting up. Micha feels suddenly rude. He introduces himself, apologises, and the man laughs, but it is not unfriendly. He says his name, too, and good evening. He has caught his breath now.

– Name? Name you are looking for, I mean.
– *Askan Boell. B-O-E-L-L.*
– Boell. Askan.

He types as he talks. The fan in the computer whirrs.

– It's searching. It will take a few moments.

Micha breaks the silence.

– *He was my Grandfather.*
– Aha.

The man doesn't sound surprised. They are silent again, and Micha waits. He wanted the man to be surprised, perhaps even to think he was brave. Micha starts to wonder whether he is being brave.

– No. No entry under that name. Any middle names?
– *No.*
– Aha.

Micha wasn't expecting this. So quick, so few questions; just a name and then nothing.

– *He was in the* Waffen *SS. On the Eastern front.*
– Aha.

The man on the phone doesn't need this information. Micha just wants him to know. To know that he knows.

– *The Russians had him. They kept him prisoner after the war, for nine years.*
– Yes.
– *So there must be a file on him somewhere?*
– The Russians. They still hold on to their stuff. We know very little about who they held and why.
– *Oh.*
– You know, it was quite normal, too. Quite normal for the Russians to keep German soldiers for many years. Some only came back in the late fifties.
– *Yes.*
– They were slave labour.
– *Yes. Not criminals?*

– No. Very unlikely anyway. No judgements against them that we know of. That they knew of, even.

He is kind, this man. Micha wants to stay on the phone to him and his slow voice. He feels reassured. Micha wants to tell him he's made him feel better. The computer is switched off. The whirring fan stops, abrupt.

– Well. Sorry I couldn't help.
– *Thank-you.*
– You're welcome.

And he's gone. Micha goes downstairs to help Mina fold the clothes. He tells her about the man on the phone and what he said.

– It was normal?
– *Yes.*
– That's good, then, isn't it?
– *Yes.*

Micha doesn't feel so good any more, though. He feels like he's come to a dead end.

– So what now?
– *I don't know. Find another man with another list.*

Micha laughs, and Mina looks at him.

– *A bigger list.*
– How big was this one?
– *20,000, I think.*
– My God, and there are bigger lists?

— Yes, I read about a man with 70,000 names.

Mina whistles.

— So many?
— Yes of course. You know how many people were killed, don't you?
— OK, Michael.

He has been raising his voice. The cellar feels very quiet now, small. Too small for loud noises.

— It takes a lot of criminals to kill that many people.

Mina folds the clothes.

— I said OK.

She feels told off, and Micha feels ashamed. *When did I get so righteous?* He carries the clothes upstairs and tells Mina he'll take her out for dinner.

———

Usually, he goes on a Sunday. Today is Wednesday, Micha's classes finish early, and he wants to see Oma, to ask her some questions. She will be surprised to see him, claim she has nothing to feed him. Micha buys cake on his way to the bird's nest.

The nurse at reception phones up to Oma as he gets into the lift. She has to repeat herself a couple of times. Oma is already halfway down the corridor when Micha gets up to her floor, her face creased with worry.

– What's happened, schatz? Micha? What's wrong?
– *Nothing, Oma. I've just come to see you.*
– Really?

She holds on to his arm, can't believe it.

– *My classes finished early. I brought cake, look.*
– And Mina is fine?
– *Yes, Oma, yes. Everyone is fine. Come on, I'll make the coffee.*

Micha feels like an intruder in his Oma's little kitchen. She stands in the doorway, watching him put the cakes out on to plates. He has thrown her routine; he knows it; it is painful to see. *My Oma is an old woman now.*

– You don't work on a Wednesday?
– *I finished early.*
– Oh, yes. You said that.

Micha carries the plates into the other room. His Oma follows.

– I have physio on Wednesday mornings.
– *Yes. Did she come this morning? Your physio?*
– Yes. That's right.

Oma settles into her chair, happier, fixed back into her week again.

– Do you have cuttings for me?
– *Of course.*

Micha lays the articles out for his grandmother, and eats while she reads. She asks him questions about them, and he answers. It's almost like a normal visit, but not quite. To Micha, it feels like they are sitting at her table with its red wax cloth, both acting out a normal visit.

He watches Oma. She is looking at the newspaper cuttings but not reading any more. Her fingers wander over them, wrists shaking gently, as though her hands are too heavy to hold. She doesn't see him watching. He holds his breath.

— Oma, where did Opa serve in the war?
— In the east, schatz.

No hint of surprise at the question, no hesitation. Just geography. Micha decides to go on.

— Where in the east?
— He was fighting for three years, a little more. The Ukraine. Russia. Belarus. It was all the Soviet Union then.

Oma smiles, sighs briefly, nods.

— Yes. Belarus. White Russia. His last year. He was there at the end.

She cuts a cake in half, and divides it between them.

— Too much for me, you'll have to help.

Micha searches Oma's expression, but she doesn't seem worried at all. He allows himself one more question.

– *Do you know where in Belarus?*

Oma swallows her mouthful of cake. One hand held in mid-air; hanging loose on her brittle wrist.

– In the south I think. There is an atlas. Wait, I'll get it. Hold on.

She pushes Micha down in his seat as she passes, makes her way to the bookshelf. Oma peers at the index and then opens the atlas on the table, stares a long time at the map.

– Wait, I'll find it. All the borders are different now. All changed.

Micha waits. The cake pulls all the moisture out of his mouth. He drinks scalding coffee to help himself swallow.

– I got letters from him. Sometimes every week. The address was always at the top. There!

She points and her finger shakes. She presses it down on the page to hold it steady. Micha sees the small town on the map. Scattered pink on green and grey. Oma pulls at his arm.

– The one beginning with S, not far from the river. He wrote about the river, and the marshes, I remember that. Do you see it?
– *Yes.*
– That's right. 1943. It must have been. After the Russians were moving west again.
– *Do you remember when?*

– Summer, autumn. He was there for a while then. And late in '43 he was fighting near there again. They moved around, went to where the fighting was, of course. But a lot of his letters came from there in that last year.

Micha looks away from the atlas, up at his Oma's face. She is excited.

– Yes. He sent his last letter from there in May, and not long after that they captured him.

She stares at the map a while longer, absorbed in thought, fingers pressed into her soft cheeks. *Thinking about her husband*. Micha drinks more coffee, gives her a little time before his next question. He promises himself it will be his last.

– *Do you still have Opa's letters?*
– No, schatz, no. He burnt them all when he came back.

Oma's face gives nothing away. Micha makes himself sit quietly at the table while she puts the atlas back on the shelf, and then he excuses himself and goes to the bathroom. His hands shake like Oma's, so he has to leave the door unlocked. He sits on the edge of the bath and wipes the sweat from his palms on to his trouser legs. He tries to imagine his Opa burning his letters. *Where did Oma keep them? Was he angry when he found them? Did he stuff them in the stove? A fire in the garden? Did he read them again before he destroyed them?*

What did he write that he wanted to burn?

Micha can't ask Oma. He is too afraid.

———

Mutti and Vati come for dinner on Friday. Micha hears them laughing on their way up the stairs. They kiss Mina at the door, tell jokes in the hallway while she takes their coats. They come into the kitchen where he is cooking, peer into all the pots on the stove. They bring smiles and noise with them and Micha is glad they are here.

– Luise will come when her shift finishes. She said we shouldn't wait.

Mutti has brought flowers and wine, and fruit salad.

– We said we'd make dinner.

Mina scolds her, searches the cupboards for a vase.

– I know. I got bored this afternoon.
– Bored? I am exhausted and my wife is bored. Something doesn't make sense here.

Vati has come straight from work. He sits down heavily at the table, pulls his tie off and sighs. Micha knows he is exaggerating for effect, but he does look tired. Mina stands behind Vati's chair and kneads his shoulders.

– You should stand up and walk around once an hour. Do neck exercises. Like this.

She steps in front of him, demonstrates, rolling her head forwards, then to one side. Vati copies her, then laughs at himself. Micha stands with Mutti by the stove.

– It's nice of you to visit Oma so regularly, Micha.
– *I like seeing her.*
– I know, I know.
– *This is preamble, yes? You're leading up to something?*
– Yes, I'm leading up to something.

Micha was teasing, but Mutti blushes. He wonders if Oma told her about his questions. He wonders if Oma was worried by them. He stops teasing and stirs the sauce that doesn't need stirring. His palms are sweating again.

– I think she was a bit confused, though.
– *Yes?*
– I think we should stick to a routine with her. Regular visiting times.
– *Oh, right.*
– She forgot about her doctor's appointment on Thursday. When the nurse came, she got quite angry. Kept insisting it was Monday because her grandson had been. She's quite embarrassed about it now.
– You didn't tell me you went to see your Oma.

Mina has been listening at the table, Vati, too. Micha turns round and finds them both staring at him.

– *There was nothing to tell.*

He turns back to the stove. *Liar.*

– Oma is an old woman, now.

– *I know, Mutti. I know that.*
– I think we forget sometimes.
– *I didn't forget. I finished early on Wednesday, that's all. I'm sorry.*
– It's OK. It's fine.

Micha serves and Mutti carries the plates over to the table. He feels like he's been discovered. He sees broken dishes, food on the floor and walls. Braces himself for the bomb. *Opa, murder, family, me.* Mutti is still talking.

– It was quite nice, actually. I haven't talked to her about Papa, about your Opa Askan. Not for years. And today we talked about him all morning.
– *Oh?*
– You talked about him, too, didn't you?
– *A bit.*
– What did she say?

Mina is asking Mutti, not Micha, and he is grateful. She is diverting Mutti. For him. He knows it. He takes a mouthful of wine.

– We talked about when Bernd was little. Family times. Lovely times I had forgotten. In the Steinweg house, when we moved in, Opa painted pictures on our bedroom walls. Wonderful. An ocean for me, and a forest for Bernd. Next to our beds. I had forgotten that. Oma told me she found him crying in Bernd's room when they moved.

Micha sits down at the table and when Mutti smiles at him, he smiles back.

– I think she enjoyed remembering. She enjoyed talking to you, too, Michael, she said so.

He pours the wine. He doesn't want to say anything to prolong the conversation. He knows he is being rude, but he doesn't want to think about his Opa and about the letters he burnt, not this evening. There is a silence and then Mina changes the subject for him.

There is some archive footage of Hitler which upsets Micha more than most images of those times.

A Christmas party, probably early in the war. At Hitler's mountain home, and everyone there: Göring, Speer, Bormann, all their wives and children. The footage is black and white, shot inside, but speckled with dust that looks like snow. Adolf Hitler sits among the children, and they look round at the camera and smile. Four and five and six year olds; shy and uncertain in lederhosen and dirndl skirts. But they also smile at him, at Hitler, and talk. It is silent, so Micha doesn't know what the children say, but he can see that they aren't afraid. *They like him.* One girl comes running into frame to tell him something, and he raises his eyebrows, open-faced and all ears while she speaks. Godfather and favourite uncle, with soft eyes and smiles. Who doesn't look at the camera, only at the child.

– Oh no.

Mina shudders when Micha shows her.

Hours later, when it is just getting light, she comes and finds him in the kitchen.

– I can bring some sleeping pills back from the clinic. Sabine will prescribe some for me, I'm sure.
– *It's OK.*

She yawns and stretches, makes tea for Micha, and massages his head, and he loves her for it. Because he knows she doesn't understand why this film clip of Hitler gives him nightmares and the pictures of Belsen, Dachau, Auschwitz don't. They make him cry; she has seen him cry. But they don't have him awake, dry mouthed, smoking at the kitchen table at dawn.

It's not right.

If Micha could choose what hurts him, it wouldn't be this.

—

Micha knows Mina won't be happy when he tells her his plans. They were going to go walking, camping. Go south to the sun.

– I've booked holiday time, Michael. I've saved money.
– *Sorry. I am sorry. We will go away.*
– When?
– *Summer. Cancel your time off, and we'll take a long break in*

the summer. Go to Turkey.

He says it because he knows that's what she wants; Micha in Turkey, Micha with her family. Mina sees through him.

– Yeah, yeah.

Later, he finds her reading the guidebook.

– Where are you going again? Minsk and then where?
– *South-east. Not far from the Pripet.*
– And Opa Askan was there?
– *Yes, I think so. It looks that way.*

Micha sits down on the bed next to her. Mina carries on reading, flicking through the pages of photos.

– Are you nervous?

She doesn't look at him. Micha shrugs. She doesn't ask again.

Belarus, Easter 1998

Micha waits at the main station door. Mina said she'd take a half day and come to see him off. He watches her wheel her bike through the traffic. It is late afternoon and the shadows are long. Mina finds the right queue for Micha to stand in at the ticket office, waits with him for a while, and then goes for a wander.

He finds her staring up at the departures board in the main

concourse.

– *I've got my tickets.*
– I've found your train. There.

Pigeons flap high above them under the roof. The station smells of bread and coffee, but also of piss. They find the platform, and the train is already there, so Micha gets on. Mina watches him find a seat, gives him a wave through the window. He knows she wants to get it over with, can't think of anything to say. He goes back to the door and tells her she should go.

– *Go swimming. Call one of your friends, have a sauna.*

She steps up into the train doorway and puts her arms around him. She kisses him.

– Your favourite.

Micha takes the bag of pretzels from her. Still warm, they smell amazing. He watches her go. Mina waves when she gets to the steps at the end of the platform, then she takes them two at a time.

—

The Ostbahnhof in Berlin is crowded, but the compartment in the new train is empty. Micha reads the paper and then sleeps for quite a while, though it is still early. When he wakes up it is evening and they are at the edge of Germany. There is another man in the compartment with him now. Older, with thick square glasses and a thin face. Micha smiles at him, and he nods. Their passports are checked with their tickets and the train lumbers on, slowly picking up speed. They are in Poland but the landscape looks no different. Micha can't believe he is doing this. Has no idea what he will do when he gets there. He eats one of Mina's pretzels and goes to sleep again.

Minsk is sticky. A hot Easter, the taxi driver says. Very unusual. Micha speaks English with him at first, tries a little German, and then goes back to English again. He tells him he is going south, but the driver doesn't answer. A few streets later, the driver points out a good restaurant. They don't talk again.

In the hotel, everything is quiet. A young woman sits at the wide desk in the narrow lobby. She wears heavy make-up, greasy in the heat. The room she gives Micha is large and bare. A bed and a TV, and a dripping shower in the bathroom down the hall. He opens the window after the young woman has gone and lies down on the bed and closes his eyes. There is no air in the room. The sheets smell faintly of smoke. TV noise leaks through the walls. Music and squealing tyres, then low buzzing voices.

When Micha wakes up it is dark and cool. He turns on the TV and then has a shower. He lies on the bed and lets himself dry off, watching the evening news, which he doesn't understand. Germany in the headlines. Pictures of

Frankfurt, the Chancellor waving at the press pack. He turns off the TV and gets dressed.

Micha is hungry. He goes out and looks for the restaurant which the driver recommended, but when he gets there he doesn't go in. He tells himself that he is looking for a bar, but when he finds one, he doesn't go in there, either. He feels conspicuous. He goes back to the hotel, orders pancakes from room service, and eats them watching a football game. Later he orders some beer, and much later he manages to go to sleep again.

—

Micha spends a long day in Minsk. He tells himself he is sight-seeing, but he knows he is just delaying. He is tired, disorientated. The city is all wide, bleak avenues under a thick grey sky. He finds the river and follows its path, keeping off the roads and in the parks as much as possible. He sees onion domes above the tree-tops and knows he has come east.

For lunch Micha finds a crowded restaurant, and orders by pointing at the food on the next table. Dumplings stuffed with mushrooms. *Real Belarussian food eaten by a real German tourist.* The waitress approves. In the main square he takes photos. Apart from that, he keeps his camera in his bag. Still feeling too conspicuous. At a kiosk, Micha buys an English guide to the city. The middle pages form a map of Minsk and the surrounding area. This map is scattered with red dots, which he looks up in the index.

Sites of Nazi atrocities; ghettos cleared, villages razed, populations executed. Micha stops walking, stands a moment in shock in the road. He remembers why he is here.

—

Two towns now where Opa was. Eight villages. The German stronghold north of the marshes where his final year of fighting came to an end.

Micha arrives at dusk, after two trains and a bus from Minsk. The sun is setting and he needs a place to stay. The town is small; no bus station, just a stop. He sits down at the edge of the road and eats the last of Mina's pretzels. It is stale, but he is hungry. It is cool here, the air smells heavy and damp. Micha pulls an extra jumper from his pack before he starts his search for a room.

He is on a main road; asphalt and wide enough for two cars to pass. The edges are paved in concrete slabs, and the smaller roads leading off it are also laid in cement. Off those roads are unmade tracks; beaten earth, hard as the concrete where dry, but with muddy dips where the rain has gathered. The street lights on the main road are lit as he reaches the edge of the town. Micha thinks there are no hotels. *This place is too small for that.*

He turns around and makes his way back towards the bus stop and beyond, although he doesn't remember seeing a hotel on the way into the town, either. The street is quiet;

no one to ask. The windows of the houses are lit yellow and white, and a truck passes on its way through the town, headlights throwing Micha's shadow far ahead of him on the pavement. A generator thumps on a side street; a mechanic working late. He has a bare bulb clipped to the open bonnet of the car he is working on, leans deep into the engine.

Micha knocks gently on the panel of the car. The mechanic smiles in greeting, speaks no German or English, and waits patiently as Micha works his way through the phonetics of his phrase book. The mechanic smiles again; he mimes sleep: eyes closed and head cocked against an open, oily palm. When Micha nods, the mechanic claps his hands together and lifts his pack.

The room is small and Micha likes it. A cot bed; wood-panelled walls painted pale green; a window with dusty muslin curtains; a chair and a small table; a huge wardrobe. It is at the back of the house, facing out on to an over-grown garden and the dark evening sky. The mechanic is pleased when Micha nods. He writes down a figure on a scrap of paper, and Micha pays for three nights.

In the kitchen, the mechanic sits Micha down with a glass of vodka, and slips out of the door. In two minutes he is back with an old woman and a heavy book. She is carrying a steel pot and a loaf. While the woman gathers plates and slices bread, the mechanic leafs through the book to a map of Europe. He pushes it across the table and points at Micha, then the map, and then Micha again. Micha points at Germany, and the mechanic nods vigorously, exchanges words with the old woman at the stove. Micha watches them both, but they keep smiling. Micha realises he was expecting a negative reaction. The old woman puts soup and bread on the table in front of him. She pats Micha's shoulder and pushes the glass of vodka closer to his plate.

The mechanic lays his palm flat on his chest.

– Andrej.
– *Michael. Micha.*

Micha holds his hand out across his plate of soup, and Andrej takes it. They both smile, half rise from their seats. Andrej introduces the old woman as his mother, or perhaps grandmother, Micha doesn't quite understand. He holds out his hand, but she waves it away, smiling, points instead at his soup. Micha eats and they watch, talking with each other. Micha knows they are talking about him, but it doesn't make him uncomfortable, and he enjoys the soft whispering noise of their words. Andrej holds up his hand, five fingers, and slips out again. The old woman smiles at Micha across the table, speaks to him in Belarussian, Russian, he doesn't know. He smiles back, and eats the bread she cut for him.

Andrej comes back with another young man. He wears greasy overalls, too, crescents of black under his broad fingernails. He speaks some German, translates for Andrej and his mother/grandmother.

– They would know why you come to our place. From Germany.

Micha can see he is flushing, aware of his halting translation. *I can't tell them about Opa.* It is too nice in this kitchen this evening. Micha tells them he is on holiday, *I am a tourist*, and they laugh. Andrej speaks, the other man translates.

– We have people from the newspapers here. Chernobyl. The Pripet has radiation and they come past here on their way. It is not so far.
– *I am not a journalist.*
– No. Good. They are happy to have a tourist. Andrej and his mother.

Micha drinks vodka with Andrej, his friend and his mother; all together and smiling around the kitchen table. Andrej starts to ask more questions, but his mother slaps his arm. Andrej looks apologetic. He does his little sleep mime for Micha again, and Micha nods. They all stand up with Micha, and Andrej leads him back to his room. He shows Micha how the light works, and where the toilet is, and they say goodnight.

Micha hears them talking on in the kitchen as he brushes his teeth and gets into bed.

—

Now that he is here, he doesn't know what to do. He should find people, ask questions, make use of his time. He has the stolen photo with him, still missing from the album Oma keeps by her bed. Opa on his honeymoon, standing in shirtsleeves in front of a lake. *Not so long, only a few years before he came here.*

Micha has four days and he is afraid.

Andrej lends him a bicycle, and a map of the area. He shows Micha the nice places to go, and his mother packs food in a bag. Micha cycles, eats his lunch, cycles some more.

In the evening, he writes to Mina, propping the photo of Opa against his knee. Micha tries to imagine him in uniform. In the doorway of Andrej's kitchen with a gun, standing at the crossroads at the edge of the town. The man in his head, with the SS insignia, he is Nazi Opa. The man in the photo is just Opa. Opa before Micha knew him, but still Opa all the same.

He tells Mina he is not getting very far. He crosses that out, starts again. *Not trying hard enough.* But he crosses that out, too. On a new sheet, Micha writes what he really thinks. *I'm a coward. I don't know what to do.*

Andrej drives Micha around in his pick-up. Micha enjoys Andrej's gentle banter with his customers, understanding nothing but the smiles, the serious handshakes. He walks through the villages past old men sitting on their porches, making the most of their warm Easter morning. He thinks about showing them the picture and saying Opa's name, but he walks on.

They could say anything. He shot my brother and twenty other men. Hunted down the Jews in the forest here. Look, here behind my house. He hated them, you see, wanted them dead.

Micha tries to imagine a voice telling him that, a face. He tries to imagine how he would feel if that's what he heard.

Andrej talks to him in Belarussian, Micha speaks German, and they get on well. At lunchtime they drink scalding tea and heavy bread with butter and jam. A German brand. Sitting on a verge at the side of the road on a fresh spring day. Cars beep as they pass, and Andrej raises his arm in greeting. Micha buys beer on the way home, to share with Andrej and his mother. They sit together in the evening, watch TV in the kitchen. Andrej and his mother laugh, and Micha, too.

I need a translator.

He goes to bed, but he can't sleep.

Micha gets up early and goes out to find Andrej's friend before breakfast. The German-speaker. The books in the library are Belarussian, he says, amused that Micha should want to read them. English books, German books, they are in Minsk. Not here.

— *I have questions, though, about this place. Maybe only people round here will know.*

The friend shifts his weight on to his other foot. Micha doesn't say Opa, he only says war, Occupation, Nazis, and he looks at the friend's collar, at his ear while he talks. Micha tries to ask him; for help, to find people, translate. But it all sounds so vague and strange. Even in Micha's head.

Andrej's friend is embarrassed for him, and Micha knows it.

There is a museum, he says. Not in this town, the next one. He takes Micha to the road, flags down a car, leans in through the open window, tells the driver where Micha wants to go. They both look at Micha briefly, and the driver smiles and opens the passenger door. Andrej's friend shakes Micha's hand.

– It's a small place. But a good museum.

—

Next to the old town hall Micha finds a wooden building with a concrete floor. Objects and photos are lined up along the walls. All done with care; neatly written tags; thin rope strung on hand-turned posts to keep the visitors at the correct distance. A young woman sits at the door on a canvas chair. Micha drops coins into the box at her feet and she smiles and goes back to her book.

Along one side are old paintings and photos of the town

in the early years of the century. The main dusty, busy
street of 1925 contrasted with the asphalt and two cars of
last year. *Bigger then, before the war. Thriving.* Houses,
people, a market place. Outside the wind is blowing.
Micha can hear it in the trees. The branches brush against
the skylight in the roof of the museum.

He has reached the first corner of the room. Opposite
Micha, in the second, stand three tailors' dummies, each
with a uniform on. SS, *Wehrmacht,* and a third he doesn't
recognise. Empty arms hang loose and thin beside the
stuffed chests. He doesn't hurry towards them. He turns
to check, but the young woman is not watching him, she
is still reading.

Between Micha and the uniforms are exhibits and pictures
of the Jewish communities who lived in the town before
the war. A small school, and a textbook written in
Yiddish. A graveyard from which the stones were stolen
to pave the streets. Micha blinks, moves on to the
uniforms.

They are creased, threadbare. *Worn.* Two are German and
the unfamiliar third is Russian. Micha sees a button
missing from the heavy SS coat. *Torn off, cut off, shot off,
dropped off.* This coat is real, not a replica. *Someone
undressed a corpse and kept a trophy. Or someone threw it off and
ran away when the Red Army came. Or someone found it and
wore it and maybe they were even glad of it, even though it was
German, because it was woollen and warm and it was winter and*

they were cold.

All along the final wall are photos taken during the war. Micha sees them out of the corner of his eye while he is still by the uniforms. He prepares himself to look closer; tells himself what they will show. *Public executions, smiling Germans, mass graves, mass shootings.* He is right. Heads hanging loose, bodies hanging long from trees. Young men aiming rifles at kneeling children. Soldiers standing, smoking in the sunshine, and behind them, the dead lying pale and naked in rows.

Micha looks at them all. Looks hard into the faces of the soldiers, checks for Opa's cheekbones, his high forehead, his deep-set eyes. A cigarette held in the fingertips, turned in towards the palm. Micha is sweating. He doesn't find him. He goes back along the wall, looks again, but still he doesn't find him.

The young woman is watching Micha. He catches her eye and she looks away. He tries to imagine what he must look like, staring so hard at these terrible scenes. He wonders if he should hurry, or stand further away, or cry. He doesn't know. He doesn't care now; he is trying hard not to be a coward today. Micha calls across the room.

– *Do you speak German?*

She looks up, frowns, hasn't understood. She says something. Micha thinks it sounds like an apology.

– *Do you speak English?*

– Yes, some. I am sorry.
– *Perhaps you can help me. Do you know if all the pictures were taken here? In this town?*
– Oh. The pictures on this wall? The Occupation?
– *Yes.*
– Oh. I think so. I'm not sure, wait.

She puts down her book, hurries to the wall, heavy shoes loud in the small room. Micha stands a little way back, while she works her way along the pictures, reading the inscriptions, the names and dates.

– These were.

She points for Micha.

– On this panel. The others were taken in Belarus, too, but further north and also west. They are there to tell you that these things happened all over the country, you see?
– *Yes. Thank-you. Do you know which SS divisions came here? Waffen SS?*
– They are listed here, I think.

She goes to the shelves in the corner by the door, brings back a book, handwritten. Micha thinks she is excited to be helping, unselfconscious. He is still sweating; his scalp, his hands and feet.

– Yes, look. Here on this page.

A long list, *Wehrmacht*, SS, Police, but Micha sees Opa's division. He thinks it must show in his face because the young woman avoids eye-contact when he looks up.

– *Thank-you.*
– You're welcome.

She smiles, embarrassed, still looking away, returns to her chair by the door and her book. Micha stands a while longer by the photos, not looking at them, and grateful, too, that the young woman is not looking at him.

This is not so bad. Micha talks to himself. Very quietly, but it helps to hear a voice. *I came here to see this; that Opa was here. I was ready for this.* He is surprised to be so calm. Micha signs the visitors' book; full name, full home address. *I was here; so was he.*

– *Do you know if there is someone I could talk to? About the Occupation?*
– A historian?

The young woman is surprised, her book held open in mid-air.

– *Or maybe someone who remembers it. Who was living here then?*
– I don't know. I have to think about it.
– *I can come back tomorrow.*
– You want to speak to someone tomorrow?
– *If you can think of someone. Today, even.*
– Well, tomorrow. Maybe.
– *Yes?*
– I think maybe my grandfather can help.

– He would speak to me?
– Well, I don't know. Maybe he knows somebody.

She doesn't sound so sure. Micha tells her he'll come back in the morning, says he would be very grateful if she would ask her grandfather. She nods, and takes Micha's hand when he offers it, embarrassed again.

In the morning, the grandfather is there, but he doesn't want to talk. He came to size you up, the young woman tells Micha. He hasn't seen a German for years. She blushes as she translates, hides her smiles behind her hand.

– He says there is a man in the next village you should talk to. Jozef Kolesnik. He will remember the Germans. You should go to him this afternoon. My grandfather will tell him you will come.
– What time? After lunch? Do I have to wait until after lunch?

Micha tries to catch the old man's eye, but he just chews at his bottom lip and nods at his granddaughter. He walks away without another glance at Micha.

———

The village is not far; three, maybe four kilometres. The clock outside the bakery says quarter to two when Micha arrives, and it takes him no more than five minutes to find the house. There was no time arranged; just afternoon, after lunch, but Micha is nervous that there is nobody home.

He checks the address again, knocks at the door one more

time, and then he is not sure what to do, so he sits down and waits.

The house is green. Wooden and painted blue-green. Micha sit on the steps leading up to the narrow veranda which runs the length of the building. There are more steps at the far end, down to a small garden and a muddy lane. Two low windows face out over the road, and after half an hour or so, Micha gets up and taps on the glass. No reply. He tries again, fingertips against the next window, cupping his hands around his eyes and peering inside. No noise or movement, nobody home.

– *Hello?*

Micha's breath clouds the glass, and he wipes it away quickly with his sleeve. The house stays quiet and still.

Micha's hello sits in his ears: a loud voice in a quiet afternoon. On the veranda, he watches his hands shake, and then slowly steady again. He stands there a while, uneasy on the steps of the silent house, then he wheels the bicycle across the road, and sits down on the low wall opposite. A safe distance, hands in his pockets, photo of Opa resting against his palm.

If he remembers Opa.

I want him to remember Opa, and I don't.

Micha gets up and walks, leaves the bicycle and walks. First to one end of the street, then the other. The minutes go by, a few people, a few cars, but none of them stop at the house. He sits down again.

He had not thought of this.

It is already late; shadows creep across the street towards him. From this distance, with the road in between, the house looks different. Not so empty, perhaps. Micha imagines a light coming on, behind a curtain, and the idea doesn't seem so strange. Here, across the road, Micha can imagine there is someone inside. Behind a door, or under a window; sitting quiet and still while the stranger called too loudly through the glass.

He doesn't have a watch, doesn't know how long he has been here. *Two hours. Three. More.*

The sun is not warm now, but it is not evening, not yet, and so not yet time to go. Micha's legs are numb from sitting. He walks up and down until the pins and needles come, and then he unlaces his boots and rubs his feet. When Micha looks up he is not alone.

An old man stands on the porch, an old woman next to him, both of them watching him.

– *Jozef Kolesnik?*

Micha picks up the bicycle and wheels it back across the road. He didn't see them coming. *They must have come through the garden. From the lane.* The old man holds a bag of shopping, and Micha thinks: *It's fine, he has been shopping. Shopping, not hiding.*

– *Jozef Kolesnik? Do you speak German?*
– Yes.
– *You are Jozef Kolesnik?*

He does not answer. Micha stops walking.

– *You did get a call? Someone told me they would call.*
– Yes.

Micha steps forward. He doesn't know what to say. Three hours he has been waiting. The sun is low and Micha has not left the street in case he missed him. Afraid he would come, afraid that he wouldn't. And now he is here.

– *I wonder if I could ask you some questions? Just a few? Would that be possible?*
– About what?

The old man is three steps up on his porch, and behind him stands his wife. Micha puts one hand in his pocket, fingers on the photo, resting against the smooth side, prints on the gloss.

– *My name is Micha.*

Micha pulls out his hand; holds it open, unsteady, and the photo stays hidden away. The old man shifts his bag of shopping from one hand to the other, but he doesn't respond.

– *I am Michael Lehner.*

— You are German?

— *Yes.*

The old man turns to his wife, and she takes his arm, says something. Micha thinks she is asking him to leave; asking the old man to ask him to leave.

— *I was at the museum. I was told you might remember.*

The old woman talks to her husband. He answers and she breathes out, a heavy sigh. Micha waits for them to speak to him, but they don't. They just look at him, and he looks at them, and Micha is terrified of what he is about to do. Of the reaction it might produce.

No.

It is too hard. He tastes salt. Panic at the back of his throat.

If he remembers Opa. Will he remember good things? Will there be good things to remember, or only bad?

Tears are on their way; Micha can feel them. In his chest now, but on their way to his eyes. The old man speaks.

— Remember what?

Micha doesn't answer; he holds still.

If I show him, then he will say, yes I knew him, or he will say no, I did not. It will be something. That will be something at least.

There is sweat on Micha's back and in his hair.

— *Wait.*

But it is too hard. The words don't come, only tears.

— *Sorry.*

Micha's mouth is thick, his eyes are full.

— *Sorry.*

He holds on to Andrej's bike and hides his face with his arm. It is dark behind his sleeve.

— *Two minutes.*

The old woman steps down off the porch. She has toilet roll in her shopping bag, and pulls off some sheets. Micha wipes his face, his nose, and the old woman pulls off more. Jozef Kolesnik looks down at his feet. His wife takes Andrej's bicycle and leans it against the fence and then she goes into the house.

He is shocked, the old man. A German boy cries outside his house. Micha thinks he is angry, too, but he doesn't speak. He sits down on the veranda steps, and Micha wants so much to sit with him, and lean against the smooth wood of the rail. His wife brings Micha vodka, and a handkerchief, but she is not friendly. Micha knows she wants him to go, and that her husband does, too. *Stop crying and go.*

— Jozef Kolesnik.

The old man holds his hand on his chest.

– Elena Kolesnik, my wife.

She nods and then he stands up.

– Please go away.

He takes a step closer to Micha, speaking quietly, one step down off his porch.

– It was many years ago. A bad time. I am an old man. Please go away.

So strange that he says please. It is deliberate, a kindness. He holds out his hand; a gesture to help Micha away from his house.

Micha is close enough to look into his eyes, but he doesn't. He could still show him Opa's photo, but he doesn't. It is dusk and it is too hard. He takes Andrej's bike and he leaves.

—

When he gets back to Andrej's the house is dark and no one is home. Micha washes and shaves and gets into bed. He leaves the light off and stares at the wall, the day gathered like a headache behind his eyes.

Later, Andrej knocks at the door, brings in a tray of food.

Micha offers him his glass of beer, and drinks from the bottle. Andrej sits quietly with him while he eats. Micha's eyes are still swollen from the day's tears; he thinks that Andrej must see that. He stays with him and Micha is glad.

In two days, I will be with Mina.

Micha cries again and Andrej lifts the tray from his lap and pulls the blankets over his legs. He turns off the light and whispers something in the dark before he goes. Micha doesn't know what he says, but it's good to hear something. A voice before he sleeps.

Home, Spring 1998

It is time for all the usual late spring things. Cycling to school now the weather is good, tackling Shakespeare with the final-year class, going for slow walks with Oma through the park.

Micha carries his winter habits with him, though, and goes to the library most days after school. Sometimes to read, but often just to sit; a quiet cushion between work and home. He is not sure why he does it, so he keeps it to himself; always back and making dinner by the time Mina gets in.

He is not ready for it, but life moves on.

—

Michael sits on the edge of the bath and Mina sits on the loo.

— *Do you feel pregnant?*
— Wait.

Mina takes hold of Michael's wrist, pulls it round so she can see the secondhand ticking away.

– Are these tests accurate?
– Better than the doctor's, Sabine says.
– Why don't they use them?

Mina shrugs.

– There. Blue line or no blue line?

She hands the white stick to Micha, and he snaps off the top like it says in the leaflet on the bathroom floor.

– Yes.
– OK.

Micha can't stop smiling. *Stop smiling.*

– What do you think?
– It's a blue line.
– No, I mean do you want to have a baby?
– I'm pregnant. I'm going to have a baby.
– Yes? I mean, are you happy?

Please be happy. Mina has her hands over her face; her voice comes out muffled by her palms.

– Are you happy?
– Yes, I am. I think I am.
– You think?

Mina laughs. Micha thinks she must be happy.

– I'm happy. It will be great. I'm happy.

She stands up and pulls Micha up from the bath and puts her arms around him, and he is so glad to be home; glad to feel so very happy here with her.

—

The letter Micha wrote in Belarus arrives a long time after him. Well over a month. Mina cries when she reads it.

– You weren't a coward. You were brave to go there and do what you did.

She says it like it's finished. Micha doesn't respond. She doesn't know about Jozef Kolesnik, the tears, and the photo he took all the way to Belarus, and then didn't show.

—

Micha can't look at Opa's photo now.

He wishes he could throw it away.

On Sunday, Oma makes coffee, and Micha lays out the newspaper cuttings for her to read. He has the picture in his pocket, waits for the right moment, standing at the window until Oma settles down. She cuts herself a slice of cake, and he slips into her bedroom.

Put it back, sit down and drink some coffee.

That's what Micha thought he'd do, but instead he stays

in there. Sitting on Oma's soft single bed, with her album open on his knees.

There is Opa as New Husband on honeymoon. Askan in shirtsleeves by the lake; slotted in place again on page 1938. Micha turns over, seventeen years later, back to back: Opa as Papa. Opa with young Karin, holding hands. Askan in a dark suit, leaning over, smiling into the crib where his baby son lies.

Micha flicks the pages back and forth, back and forth. 1955; Opa has less hair, more lines; his waist is thicker, his arms are thinner. *And in between?* Two children, nearly two decades of faithful marriage. Seventeen years have passed, but if Micha didn't know, he would never guess there had been war and prison, too.

Micha shuts the photo album, tells himself, *he was a soldier*, but in his head, he inserts the photos from the museum. Thick pages; a whole album of atrocities between the honeymoon and the newborn boy.

– Bring it out here, schatz. Sit out here. I see you so rarely.

Oma is at the door. Her head shakes a little now, with age. And she is smaller again, bones folding in on themselves, head well below Micha's shoulder when he stands.

I went to Belarus and I came back.

A museum and an old man; *wasted days*; nothing more. Micha could cry again. Here, now, in the bird's nest, on

Oma's bed. Rage about those days. That he let them pass like that.

— We're going to have a baby. Mina and me.

He needs Oma to smile now, be happy. Something to stop him being angry.

— Micha! I am hearing things! Say it again!

She holds out her hands. Micha knows he should take them, but he can't.

— You mustn't say, though, Oma. Please. It's a secret still, you know?
— Yes yes, of course, schatz. I know. A baby!

She puts her hands on his face and kisses him. Micha can cry now, so he does, because he doesn't have to explain. Oma brings tissues, cake and smiles; baby books from the drawer where she has stored them.

— Just in case. I always hoped, you know. For you and for lovely Yasemin.

My Oma.

Micha's family map. The one that leads to Opa. It always stops with her.

———

Micha carries Opa's honeymoon photo on trains and buses, around the school, the supermarket, the cinemas and bars. It creases, and he buys a plastic wallet to keep it from tearing along the deep fold across Opa's legs.

At school, they commemorate the liberation of the camps, and the children make speeches. Many of them cry. The history teacher explains the day to the silent hall, crowded with parents, older and younger brothers and sisters. Michael sits with his shame and his fury at the back with the staff.

Mina sits up in bed, Michael smokes at the door. Not sure how he can describe it to her; his anger; how he saw this day.

– *Every year it's the fucking same. The students read survivors' accounts. Everyone cries these 'we didn't do it' tears. Then the essays get marked, the displays are packed away, and we move right on with the next project.*
– Why don't you say something then?
– *I can't talk to the other teachers.*
– Why not?
– *They just wouldn't want to hear it.*

Micha thinks Mina doesn't want to hear it either. He carries on.

– *It's taboo, untouchable. It says our school is open and good.*
– I think it is. I think it's good. The students should learn about it.
– *But it's perverse, Mina. They identify with the survivors, with the victims.*

– How do you know?
– *Those are the words they are taught. Those are the words they cry about.*
– And they shouldn't cry?
– *Yes they should cry! But they should cry that we did this. We did this, it wasn't done to us.*

Mina sighs and punches the pillow into shape behind her head.

– *They shouldn't only cry about the things that happened, they should cry because we made them happen.*

Micha tries to keep it quiet. Mina doesn't like it when he shouts, and he has been doing so much shouting these days.

– *Do you understand what I mean?*
– I think so, Michael. Yes. But 'we' didn't do it. It was another generation.
– *But we're related. It's still us. I mean, I can't be the only one. There must be others in that hall every year with grandfathers like mine.*
– Not everyone. Some of your students are Turkish, aren't they? Greek? Iranian?
– *OK, then I'm talking about the ones with German parents, grandparents.*
– But they *didn't* do it, Michael. They really didn't. The children, the students. Even the very purest of the pure German ones.

Micha stops. Mina has her eyebrows raised, angry.

– *They are being taught that there are no perpetrators, only victims. They are being taught like it just happened, you know, just out of the blue people came along and did it and then disappeared. Not the same people who lived in the same towns and did the same jobs and had children and grandchildren after the war.*
– I don't think that's true.
– *It is, Mina. I never made the connection before, and it was there in my home. He drew me pictures, I sat on his knee.*
– But you don't even know if he did anything!

Mina has her hands over her face. Micha covers his eyes, too.

– *No. OK. I just think they should read about the people who did it, too. The real, everyday people, you know. Not just Hitler and Eichmann and whoever. All the underlings, I mean. The students should learn about their lives, the ones who really did the killing.*
– I think you're the perverse one here.
– *I'm serious.*
– Michael, you are fucking sanctimonious and you're fucking obsessed. Please, can we talk about something else now, or can we just go to sleep?

Micha knows Mina is waiting, but he can't think of anything else to say. She turns the light off and Micha finishes his cigarette in the dark. When he gets into bed, he turns his back to Mina, closes his ears to her breathing.

Tries to shut himself away, but the rage and the shame both remain.

Mina said it. There is no place for sanctimony here.

—

Micha's uncle is surprised to see him. He tells his secretary that he won't be long, and then he looks up at his nephew, awkward, clears his throat.

– We can be as long as you want, Michael. Of course.

He says he'll buy lunch.

Micha doesn't know where to start, and there are awkward silences until the food arrives, but Bernd relaxes when he asks his questions.

– He drank. I think he probably drank all my life, though I only remember him really drunk two or three times.
– *Why do you think Opa drank?*
– I don't know, Michael. Maybe in Russia, in the prison, perhaps that's where it began.
– *Not earlier?*
– Before he was married?
– *No, the war.*
– Oh.

Bernd takes a mouthful of his food. Micha thinks he's stalling.

– *I mean, do you think something might have happened to him.*

Or he might have done something in the war, and that made him want to drink?
– Perhaps. Perhaps.

Maybe he just doesn't know.

– He did drink, and I remember there were times he got so drunk and angry we had to leave the house. Mutti, your Oma, she took Karin and me outside, and we went to the park and waited until it was over.
– *He smashed a window once, didn't he?*
– Yes. Did your mother tell you that? He did.
– *Why?*
– Why? I don't know. Because he was angry, because he could.
– *What happened?*
– He smashed the kitchen window with his fist and Mutti took us outside. That's not how I remember him, you know? It's not really what I remember him for.
– *How do you remember him?*
– He was a very good father.

Bernd blushes. Micha smiles, despite himself; he enjoys hearing it, seeing his uncle's love.

– He was gentle. My schoolfriends, their fathers had rules, seen and not heard and so on, but Papa wasn't like that. He let us run around the house and sing, he let us make a mess. He liked it. I think he really enjoyed it.
– *So, when he drank, or when he was drunk. Was he a different man?*

– I don't know. I suppose so. Maybe that's one way of seeing it.

– But that's not how you see it?

– No. I don't know. I've never really thought about it, Micha.

– Do you think he might always have had it in him?

– Alcoholism?

– Violence.

– He wasn't a violent man.

– But he smashed the window. You had to leave the house. I mean, you must have been scared, Oma must have been scared.

– Listen, Michael. What he did was three, or at most four, times over a period of, I don't know, years. He got drunk, and he got angry and we were there, we were there to take it out on. That's all. It was a shock, as I said, but that's all.

Bernd smiles, exasperated. They sit and eat and Micha thinks.

Perhaps he is right.

I am finding connections because I am looking for them, not because they exist.

Opa drank because he killed. Opa killed because he drank. Opa drank because the war was lost, because he was wrong, because he was in prison for so long. Opa drank.

– Do you think Opa killed anyone?

Micha's uncle looks at him. Micha takes a mouthful of

food. It occurs to him that his uncle could do the same, and that they could pretend he never said it. But then Bernd speaks.

– He was a soldier.
– *He was in the SS.*

– The *Waffen* SS, Micha. A soldier.

Micha waits a little longer, but knows that that is the only answer he will get, and he doesn't dare ask anything more.

—

It is the weekend. A first day of summer with sharp green leaves. Mina buys fresh bread for breakfast and says they should get out of the city, maybe stay somewhere overnight.

– Haven't been sick this morning. Don't even feel sick.

She smiles, puts on another slice of toast, pours another glass of juice, rests her feet up on Micha's lap.

– *Taunus?*

He thinks how nice it will be to watch Mina enjoy a picnic lunch.

– Oder Vogelsberg? We could borrow Cem's car. Find a hotel, come back tomorrow evening.
– *Let's camp. We won't be able to camp for a while after this one is born.*

Micha rests his hand against her still-flat stomach. She smiles.

– If you like.
– *OK, good. I'll get the tent out of the cellar.*

When Micha gets back upstairs, Mina says:

– This is nice. This is nice isn't it?
– *Yes, of course it is.*

He kisses her. He knows what she means; leave Opa Askan at home.

Micha doesn't talk about him, and he laughs and smiles all weekend. And he does feel lucky and happy, too, with Mina and with the baby. But he doesn't leave Askan at home. Even while Mina builds a campfire and Micha reads out his list of names for their child, Opa sits next to him on the cool evening grass.

—

The phone rings and Mina takes Micha's hand, pulls him back down on to the sofa.

– It's after ten. No one should phone after ten on a week night.

Micha folds his fingers around Mina's hands. Luise's voice is loud on the answerphone.

– Listen, brother, I don't know what you are up to, but I wish you would just be careful, just a little bit more careful, you know. And you better not be asking Oma the same stupid questions as Bernd, because if you are, then you are even more heartless than I thought. And if you are listening to this, which I bet you are, then you are a fucking coward, too.

She breathes a moment or two, and then she hangs up.

– My God, Michael. What have you done?

—

In the kitchen, Micha helps his mother with the food. He is nervous. His mother brushes the hair back from her face, and he can see how tense she is. It shows in her skin, around her eyes.

Bernd told Inge, who would have told Luise, and probably also Mutti, because Mutti knows.

Micha isn't sure whether he is supposed to speak.

– Michael?

He stops chopping and looks at her. His mother holds his gaze and then turns away, opens the oven door.

– *I just started wondering why he was away so long. Why the Russians kept him.*
– Lots of men were kept away. It was normal. Almost all my schoolfriends. If their fathers weren't dead, they were prisoners of war.
– *I know. But maybe not all of them were prisoners of war. Not*

normal prisoners.

Micha's mother closes the oven door.

– He didn't do anything, Michael.
– *How do you know?*
– I know.
– *Have you ever been curious?*
– No. Of course not.
– *Did you ever ask him?*
– I didn't have to.
– *How do you know then? How can you know?*
– Because I knew my father. You never really knew him Michael, you were too small.
– *It's that easy?*
– Yes.
– *Yes, of course it is. Because I can't dispute that, can I? I can't ever know him like you did, can I?*

He can feel the pulse in his throat. They have never spoken like this before. Micha's mother frowns.

– No. You can't.
– *You were thirteen when he came back.*
– Twelve.
– *You didn't know him then. He'd been away all your life.*
– He was my Papa. Always Askan. Just the way he was.

Upset. Voice raised, hand raised.

– He wasn't capable, Micha.
– *But everyone would say that about their father, wouldn't they?*

No one would think their own father could murder.
– I don't know about that, Michael. Perhaps you should ask someone whose father is a murderer.
– *You can't be sure. If you've never asked, you can't be sure.*
– He didn't do anything.

Micha's mother carries the pots out to the dining room. He follows with the salad. His father has opened the wine and is sitting at the table with his hands in his lap. He has been listening. He doesn't look at Micha and he doesn't speak. Mina sits opposite him. She looks up at Micha as he comes in to the room. Embarrassed, angry. He can't tell, can't read her expression. Her eyes are dark and her lips drawn tight. They eat.

But Micha is furious. He puts the food in his mouth, chewing and chewing. He swallows, puts his knife and fork down.

– *Will you want to know?*

His mother looks at him. *She wants me to stop.* Micha doesn't want to. His father stands up.

– *If I find out. Should I tell you?*
– Shut up!

Micha's father shouts, his mother looks away. He thinks she might cry now, and he still doesn't want to stop.

– *Will you want to know?*

Mina stands up and leaves the room. Micha's father slams

the wine bottle down on the table, dark splashes on the blue linen. Micha stops. His father presses his palms flat on the cloth, breathes in loud and long. Micha can see him searching for something to say; too angry. His mother still doesn't speak.

Micha leaves the room, finds Mina in the kitchen. She is standing by the sink with a glass of water.

– *We should go*.
– Right.

She walks past him, takes her coat from the chair in the hall, and goes in to the dining room. Micha can't hear what she says. When Mina comes back again she is crying. He holds the door open for her, and she walks out. Without looking at him, and she stays ahead of him up the street.

Micha doesn't get on the train with her. He stays in the station, drinks a coffee, eats a pastry. Sweet and sticky on his tongue. He lets himself sit alone and quiet for a while, not think about what he has done.

When he gets home, Mina isn't there. Her swimming costume is gone from the hook in the bathroom. Micha calls his parents and gets the answerphone. He says *hello it's me, just calling to see how you are*. He doesn't say sorry.

—

– You think I've come to tell you off, but I haven't.

Luise's voice on the intercom. She hauls her bike up the stairs, sweat on her upper lip. Splashes her face at the sink in the kitchen, leaves it wet, sits down at the table to get her breath back. Micha waits by the fridge for her to speak.

– You didn't have to tell them what you are doing.
– *I thought you weren't here to tell me off.*
– Sorry. Sorry.

Luise has wine in her bag. She gets it out, puts it on the table.

– *Too early in the day for me, Luise.*
– Yeah?

She looks at the bottle, pushes it away from herself.

– I tried to find out about Opa, too.

The blood rushes in Micha's ears. He hears its high-pitched singing over the hum of the fridge. They are silent for some time. Luise takes her hands away from her face. She looks like she will cry. *Don't cry.* Sweat prickles under the skin on Micha's back.

– *When?*
– While I was studying in London. There is a library there, set up by a Jewish man. German. He fled, in '33, I think. Anyway. They hold lots of information. About the camps, survivors. About Nazis. They were very helpful, very kind. I used to go there every week. It made me feel better.

She is crying. Her voice is tight. Pushed out of her throat.

– *Better?*
– Yes. Like it was OK. No, not like it was OK. I don't know. It helped.

Luise smiles, wipes her face with her hands.

– *And?*
– What?
– *What did you find about Opa?*
– Oh. Nothing.
– *Nothing?*

Micha can't believe her.

– He wasn't on any list. There were a couple of readers at the library. People with lists of war criminals, Nazi officials. They didn't have him.
– *I called up about one of these databases, too.*
– In London?
– *No, in this country.*
– Yes? And?
– *Nothing.*

Luise nods. *Nothing.*

– *You think that means he didn't do anything?*

She breathes out, hard.

– Mutti and Vati don't need to know.
– *That's your opinion.*

— Yes that's my opinion.

Luise stands up, takes her coat and bag.

— *This conversation is over now, is it, Luise? Because you say so?*
— It has to be their choice, Michael. You can't inflict it on them.
— *They would just choose not to know.*
— What's wrong with that? How does it help them to know?
— *Why should we protect them from what he did?*
— We don't know what he did, Michael. If he did anything.
— *But you think he did do something?*
— I don't know. I don't know and you don't know.

Luise screams at him. Her finger points sharp at his chest. They stand about a metre apart in the kitchen. *She will tell Mina that I didn't even blink when she screamed.* Micha sets his face hard. He doesn't want to show her what he feels. Doesn't want to have to show her.

— You know a lot of treatments we use now are based on research from the camp hospitals?
— *No, I didn't know.*
— They are. I used to get sick thinking about it. I'd get sick thinking about the doctors in the camps.
— *And now?*
— Christ, Michael. It still makes me sick.

Micha wonders how long she's been here. It feels like ages. Time for Mina to come home. *She would talk to Luise and I could go and lie down.* Micha is ashamed of his thoughts, but he still wishes his sister would go.

– Shall we open the wine?
– *No. I'll save it for when you come again.*
– You want me to leave, don't you?

Micha shrugs. He knows he's being cruel. Luise stands for a couple of seconds, and then she smiles and Micha smiles back. *She's sad. So am I.* Micha doesn't tell her, but he hopes she knows.

– If you find anything, you will let me know, won't you?
– *About Opa?*
– Yes.
– *You want to know?*
– Of course I do. You think you have a monopoly on honesty, Michael?
– *No.*
– Yes you do.

They're in the hallway. Micha holds the door while she wheels her bike out.

– I don't think Mutti and Vati need to know, that's all. That's all I wanted to say.
– *OK. You've said it.*

Luise lifts her bike, starts walking down the stairs. Micha stays in the doorway, and she doesn't look round.

– Tell Mina I said hello.
– *I will.*
– Tell her I think my brother is an arrogant shit, too.
– *I will.*
– Of course you will.

He hears her blow her nose at the bottom of the stairs and then he closes the door.

— ·

We fought a lot when we were children, my sister and me. Vicious, with scratching and kicking, and blood sometimes, too.

I remember one fight at Oma and Opa's house. I got into a real rage. We were at the top of the stairs, and I was lying on the floor. Screaming, hiccups, that kind of thing. I kept trying to kick her, but Luise was just out of reach. She was on the top step, crying too, and she had her mouth wide open. Her lip was split and her teeth were red. I must have done that.

And then Opa was there, up on the landing with me, holding me inside his arm, against his chest, and pressing his cheek against my hair. I can remember his smell; soap and smoke.

He held Luise inside his other arm. I remember he pressed his cheek against her hair, too, but I didn't mind. Later, maybe, I was jealous, but not at the time. Opa was there and you couldn't be angry. When Opa was there you were fine.

—

Micha cycles home from school and it rains. So hard he

has to take his glasses off and squint to see the road. Cars loud next to him in the spray. Soaked through when he gets home, he undresses and climbs into bed. For a long time he doesn't sleep, he just lies and watches the light leave the day. He gets hungry, and Mina is still not home, and he can't get warm. He thinks of Opa Askan's photo: in his pocket, in his wet trousers, lying with his other wet clothes on the bathroom floor.

It is dark in the flat when the phone goes. He has been dozing, unsure of the time, and the bell rings loud in the cold quiet of the hall.

– What do you want?

The question comes before he has even said his name.

– What did you want to ask?
– *Sorry? Who is this?*

But Micha knows who it is, and already his hands shake; even before he can think, before he can speak. *No.*

– This is Jozef Kolesnik. Calling from Belarus. I want to know your question.

There is silence on the line, then a long breath. *In or out?* Micha remembers the old man was kind. Polite. But he is angry now.

– *Sorry. Mr Kolesnik, you will have to forgive me. I have been asleep. I lost track of time* —
– Are you a journalist?

– *No.*
– You want to know about me?
– *No.*
– No?
– *I'm not a journalist.*
– Who are you?
– *Michael Lehner.*
– So you said.
– *I'm a teacher.*
– What do you want from me?

Micha can't think of a reply. Not one which doesn't include Opa, and he doesn't want to include Opa.

– What do you want from me, Mr Lehner?
– *You remember the Germans, the Occupation. I was told that.*

No reply, just the same breath. Difficult, frightened; a deep breath in.

– *I wanted to speak to someone about what happened. In your town, when the Germans came.*
– You are Jewish.

It's not a question.

– *No. No. I am German. I mean. I am not Jewish.*
– So what is your question?
– *Mr Kolesnik, I'm not sure the telephone—*
– Your question!

He shouts, hoarse. His voice rips into Micha's ear.

Micha hangs up the phone.

———

Micha is shaken by the phone call, and by Kolesnik's anger, but he prays for him to phone again.

———

Micha takes time off school. He calls in sick after Mina leaves for the clinic, then he sits in the kitchen with the phone.

After four days of silence, he goes back to work, and when he gets home on the fifth, a letter has arrived.

———

Herr Lehner

Please accept my apologies. I lived through it here, and I think you know it was a terrible time.

Please understand. I don't think I can answer your questions. It is painful to remember those years. I prefer not to talk about them.

Jozef Kolesnik

Michael reads the precise, cautious constructions over and over again. The careful, sloping hand.

———

– Why didn't you tell me about him?

– *Because I cried, Mina, and I didn't show him the photo.*
– Why didn't you tell me he phoned?
– *Same reason. I hung up, ran away. I don't know.*

Mina sighs and the blood rushes to Micha's face. She pushes the letter away from herself across the table, leans forward and presses her fist into the small of her back. The weight of the baby is already changing the way she moves and stands.

– What did you say to him? When you were in Belarus, I mean.
– *Nothing. I wanted to ask him questions, and then I didn't have the courage and then he told me to go away. Asked me.*
– Is he Jewish?

Micha shakes his head.

– *All the Jews were killed.*
– No. I can't deal with this any more Michael.

Mina shakes her head, opens her mouth to speak again, but Micha cuts her off.

– *I think I will go back.*
– What?
– *To Belarus, talk to him.*
– But he says he wants to be left alone.
– *I will leave him alone. I only want to know about Opa. I won't ask anything about him.*
– He'll just tell you to go away again.
– *Maybe, I don't know. I'm going to write to him, try to go.*

Next holidays, next month sometime.
— Fuck. Michael.

Mina stands up and walks across the room. She faces away from him, leans against the door.

— *Mina.*
— I can't deal with this any more. It's disgusting, Michael. I don't want it in my home.
— *I'm sorry, Yasemin. I am, and we don't have to talk about it any more. I'll just go and then I'll know.*
— Why do you have to know? I don't understand that. Really. Why do you have to know?

Micha shrugs. She has her back turned, she can't see.

— *I just do.*
— What good will it do?
— *I don't think you can really look at it that way, Mina.*
— I can. And I think you should. Look at it from someone else's perspective, you know. Mine, your mother's, Mr Kolesnik's. Think about other people.
— *I do.*
— Liar.

Micha stares at her back, furious, knowing that she's right.

— This is my grandfather. Do you remember him shooting the Jews in your village?
— *Fuck off, Mina.*
— What? That's your question. It's what you want to know, isn't it?

She kicks the door, and jams her fists into the small of her back again. Michael sits at the table and starts to cry.

— I'm pregnant and you want to go away to Belarus and talk to an old man who never wants to see you again about something that he doesn't want to remember. That's the way it is, Micha, you see?

He doesn't answer; doesn't trust himself. He wishes she could come and put her arms round him, but he knows she can't. He can see that in her fists and shoulders.

Micha cries because he knows she is right. It is unfair to leave her alone and pregnant. He is hurting her, his mother, father, uncle, sister, Kolesnik and Oma, too.

But he also cries for himself.

This is my Opa. Do you remember him killing the Jews in your village?

Mina asked the question, and he can still barely say it inside.

———

Micha writes to Kolesnik, and Kolesnik writes back.

The old man says again that he doesn't feel able to help, but this letter, too, is polite, and a phone number is printed clearly at the top with the address.

Micha refolds the letter carefully and puts it away before Mina gets up for work.

—

Micha thinks about phoning, but in the end he writes again. It is easier, he can be calmer, the request more composed. He can lie.

It is a research project about the German Occupation of Belarus, to be used in teaching materials covering the war and Holocaust. To complete it, I need details of the daily lives of the German soldiers and policemen who served in the area. I think I can understand your feelings about the time, Mr Kolesnik, but I believe you can help me, and perhaps help future generations avoid the mistakes of the past. I would therefore be very grateful for your time.

Micha says nothing about Opa. Another lie. Indirect, by omission, but a lie all the same. And if he is honest, Micha knows it is not there to protect the old man; only to protect himself.

He promises Kolesnik that he will ask no questions, look for no details about his own life.

Anything you don't want to answer, you can just say so, and that is fine. And if you want to stop, at any time, then I will go away.

Micha tells himself that this goes some way to make up for the lies.

—

– Have you thought about what will happen here if you go?

– *What?*

– You haven't, have you?

Mina cuts a slice of bread and watches Micha cook for a while.

– Your family, Michael.

– *I know.*

– You don't. You don't know what you are doing.

Mina flattens the bread with her fingers, leaning against the fridge. Micha wonders who she has been talking to. *Mutti, Luise.* What they have been saying. *I should ask.* He can feel Mina waiting. *I should want to know.*

– You think maybe your Opa drank because he was guilty?

– *Maybe.*

– It could just have been the camp he was in. Or the prison. Wherever the Russians kept him.

– *Mina, please. Please don't try to persuade me not to go.*

– I think a camp would have been enough for me.

She stops talking, eats her squashed bread. Micha wills her to look at him, but she doesn't.

– I don't know what they did with German soldiers, but they were terrible places, Michael.

Micha watches her eat a bit more bread.

– I treated an old man who'd been in the Gulag.
– *You never told me.*
– It was before I knew you. He'd been out for twenty years, but his body was still affected. Malnutrition, beatings. He was an alcoholic.

Mina eats the rest of her bread and then she stirs the food on the stove. She stands very close to him, but Micha feels she doesn't want to be touched.

– *But I saw the pictures of what they did there, Mina. Where Opa served.*

Mina carries on stirring.

– *I have to know if he did those things, too.*

– Why?
– *I just do.*
– That's not good enough for me, Micha.

She is not angry, though. This time it is Mina who cries. Micha stands with her. He tries, but he still can't explain.

– *I love my Opa, Mina. I don't know what else I can say. He might have done something terrible. It's just important for me to know.*
– Will you still love him if he killed people?
– *I don't know.*

She stares at him. *I did think of that, Mina, and I really don't know.*

– He might not remember. This Kolesnik. He might not know, Michael. You might never know.

Micha reaches out, rests his hand on the small of her back. She turns and puts her arms around him. She cries. The baby is a small, proud bulge between them. Micha pushes his face into Mina's neck.

———

Herr Lehner

I have given your request some thought, and in the light of your assurances, I think I can offer my assistance.

Kolesnik

———

– *I thought, if you wrote it out for me, then I could copy it.*

She is amused by Micha's request, Mina's friend of a friend. She offers Micha a cigarette, reaches over to pick up the ashtray from the next table.

– Who are you writing to anyway?
– *Andrej? He's a friend.*
– You speak no Belarussian? No Russian?
– *No.*
– And you have a Belarussian friend who speaks no German?
– *Yes. I stayed with him.*

– I see.

Micha is still nervous, despite the woman's smiles.

– *Coffee? Cake?*
– Coffee would be great.

He leaves his letter with her on the table and goes up to the counter to order. When he gets back, she is not smiling any more.

– You want to tell your friend that your grandfather was a Nazi in his country?
– *Yes.*
– Over one and a half million killed, you know that? Two million?
– *Yes.*

Micha nods, but he didn't know. *Why did I not know that?*

– A whole generation of my family.
– *By the Nazis?*
– By the Nazis.

She is holding out Micha's letter, but he doesn't take it back. He thinks: *she is married to a German.* He is amazed.

– *You are married to a German.*
– Yes.

No explanation. *Why should she explain to me?* She reads the letter again.

– I hope your friend is understanding.

— *I have to tell him the bit about Jozef Kolesnik. It's a small place. He will find out I am talking to him anyway, and I would rather he knew from me.*
— OK. If you say so.

She writes for a while, then she stops.

— You don't know him very well?
— *No.*
— You don't know about his family?
— *No, but he knows I am German. He was very welcoming. His mother, too.*

She shrugs and writes some more. Micha feels uneasy now, not sure at all.

— Listen, you can send what you like, but if you change your mind, just leave out that bit.

She circles five sentences.

— Those are about your grandfather. It is up to you, but the letter will still make sense without them.

———

Micha is late. He gets to the station in plenty of time, but first one train doesn't come, and then another.

The people on the platform turn to each other and whisper, filling the unexpected time. Micha thinks of his father, who is always early, and how he will be waiting for him. And he thinks: *why today? Why did the trains go wrong today?*

– Sorry. It was a long meeting.

Micha's father shrugs, buys him a coffee. They stand at the kiosk, and commuters hurry down their snacks around them. Micha wasn't planning to lie; *I could have told him about the trains*; but it just came out. And it sounds flippant, thoughtless; just exactly like a pointless lie.

He thinks I came late to hurt him.

Micha has hurt his father, before he even opened his mouth.

– I don't want to say much, Michael. I will be quick.

He looks around the station concourse.

– My father was a soldier. He died at Stalingrad, and I never knew him, but I know that he fought soldiers, not civilians, and so I can live with that. It was a war. I can live with that. Askan was in the SS. Waffen SS, but SS all the same, and he served in the east. This means. To me. This means that there is always the possibility. That you are right.

Micha stays quiet. *He said it.*

Micha looks at his father, watches him shake his head. Vati coughs, and then he goes on.

– I knew Askan for many years, ten years. I loved him, I love your mother, and she loved him very much. In my heart, you see, I can't believe that he could kill. In a battle

yes, but not what you think. Not murder.
– *Himmler said it was a battle. A war against the Jews.*
– Michael. Let me finish.

Micha nods. He is sorry. He lets his father choose his words.

– However much I don't feel he could do that. However much. There is always this possibility.

Micha looks away from his father, down at his cup, allows him to continue without his son's eyes on his face.

– I have never told your mother that I think this, and I never will. I am only telling you now because I want to explain. I wanted to stop it with our generation. Yes? Bernd, your uncle, was already born after the war. Do you understand? I didn't want you and Luise to be touched by it. Askan loved you both. That's the part of him I wanted you to have.

Vati gathers his briefcase and coat. Micha can't look at him, so he doesn't know if his father is looking at him.

Mina is right. I don't know what I have done.

Belarus, Summer 1998

It is embarrassing, being here again; Micha hadn't expected that. The last time he saw Elena Kolesnik, he cried outside her house, and she gave him vodka and wanted him to leave.

She has made food, good heavy bread, and Micha occupies himself by looking at the photos on the windowsill while she lays the table. One is of Kolesnik and his wife, when they were younger, middle-aged. Both wearing overcoats, buttoned up against the cold. Shoulders hunched, standing on stone steps covered in snow. Arm in arm, hands in mittens, Kolesnik's wife holds a small bunch of flowers to her chest. Both are looking past the camera, at the ground. Both smiling, but self-conscious, too. When Micha looks up, he finds Kolesnik standing in the doorway.

– *This is the two of you?*
– Yes. Our wedding. We were quite old already when we married, you see?
– *Not so old, really.*
– Yes, we were. Lucky to find each other.

The old man smiles. He speaks to his wife, and she smiles, too. At Micha. She says something to her husband.

– Elena says it is our only photograph together. It is true.

His wife speaks to him again and he nods.

– We have known each other almost all our lives, and only one picture.
– *Please tell your wife I will take a photo before I go. I will send it to her from Germany.*

Kolesnik translates and his wife nods, blushes, pleased. Micha is pleased, too.

He watches Kolesnik while they eat. The old man's hands are broad and hard. Thick skin over large bones; creased fingers with heavy knuckles and wide, flat nails. They move slowly, the hands, from plate to mouth, rest on the table while he chews. Micha looks up at his face, looks away. The old man's eyes were on him, too; watching him watching.

After they have eaten, Micha and Kolesnik drink vodka together in the kitchen. The old man watches while Micha sets up the tape recorder, loading the batteries, setting the levels. Micha wrote to him about it; told him he would want to tape their conversations, but he can see that Kolesnik wasn't expecting this today. *Shit. Not on the first day.*

– *I thought we could just get used to talking? With the tape running?*
– Yes. Good idea, good idea.

Micha stops the tape, rewinds a little and presses play. Kolesnik's Good Idea hisses back into the room, tinny but clear. The old man smiles, but his eyes flick quickly away from Micha's. Shocked at the sound of his own voice.

They sit together in the kitchen among the pots and pans and plates, and the tape turns, recording the silence. There is a new loaf of bread on the stove, and onions in a box on the floor. Everything in its place; heavy boots by the door, leather mittens hanging from a shelf painted the same colour as the wall. Elena Kolesnik walks through every so often, moving between house and garden, ignoring Micha, the rolling tape, working around him, as if he weren't there.

– We will stick to our arrangement.
– *Yes.*

Micha answers, although it wasn't a question. Kolesnik nods. The skin around his eyes creases; resting somewhere between a squint and a smile. Micha knows it is a caution. The old man is drawing a line which both of them can see.

Micha puts the batteries on charge before he goes to bed, the red light glowing in the black night. He makes a mental note to give Andrej extra money for electricity before he goes home.

—

– *Can you tell me about what happened? While the Germans were here?*

Kolesnik frowns, tilts his face up a little.

– So many things happened here.

Micha thinks he might be mocking him.

– *Yes. I know. But please, if you could tell me what they did here.*

Micha shuts his eyes, briefly. He knows what they did; *they killed.* His request sounds naïve. He knows it will sound even more naïve when he listens to the tape again tonight.

– You could start from when the Germans arrived, perhaps?
– Yes.

The old man clears his throat.

– So. From when the army came?
– Did they come first?
– Yes.

The old man's shoulders are not set so squarely now, and he takes the cigarette Micha offers him. Kolesnik looks at Micha; old man at young. He has the same heavy skin on his face; thick folds hanging between cheekbone and jaw. It is paler, finer around the eyes, and it puckers there as he smokes.

– 1941, in the summer. We saw the planes and then came the army. And later the SS came with the police, and they stayed. We had a police station and a barracks, and they set up a new government here. Before it was the Communists, you see, so the Germans found new people and made a new government.
– New German people?
– Belarussians and Germans. The Germans were in charge, but they had Belarussians who worked for them here, of course. It was the same in the police.

– And after that?
– We had curfews, new laws. They changed everything. Schools, roads, farms. We didn't have the old collectives any more. The farmers had to work for the Germans instead. To feed the army in the east. Those sorts of things, you see. That's how they changed it.

Micha waits again, but he doesn't think Kolesnik will say more of his own accord.

– And then?
– What do you want to know?
– There were Jews living here?
– Yes, there were Jews.
– What happened to the Jews?
– They were killed.

Kolesnik's face is blank. He looks straight at Micha while he speaks.

– Can you tell me who did the killing?
– Depends who was there. Sometimes just police, sometimes police, SS, army.
– Waffen SS?
– Everyone.
– Germans?
– Germans, Belarussians, Lithuanians, Ukrainians. Germans mainly.
– Can you tell me about them?
– What do you want to know?
– Who were they? What did they do?

The old man's eyes are on his face.

— I just want to know who the people were, what they did.

Kolesnik nods, smokes.

— You don't have to tell me if you don't want to.
— No. I know that.

Kolesnik's words are hard, but his face isn't. Not so blank any more.

— I only want to know about the Germans.
— Yes, you said. What the Germans did to the Jews.
— No details. Just people. Events.

Micha lets the old man think about what he might say. Stretches his fingers, rubs at the blue-red crescent-moons left by his nails on his palms.

— First they made a ghetto. That was the first thing they did. And they stopped the Jews going to school, and also they didn't let them work, they weren't allowed to work for themselves any more, you know. Perhaps that came first.

Kolesnik shifts in his chair. Micha waits and the old man goes on.

— Quite soon after they came, they killed all the men, or nearly all the men. All the old ones, sick ones, the boys. They left enough to keep the work up. In the sawmill, other places. Shot the rest.

– *Shot them?*
– Rounded them up in the town at night and in the morning they shot them. They thought the men would be the ones to fight back, you see.

Kolesnik coughs, briefly; wide palm covering his mouth.

– More Jews were killed again in the spring, and then they brought Jews from all around, all the villages, and put them in the ghetto. They used some to work and the rest they killed. It went on like that, you see?
– *How long? How long did that go on for?*
– The last shootings were in 1943.
– *Who did the shooting then?*

The old man frowns, irritable.

– Like I said, police, SS, everyone.
– *Waffen SS?*
– Don't remember. Probably. It was in the woods, to the south, beyond the river. They were buried there.
– *When in '43?*
– Late summer.
– *Late summer.*

Kolesnik stops speaking, Micha is thinking: *Opa was here. Same time, same place.*

– No. Early autumn. There were haystacks in the fields.

Micha looks up. The old man is looking out of the window.

Such a strange thing to remember. Killing and haystacks: they murdered and the seasons changed again.

— After that. The Jews that were left, they were hiding in the villages, in the marshes, with the partisans. And the Germans, they went looking for them there.

Micha stares at the old man in front of him. *He saw all that. Remembers it.* Murder, summer, autumn, winter, spring. The ghetto being emptied and filled and emptied again.

Micha opens the notebook in front of him. It is reflex, something to do.

— What are you writing?
— *Nothing.*
— Will you be writing things down while we speak?
— *I don't know. I thought I might. Do you mind?*

Kolesnik blinks.

— No. No.

They sit in silence. The old man waiting dutifully for Micha to speak.

But Micha can't say anything, he can only think: *Same time, same place. Summer, autumn 1943. He remembers it all.*

Micha closes his book again.

— *Sorry. Do you mind if we stop? I don't think I want to go on today.*

—

In the evening, Micha cycles between the villages. Fast at first, but then slowing down.

When he gets back to Andrej's, he takes out the photo of Opa and lays it on the small table in front of him.

Micha knows: he could take this picture with him to Kolesnik's tomorrow, show him, be direct.

This is my Opa. Do you remember him killing the Jews?

Micha listens to the tape again. *Same time, same place.* He tries to bargain with himself.

I don't even need to tell him. Kolesnik doesn't need to know. I don't have to say Opa. I can just say Askan Boell.

In bed, however, he thinks of Kolesnik. The old man's broad, slow hands, the soft skin around his eyes. His blunt answers. Micha is still too afraid.

—

– *Can you remember any of the Germans?*
– Yes.
– *Can you tell me about them?*
– What do you want to know?
– *Doesn't matter. Anything. Just whatever you remember.*

Kolesnik is unsure. Micha thinks he looks almost embarrassed for a while; struggling for words.

– *Anything. Start anywhere. Please.*
– I remember one.

— *What was his name?*
— Tillman. A doctor with the police. He taught them. How to shoot people. The cleanest way, you see. But you didn't want details.
— *No.*

Kolesnik looks relieved. Micha is relieved. They both sit in silence again.

— *If you can remember the German names, maybe? I thought you could just tell me those?*

The old man remembers a few, quite a few. He lists them slowly, and Micha listens, writes, waits. Surnames and some first names, too, but Askan and Boell are not among them.

— *There were more than that, though? There must have been more?*
— It was a long time ago.
— *Yes.*

Micha thinks while the tape hums. *Two more days.* He decides to allow himself two more days before he shows the photo.

— I remember one who shot himself.

Not Opa.

— *He killed himself?*
— Behind the barracks. After one of the shootings.
— *He thought it was wrong?*

– Yes, I think so. I remember they shot the Jewish children, and then the next day he shot himself.
– *He did it, though? He shot the children.*
– Yes. He did.

There are long, empty seconds while Micha can't speak. Kolesnik is watching him, and Micha knows it.

After a while the old man gets up. He pours vodka, one for each of them, and sets a small, full glass on the table in front of Micha. His hand shakes. Micha looks at him.

– *Sorry.*

Kolesnik nods. He waits until Micha drinks, and then he drinks, too.

– *I think it is better without details. That would be easier for you, probably?*

Kolesnik nods again. Micha thinks the old man might say something, too, and he waits, but the moment passes.

Kolesnik points at the tape recorder, and though he is feeling braver now, and warmer from the vodka, Micha stays true to his word and turns it off.

—

Late afternoon and Andrej plays cards with Micha, the rules of the game clarified through mimed agreement. Give and take: some German, some Belarussian variations, and some confusion and laughter too.

They drink vodka and Micha's stomach burns. He thinks of the paragraph left out of his letter, still unsure whether it was cowardice or good sense not to write those lines. Watches Andrej warm soup on the stove and cut bread. *How to explain now. Where to start?*

He wanted to call Mina tonight. Walk to the phone box in the main square and speak to her. Instead he eats his food, brushes his teeth and gets into bed.

—

Kolesnik is standing out on his porch when Micha turns the corner on Andrej's bike. The old man holds a hand up in greeting as Micha cycles towards the house, and Micha raises his hand, too. A silent hello.

Kolesnik comes down the steps while Micha unties his bag from the handlebars.

– Listen, Herr Lehner, I have been thinking.

Micha stops. He looks up at the old man.

– *You want me to leave?*

Kolesnik looks tired. Deep sleep creases in his face.

– No. No. I was just wondering. Can I ask you something?
– *Yes. Of course.*

Micha leans the bicycle against the house, faces forwards, smiles.

– They didn't tell you about me. The people at the museum. Did they?
– *They said you remembered the Germans.*
– Yes, but they didn't tell you what I did while the Germans were here.
– *No.*
– No. I thought they had, you see, when you came before. But your questions. I just started wondering.

Kolesnik stands very close, and his voice is soft. Micha holds his breath. The old man is so close, it's like being touched.

– I think I should tell you.
– *Yes?*
– Yes.
– *I'll set up the tape then?*
– No, I'll just tell you here.

Micha is confused. The old man is too close. Micha puts his hand out, holds the bike frame. He wants to turn away.

– My father was a teacher. He taught me languages, Polish and German, and when the Germans came I worked with them. I collaborated. That is the word for it, yes?
– *Yes.*

Micha tries not to let the shock of it show in his face. *He can see it.* Kolesnik nods, he goes on.

– Everyone knows. Here, around here. I thought that's why you came to me, you see?

— *Yes. I see.*

Collaborated. It never occurred to Micha that it could have been that way.

— I knew German, so I translated, for one and a half years, nearly two. It wasn't regular, the work. But I translated for the SS, for the police. So I knew, you see? What they were doing.

The old man nods to himself, briefly.

— And then I shot Jews. Other people too, partisans, but mainly Jews.
— *I see.*
— I know what we arranged. I said I didn't want to talk about it, but that was when I thought you knew. I realised it is impossible to talk about these times unless you know. So I thought I could tell you and then we could go on.

Micha nods. He unties his bag from the handlebars, fingers struggling with the knots. He can't stand still. He busies himself with the buckles and straps and the bike, climbs up the five steps to the door. *Get on with it.* Get a few feet of air between himself and the old man, too.

Micha is shaken.

Micha thinks: *I didn't want to know.* But it is too late.

—

— You were interviewing today?

It is Micha's first phone call home, and Mina sounds happy to hear from him.

— Kind of. Couldn't really get very far.
— He didn't want to answer your questions?
— No. It was me. I just couldn't do it. I left after about ten minutes, cycled around all day.

Mina is quiet for a while. Micha squats down on the floor, leaning his back against the phone booth.

— Does he remember your Opa?
— I haven't asked him yet.
— Oh.
— He murdered Jews.

Micha listens for her reaction. Nothing.

— Kolesnik, I mean. Not Opa. Maybe Opa, too. Probably. Mina. He killed people. He told me today. I just couldn't stay, after that. I couldn't speak or look at him.
— Are you OK?
— No.
— Micha.
— It's fine, Mina, sorry. I'm not OK, but it's fine.
— Micha. Why don't you just come home?

He knows he could. When he started the phone call, he thought he would. Now that Mina has said it, he's not sure any more. He keeps quiet, hears Mina sigh.

— What about you? Are you OK?

– Yes, I'm fine.
– *Any news?*
– Signed up for an antenatal class.
– *Really? When does that start?*
– Next week. Wednesday night. For mothers and partners. Will you be there?
– *Next Wednesday. Don't know. The one after, though. They'll go on until the birth, won't they?*
– Yes.

Micha stands up, pushes more coins into the slot in the phone.

– Listen, Micha, I think I'm going to go. I've got an early start.
– *Oh.*
– If you're OK.
– *Yes, I'm fine.*

Micha listens for noises in the background on the phone, tries to imagine where Mina is standing in their home. No fridge hum, no traffic, no TV. *In the hall, lying on the floor with her legs up against the wall. No slippers, just socks on.*

– *Look. I would come back for the class, only it would mean leaving tomorrow probably, because of the train connections. And that's a bit soon, you know.*
– Yes. I know. We'll catch up.
– *Yes.*
– You don't have to go back to see that man, if you don't want to, you know.

– I know.

– If he upsets you, I mean.

– Yes. I know. I just think I'm so close to finding out.

He says it; he knows it; what he heard today doesn't change it; the question is still there.

– There must be other ways. Other people to ask.

– I don't know. I've been thinking about that. What he did. I mean, it's terrible, but it probably makes him the best person to ask.

Mina says nothing at first and then she sighs.

– I see. Yes.

Micha hears Mina tapping the phone. With her finger-nails, or with a pen. He wonders if she's drawing on her hands.

– OK. Well, if you're OK, I'll say goodbye.

Micha is quiet. He doesn't want her to go.

– Bye, Micha.

– Bye, then.

– Bye.

———

The old man talks half into the microphone, half to Micha. He is nervous today. First day back in the kitchen. Micha finds it hard to look at him.

– I live here in the village now, but I was born in the next town, and I grew up there, in the first Communist times, before the Nazis came.

Kolesnik lights another cigarette.

– I was nineteen when the Germans came. I translated, and then when I was twenty-one I joined the police.

Micha looks at the tape recorder, eyes fixed straight ahead.

– After that, when the Communists came back, I was in prison.
– *Here?*
– In Russia. For seventeen years.

Eight more than Opa.

There is silence.

– We can stop.

The old man blinks. Outside a car passes.

– Maybe it will be easier tomorrow. Another day to get used to it. You can think of some questions, what you want to know from me. Write them down, and you can ask me tomorrow.

———

Micha has the window open because it is a hot night. Lies on top of the blanket, scratchy wool against the backs of his knees. Insects bat around the light, swarm in the pool of light on the wall.

He can't sleep. The dark is too full and close, he can't rest: he closes his eyes and it is all still there.

Micha is grateful for dawn.

—

– *The man who killed himself. The German. I was thinking that you said he was ordered to kill the children.*
– Yes.
– *What happened if you disobeyed? I mean, could he have refused to do it?*
– Yes.
– *Yes?*

This morning, Kolesnik was ready for him, waiting. Cigarettes laid out on the table, vodka and two glasses. No sign of Elena.

The old man shifts his chair forwards, now. A few centimetres closer in to the table. He thinks a moment or two.

– There were orders, but we were also volunteers.
– *You were ordered to volunteer?*
– In a way. Yes.
– *In what way?*

Micha can be impatient now. He can show it, and he knows the old man will still answer.

– You could say if you didn't want to. If you didn't want

to, you didn't have to.

– *There was no punishment?*

– No.

– *So you think he wanted to kill the children, this man?*

– No, I don't think so.

– *No?*

– No.

– *But if he didn't have to, if he didn't want to, why did he do it?*

Kolesnik doesn't answer. Micha takes a cigarette, slides one across the table to Kolesnik. The old man lights it using the end of his old one.

– *Couldn't he have shot to one side, even? Pretended to shoot them, but miss?*

Kolesnik shrugs. Micha thinks: *You, Kolesnik. Did you aim to kill or aim to miss?*

– Someone else was always responsible.

Micha looks across the wide kitchen table at the old man, and Kolesnik shrugs again. Not a dismissive gesture; defeated. Micha thinks: *aimed to kill.*

– *What does that mean?*

– Someone else said it was the thing to do. Even if they didn't order it, not really order it, they still said it was the thing to do. So you weren't responsible, you see? And then you did it, even though they didn't order you to do it. So you did it voluntarily. And that way, the ones who gave the orders weren't responsible either.

Kolesnik draws the circle, and Micha follows it round and round.

And then he just sits.

And then after a while, Kolesnik speaks again.

– It is difficult for me to tell you. I can never explain and you can never understand. I was thinking today that this is good. It is good that you cannot know what was in my head. You are too different.

And Micha thinks: *that is too easy. It is too easy to say that.*

– *Are you different now?*
– Maybe so, maybe so. I can't really say. I am not the one to say that.
– *Does it still make sense to you now? What you did?*
– No. No. But I do remember that it did back then.

—

Micha writes to Mina. He can't phone and tell her what he wants to say. Afraid to say it out loud. That that might make it true. He knows it will disgust her. She might not read it, but he will at least have written it down.

Maybe it was easy. In the circle, like Kolesnik said.

Micha thinks about Opa. *Holding a gun.* A trench in front of him and the black-green of the trees behind.

Did he aim to miss? If he did, even once, does that make him different? Less bad? Why?

Same time, same place. They came here to kill. That's what he was here for.

Micha puts the letter in an envelope and seals it. He feels sick; the need to lie down. He takes the letter with him to the toilet, tears it up and flushes it down the pan.

—

For two days Micha doesn't go back. He doesn't plan it that way, but first one day goes by, and then another.

—

The line is not good, and Mina's voice is tiny in the noise. Mutti has been calling her again. Micha knows Mina is angry with him, but he has to keep asking her to speak up. He interrupts her; unwittingly; bad timing; his words overlapping with hers. Each time, he makes it worse.

– She'll think I'm not passing on the messages.
– *No, she'll just think I'm being lazy. A bad son.*
– Why can't you just phone her, from there?
– *I can't.*
– Why, Micha?
– *Pardon?*
– I said why.
– *She'll know it's long distance, I'll have to lie to her.*
– You're making me lie to her. I don't want to lie to her.

– Has my father called, too?

– I spoke to him last week, I told you.

– Yes.

– How much longer will you be there?

– Mina, I can't hear.

– How much longer?

– A few days, maybe. I can get a train at the end of the week.

– A few days.

– Yes. You're OK aren't you? The baby's OK?

– Fuck yes Michael. Still pregnant, still fucking fine.

She is quiet then. So is Micha. Letting the dust settle.

– I'm leaving the answerphone on. If your parents call, I won't pick up.

– Will you pick up when I call?

– You'll be back soon. You don't need to call again.

Micha holds his breath. Mina can be cruel. So can he.

– My money's running out.

The pile of coins stands crooked on the shelf by Micha's fingers. He looks away from them, pretending to himself they are not there.

– Yes, OK. See you soon.

– See you soon.

They wait in silence for the line to go dead. Mina hangs up before the click and burr.

—

Kolesnik has braced himself against the chair. Ashtray and matches lying ready on the polished wooden arm. Micha hands him the day's cigarettes and he smokes.

— *Did you hate the Jews?*
— Yes and no.
— *What does that mean?*
— It means I found someone to hate.
— *Yes?*
— I was angry. About my father, about the villages, the farms, the hunger. The Communists.
— *What about your father?*
— They killed him.
— *The Communists?*
— Yes. I remember they took him away with five other men.
— *What for?*
— He was a teacher. He wouldn't teach what they said. They had taken him away before, but this time he didn't come back.

Micha looks at the old man. There are no tears, his voice betrays no sadness, he just sits still in his chair, across the kitchen table from Micha.

— *So you hated the Jews for that? For your father?*
— Yes, you could say that.
— *Were the men who took your father Jews?*
— No, they were not Jewish. The Communists who took my father were not Jewish.

Kolesnik raises one hand, broad palm held open in emphasis.

– So why didn't you hate the Communists?
– I did hate them, but they got away. Before the Germans came. Without being punished for what they had done.
– So you wanted to punish someone?

Kolesnik shrugs. Defeated again.

– You wanted to punish someone for what the Communists had done, and the Jews were there, so you punished them?
– I'm sorry. I know that doesn't sound right. I know it was wrong, you see? I can't explain it better than that.

Micha repeats, to himself: *I know it was wrong.* The room is blue with smoke.

– Did you know it was wrong even then?

Kolesnik nods.

– So why did you do it?

Kolesnik sits in silence and stares at the floor. Even after Micha asks him again, he doesn't reply. Micha turns off the tape and goes outside and stands in the summer air. When he gets back, Kolesnik is still in the chair.

—

– You are recording?
– Yes.
– They took my father from me. I was angry and hungry,

my whole family, and then the Germans came and they
told me the Jews were to blame. They told everyone that,
you see. All Jews are Communists. Which wasn't true.
— *No?*
— No. Some of the Jews here were Communists. But the
Belarussians were, too.
— *So it was a lie?*
— Yes.
— *And you believed it?*
— No.
— *You knew it was a lie?*
— Yes. But it was a lie that made sense.
— *What does that mean? Can you explain that?*
— I know it is bad to say it. I know it is wrong. I knew it
then, too.

Kolesnik looks at Micha; Micha looks past him. He
doesn't want to hear this. *I don't need to know. Not him.
Opa. Ask him about Askan Boell.*

— *The first massacres were in 1941.*
— Yes.
— *And you were translating then. For the Germans.*
— Yes, but I saw it all.
— *You saw the Germans in 1943, too?*
— Yes, and I killed.

Micha can feel the old man looking at him, looking for
eye-contact. Micha is thinking of a new question, but the
old man speaks first.

– I made the choice, you see? I watched the Germans kill the Jews for almost two years and then I killed, too. It was my choice, do you see?

Micha doesn't want to answer. He thinks he might turn off the tape, go outside again. He doesn't know why Kolesnik is telling him this. Not sure he wants to hear any more today.

– Do you see?
– *Yes. Well, no. You said you were angry. About your father.*
– Yes.
– *You thought that killing the Jews would help.*
– You're not listening.

Blunt. Composed. Micha looks at Kolesnik, briefly. Meets the old man's eyes.

– *You thought it would help, but it didn't.*
– It is hard to say this, Herr Lehner, even after so many years. It is difficult to know this about myself, do you see? I can give all these reasons. I lost my father, I was hungry, I wanted to help my family, orders were orders, I was not responsible, they said the Jews were Communists, Communists caused my pain. Over and over I can say these things. Nothing changes. I chose to kill.

Micha can feel the old man looking at him, but he can't see him. He presses his fists hard against his eyes, lifts them again, lets the black blood-ache slip away.

Nothing changes.

The old man smokes and looks at the floor.

—

Micha writes to Mina in his notebook, knowing he won't tear the pages out to send. Knowing he should take the paper to Kolesnik, be brave enough to read it out to him.

Did Opa kill? Because he thought he had to? Or just because he could? Did he feel sick, or sorry? Did he hate? Did he cry? Did he think it was right?

—

— *Did they talk about it? Afterwards. Did you hear what they said?*
— I wasn't one of them. I mean, I was Belarussian.
— *You didn't talk with them?*
— I was only there if I was needed to translate.
— *So you didn't hear what they said?*
— No. I'm not sure they did discuss it.
— *Why do you say that?*
— Afterwards. It was always quiet when we drove back. They drank a lot in the trucks and nobody said anything very much. I think the ones who stayed behind in the villages didn't want to hear about it, and maybe the ones who went to the forests and did the shooting didn't want to speak. I never wanted to speak.

Kolesnik's cigarette has burnt down. He flicks the long ash into the ashtray, lights himself another.

– Even before I did it. The first killings, people talked about them, in the town here, Belarussian people, but then they stopped. Everyone knew it was going on and no one spoke about it. I knew it was happening and I never said anything.

– *And after you did it?*

– I got drunk. There was always lots to eat and drink in the evenings afterwards. Lots of music. You didn't want to speak. Just drink and eat, hear the music, really loud.

—

Today we just sat, Mina. It was the same yesterday, too.

Micha could find no courage to ask; Kolesnik stayed with him all day. Let the young man be silent in his kitchen, gave him vodka, bread. Found him rags for his tears. They sat for hours, and the tape rolled on and on, and then it stopped, and Micha turned it over, started the recording again.

—

Micha cycles towards Kolesnik's village, but past it, on towards the town. He has the tape recorder with him, but he knows the day will be silent again, so he goes instead to the museum.

The girl on the door doesn't recognise him at first, but after he smiles and says hello, she nods and points to the visitors' book.

– Yes. In the spring.

Micha doesn't go to the uniforms or the killings this time. He stays on the other side of the room. Spends the morning with the photos of families, their houses, objects from their homes. A pair of gloves, a bolt of cloth, a small silver cup. Handwriting in a ledger, pencil-scribbled lists, personal notes in the margins of a book.

A man's leather shoe, good and heavy. Heel worn down on the outside, moulded by the wearer's step. As he walked around the village, from town to town. And then later only around his home or perhaps just as far as his neighbour's house; pacing out the narrow limits of the ghetto.

Micha doesn't cross to the other side of the room; he doesn't dare risk seeing the same faces again over there.

—

When Micha gets back to Andrej's, Kolesnik is there, sitting outside on the wall. He stands up as Micha cycles down the lane.

– I was worried. You didn't come.

Micha doesn't know what to say.

– Your friend said you were still here. I thought I'd wait.
– *I'm fine. I didn't feel like talking today.*
– No.

Micha stands outside the door, the old man looks like he doesn't want to go yet.

– *Listen. I can't really invite you in. It's not my place, you know.*
– No. I know. I was just thinking. Will you come tomorrow?
– *Yes. If that's OK?*
– Yes.
– *I just needed a break today.*
– Yes. My wife, Elena, I asked her if she would talk to you. She didn't collaborate. I thought it might be interesting for you to hear her story, too.

Micha is surprised.

– *She doesn't mind?*
– No, no. She wants you to hear.
– *OK.*
– I'll tell her you will come tomorrow?
– *OK.*

When Micha goes into the house, he finds Andrej's mother in the kitchen. She has been at the window, watching him talking with Kolesnik, and she looks angry. She says something to Micha which he doesn't understand, but her tone frightens him. She spits into the sink and leaves.

—

Micha sits at the table with Jozef and Elena Kolesnik.

Three of them, around the microphone; tape humming quietly on the table. Kolesnik will translate for his wife. Elena watches his face as they speak, but he stares only straight ahead, hands flat on the table in front of him. *He's pretending he isn't here.*

– *What do you think of what your husband did? While the Germans were here?*

Elena replies first to her husband and then to Micha.

– She feels sad.
– *Sad?*

Elena nods, rubs her fingertips against the table top. She speaks again.

– One of her brothers did the same.
– *He did?*
– Yes. She says the Germans ordered it, and he did it.
– *Did she think it was a good thing? Back then?*

Kolesnik asks his wife, and she shrugs while she speaks. A short answer.

– She can't remember.
– *No?*

Elena looks at her husband. Her lips move, but she doesn't speak. Micha waits, but he doesn't think she will answer. He finds another question.

– *What happened to her brother?*

– She had two brothers. One was killed by the Germans, and the other was executed after the Russians came back.
– *By the Germans?*
– Yes. He was killed with ten other men in her village. A German soldier was shot in the square. It was a punishment.
– *Who shot the German soldier?*

Micha watches Elena while she thinks.

– She doesn't know. A partisan, maybe.
– *But her brother wasn't a partisan?*
– No, but they shot him anyway. She says she wants you to know it was a cruel time.

Elena scratches at the table top with her long thumbnail. Her mouth is drawn tight, eyes wet. Micha stays quiet in case she says more. When she does speak, Micha sees Kolesnik nod, blink; the change in his eyes. It is the first time he has shown any response.

– By the end, she says she could only tell them apart from their songs.
– *I don't understand.*

Elena spreads her hands flat, turns them palm-up. Short fingers, fleshy pads, deep lines scored into her skin. She speaks. Stops. Her husband translates. She speaks again.

– At the end she saw no difference.

– After the Jews were dead, the Germans came and killed

and burnt and stole from her family instead. The partisans, too. They came in from the marshes with their guns when they were hungry.

– Her father locked the doors, nailed them shut, but they came in anyway.

– She says she was afraid. All the time afraid. Women were raped, men were taken away. No one trusted anyone. Every week, every day it was another thing.

– She hid in the barn. Sometimes she lay in the corn. Also in the reeds by the stream.

– She remembers when her mother was crying and crying, and when the men stole their food. Their cow. Which was all they had left.

Elena stops now and rubs her face dry. Deep breaths into old lungs. Kolesnik glances over at her, then looks ahead again. When she speaks, he looks down at his fists.

– In her village, after the houses were burnt, people lived in holes in the ground.

– When they came and did these things, she didn't know who it was. She just ran and hid.

– When she heard them singing, their language, then she knew. One day Germans, next day partisans. Later it was Russians, too.

Micha interrupts. He wants to know.

— Who was the worst?

Elena looks at her husband and he repeats the question for her, and then she looks at Micha, but doesn't speak.

— I mean, the Communists, the Germans, the partisans, the Red Army? Who was the worst?

Elena has tears on her cheeks. Micha can see them in the lines around her mouth when she moves her face into the light. *She won't answer.* Micha wonders if she is just being polite, even now, when he wants her to be honest. *The Germans. The Germans were by far the worst.*

He lets her sit for a while, and then he asks her.

— Is it enough to feel sad?

Kolesnik translates and Elena looks at Micha, angry now. She directs her answer to her husband.

— She doesn't know what you mean.

Micha tries to find another question, but he can't. Elena stands up and speaks; not to Micha, only to Kolesnik. She reties her headscarf, hands making tight, swift movements under her chin. Elena is crying. Her husband speaks for her.

— She says she can't feel anything else.

———

Micha packs his bag, looking out on to the darkening

street. Elena sits out on a chair on the porch, hands folded
tight in her lap. Micha can see her through the window,
but can't see her expression.

– She's remembering. It's hard for her. She'll come inside
in a while.

Kolesnik stands watching Micha watching his wife.

– *Elena said she is sad.*
– Yes.
– *Sad for what you and her brother did.*
– Yes.

Micha waits while Kolesnik pours a vodka for each of
them to drink.

– We have no children. When I came back, when we
married, she was too old. Elena thinks this is a punishment
for those times.
– *What do you feel?*
– What?
– *Do you feel sad?*
– No.
– *No?*

Kolesnik looks up at Micha. His eyes are steady. Micha
understands this is a challenge.

– *Do you feel sorry?*
– How can I apologise?

Micha knows it was the question he wanted. That the old

man had the answer already.

– How can I apologise? Who can I apologise to? Who is there to forgive me?

Kolesnik looks at Micha. *No one. No one left alive.* Micha thinks it, but he doesn't say it.

– I don't feel sorry for myself.

Micha watches for weakness in the old man's face, finds nothing. *No tears.*

– *Do you think you have been punished?*
– No.
– *Not in prison?*
– No.
– *Without children?*
– No.

Micha looks at Kolesnik. He can't understand this man. His blunt words.

– *Your wife cried when she talked to me.*
– I cried in prison. I cried some nights after we had shot Jews. Others did, too. I was wrong to do it and I was wrong to cry.

Kolesnik's voice comes in hoarse barks.

– *Is Elena wrong to cry?*
– Elena did nothing. She was a girl. She ran from everyone and she stayed alive.

His words are clear and hard.

— *Your wife is being punished, though. She has no children.*
— Elena thinks that is punishment. Not me. I think there is no punishment for what I did. Not enough sadness and no punishment.

—

In the morning, Micha leaves the tape recorder behind on the table in his room at Andrej's place. He packs his camera in his bag and cycles to Kolesnik's house. Elena Kolesnik stands when her husband brings Micha into the kitchen, and he takes his camera out, so she can see. She smiles and nods, speaking quietly to her husband as she tucks stray hairs away under her headscarf.

— Thank-you, Herr Lehner. My wife says it is very good of you.
— *No problem.*

Elena Kolesnik arranges two chairs by the stove, against the far kitchen wall, and Micha sets up the camera in front of them. Jozef Kolesnik helps him, holding the tripod, standing still while Micha focuses on the weave of his jacket. It is strange to work in silence, so Micha talks.

— *It's a good camera.*
— Yes?
— *A new lens, too. It's a zoom, but very sharp. The pictures should turn out very clear.*

Kolesnik looks through the viewfinder at the empty chairs, and Micha steps into frame for him. So he has something to see. Kolesnik smiles, and Micha smiles into the lens. He doesn't feel as though he is smiling at Kolesnik, exactly, but the old man laughs a little, pleased.

Elena Kolesnik sits upright next to her husband, and the old man holds her hands. Palm against palm, they wait while Micha opens the curtains wider, judges the light levels again.

– I might take three or four exposures. To be safe. If that's OK?

Kolesnik nods, stiff-necked, looking straight into the lens. He stays still like that until Micha takes the photo. Then, at the last moment, he looks away. He looks at Elena, as if she were the only thing worth seeing. Elena looks ahead, at Micha, at the camera, into the lens, but Jozef looks away.

Just like Opa.

Micha takes two more photos. He doesn't ask Kolesnik to look at him; he doesn't say anything at all.

When he has finished, Elena stands up, steps behind the camera with Micha. She smiles at him, gestures for him to sit down next to her husband, signals that she wants to take a photo of the two of them now.

Micha looks over at Kolesnik, who is staring at his wife. She carries on talking, excited, urging Micha gently over to the chair.

– *If you don't mind, I'd rather not.*

It feels rude, cruel, but Micha really does not want to have his photo taken with the old man. Kolesnik translates, and Elena stops. She is hurt, but not as much as he is. Still sitting, large hands lying motionless on his narrow knees.

Micha apologises. He packs up his camera quickly and leaves.

—

Andrej's friend stands with him in the kitchen doorway, both men looking angry and embarrassed. Micha stands by the sink, scrubbing his hands. The bicycle chain broke on the way back to the village, and his hands are grimy with oil and rust; brown-black under his nails. Still shaken from taking the Kolesniks' photo, Micha's hands feel weak under the icy flow of water from the tap. He turns round from the sink when the two men step into the room.

– Andrej says you shouldn't have brought the old man here.

Micha already knew this would be said.

– *Please tell him that I didn't invite him. He came here to find me. I am sorry.*

Micha listens to the murmuring translation, looks down at

his soapy-greasy hands.

– Andrej says that this man is a murderer.
– *I know. Please tell him I know that.*

Micha thinks: *it's over.* Friendship. The visit.

– *I will leave tomorrow. Please can you say I will leave, and that I am very grateful for the time here? His hospitality, and his mother's.*

Micha sees Andrej nod, sees the relief. *He doesn't have to tell me to go.*

Micha turns away. He is angry; tears smarting at his eyes. He turns the tap on again, scrubs at his fingers under the cold jet, but the oil just spreads under the soap.

—

– *Do you remember him?*

It is evening and Micha is back. Elena Kolesnik let him into the house and left him alone in the kitchen with her husband.

– *This man?*

Micha has put the photo on the table, so the old man won't see that his hands are shaking. Raw from scrubbing, from gripping the handlebars against the chill evening wind. Kolesnik pulls the picture closer to him.

– *This is here in Belarus?*

– *No, in Germany 1938.*
– I know this face.

Micha was ready for that. Preparing himself all day. All of these days.

– *Who is he?*

Micha doesn't know how to answer. He wanted Kolesnik to know; he didn't want him to know; he wanted Kolesnik to know without having to say the name. He says it.

– *Askan Boell.*
– Yes. He was Boell and he was SS.
– *Waffen SS.*
– Yes, *Waffen* SS. I remember him.

It is like relief. What Micha feels is like relief.

– *What do you remember?*
– They were fighting here for weeks and then it all went very quickly. It was early morning and suddenly the Red Army soldiers were here. In the town, just by the church.
– *1944.*
– Yes. They held me there, with the others like me, and then they brought the Germans there, too. Not all of them, some were dead, some were gone already, but they brought the ones that were left. Like clearing the ghetto, the Nazi ghetto. They stood them there with us and I remember Askan Boell was one of them.
– *You saw him?*

– Yes. The Russians pulled him out. They went down the line, and they pushed him down, made him kneel, you know. In the main square. They had guns, of course. A gun at his head, and they said his name, this Boell.

Alles vorbei. All over. Opa Askan Boell.

Micha doesn't know what to say. He thinks: *I should be recording this.* The tape deck is wrapped in jumpers at the bottom of his pack by the door in Andrej's house.

– *Do you remember anything else?*
– The Russians wanted to shoot us. Some of them wanted to shoot us straight away. That's why they stood us there so long, arguing. I remember that.
– *He was my grandfather.*

Kolesnik stops speaking. He looks at Micha, and Micha thinks, for a moment, that the old man looks angry. He hadn't expected to say it like that, but that is how it came out. Micha shifts under Kolesnik's gaze, sits up straighter in his chair.

– *Why did they want to shoot my grandfather?*
– They wanted to shoot us all.

Micha sits for a long time. For what feels like a very long time, and he tries to work out what it is that he feels. And he tries to work out if he can ask what he really needs to ask. Kolesnik sits opposite him and Michael can hear him breathe, and he thinks he can feel it when Kolesnik looks at him and when he looks away.

– *He was here. Summer, autumn 1943.*

Kolesnik moves. Micha sees that out of the corner of his eye. He tries again.

– *Did you see my Opa do anything?*

Micha doesn't look at Kolesnik when he says it, and he waits, but Kolesnik doesn't answer, so Micha has to look at him.

The old man has his head in his hands.

Kolesnik has pushed the photo away, too. The light from the window shines on the gloss, and Michael can't see his Opa, just the many tiny folds in the surface of his picture. The deep crease across his legs.

– *Jozef?*
– He killed people. I am sorry, Michael. He killed Jews and Belarussian people.

Micha is glad he can't see his Opa, glad that Kolesnik looks away.

– *You saw that?*

Kolesnik rubs his eyes.

– I know that he did.

He knows.

Micha looks at Kolesnik, but the old man looks out of the window. *He knows.* Micha can't see into Kolesnik's eyes, but he sees the crease in his forehead, and the shadow across his face.

– *How do you know?*

– 1943. The ones who were here then. That's what they were here for. All of them, all of us.

– *But you said. Yesterday, you said not everyone did. The man who shot himself.*

– I remember him because he shot himself.

– *What do you mean?*

– I am sorry.

Micha watches as Kolesnik rests his face in his large hands. He listens to the voice which comes through the gaps in the old man's fingers.

– There were so few who didn't do it. I could tell you all the names and faces who didn't do it because they were so few.

He knows this. Micha knows this is true.

– You understand?

He does, but he doesn't say anything. Fists pressed hard into his eyes.

———

Micha goes past Kolesnik's house with his bags on his way to the bus. Kolesnik is in the garden, standing under the tree, when he sees Micha at the gate.

– Michael!

Kolesnik is pleased to see him, hurries up the path with smiles. Micha thinks he will never get used to it; that Kolesnik likes him.

– Something to eat? You have time to stay?
– *No, sorry. I think the bus will be there soon.*
– I will walk with you then, yes?
– *Yes. Thank-you. That would be nice.*

At the bus stop, Micha leaves Kolesnik with his bags while he buys apples for the journey. He doesn't need apples, he doesn't need anything for the journey but he can't stand the silence of waiting with the old man next to him.

Micha is glad to be leaving. He tries to be, but he is not sad to say goodbye to Kolesnik. And though Micha knows Kolesnik likes him, he thinks the old man is also not sorry to see him go.

Kolesnik doesn't wait for the bus to leave. He nods at Micha through the window, presses his broad, dry palm to the glass and goes. Micha sits and waits alone, willing the bus to move.

Home, Winter 1998

Mina keeps laughing and crying and saying she is so tired. More tired than she's ever been. Micha lies down on the bed with her, although he can see that the nurse doesn't like it. Mina laughs again when the nurse leaves the room, and Micha folds the white blanket back over her arm, looks into his daughter's tiny face.

– *What will we call her?*
– I don't know. I don't know.

Mina lies the baby girl on Michael's stomach, and he can feel her faint warmth through his shirt, but no weight.

– *What's your name?*

Micha sees Mina smile at him and he laughs.

Mina sleeps, but Micha stays awake with their girl. At least he thinks he does, but Luise wakes him up when she comes in.

– I have champagne.

She has flowers, too, and Mina's parents bring baby clothes that are far too big, and then Micha's Mutti and Vati come. It is awkward; the crowd of family in the hot hospital room, and Micha gets drunk quickly on Luise's champagne. It is a long time since his last meal. He stands outside in the corridor and watches as his tiny girl is passed from hand to hand around the room.

– Will you phone Oma?

Mutti asks as she leaves.

– *No.*

Micha watches his mother's face contract; and out of the corner of his eye, he sees his father turn his back.

Luise stays on after the others have left.

— I'll phone her, then. If you like.
— *Whatever.*
— Micha.
— *What? I don't want to see her. She knew about it. She covered it up.*
— You don't know that.
— *He wrote her letters. He burnt them all afterwards. What do you think they said?*
— Not now, you two, OK?

Mina gets out of the bed and takes the baby from Luise. Micha watches his sister, but she won't look at him. He thinks she might cry again, wailing like the day he came back from Belarus; at the kitchen table, fists balled, knuckles pressed hard against her teeth. But Luise is quiet today. She takes a deep breath, watches Mina sit down on the bed with her new daughter, and then she stands.

— I should go anyway. Let you get some rest.

Micha shrugs. Mina lies back against the pillows, and smiles at his sister.

— Come back tomorrow, won't you? It was good to see you, Luise.

After Luise has gone, Micha sits down. He leans his head

back against the wall and closes his eyes.

– I was thinking you could maybe go, too.

Micha opens his eyes.

Mina is trying to feed their daughter, coaxing the small mouth through the folds of blanket and nightshirt to her breast. She shifts forward, tries to find a more comfortable position. Micha sees the hair at her temples, damp with sweat. Dark rings under her eyes.

– Go home. Come back tomorrow. Don't come when Luise is here.

———

It is Christmas again, with a new baby this time. Days and nights of rain-soaked windows and coloured lights. Milky baby smell and spicy biscuit gifts from friends.

Micha often wakes angry, but it takes him some minutes to remember why. The events of the summer impossible to connect with the small body he wraps in nappies and blankets. Tiny creased fingers, long legs, black hair. *Opa's great granddaughter.*

School holidays, night feeds, dark days. The weeks slide by. Passing their daughter between them, Micha and Mina smile at each other. He pulls her close as soon as he is allowed. After a while, she puts her arms around him, too. Everything is different again.

Michael Lehner, thirty-one: brother, nephew, son and grandson. Schoolteacher. Boyfriend, and now father, too.

In the months since he has been back, Micha has barely seen his family. Has told them nothing, only Luise. He has not been to visit Oma, and has had only two conversations with his mother. One at the hospital, the other on the phone, when she asked him to please go and visit his grandmother.

— Just for an hour or two, Micha. She doesn't understand.
— *No.*
— She keeps asking if you've gone away. She thinks something dreadful has happened.
— *It has. It did.*
— To the baby, I mean. She thinks we're hiding something.

Micha holds his tongue. Thinks of a thousand retorts. All of them angry. All of them obvious.

— Michael?
— *No.*

Micha and Luise fight about whether to tell their parents. Every time she comes to see Mina, and also in cafés, parks, on street corners. They meet to talk, and always end up shouting.

— They know anyway. Over a month you were away. You think they didn't notice that?
— *They don't know where I was.*

– Don't be so naïve. They can guess. They can fill in the details. They're not stupid.
– *So I can tell them, then? Fill in the details for them, save them the effort of speculation?*
– You're such an arsehole.
– *Fuck you, Luise. They're still not facing up to it.*
– Why? Because they don't scream and shout about it all day, every day?
– *Like me you mean?*
– Yes, like you.

Micha turns away and unlocks his bike. Luise wheels hers around him, so she can see his face.

– They know anyway, Micha. Just leave it alone now, OK?

—

– What do you want to call her?
– *I don't know.*
– I thought of Dilan. My Dad's mum was called Dilan.
– *That's nice.*
– Really?
– *Yes. Yes, really. It's beautiful.*

Micha looks at his daughter lying on his knees: soft, dark eyes, unfocused.

– *Dilan.*

He moves his face closer, and she widens her eyes. He

touches a fingertip against her palm to feel her grip.

— We can give her a German name, too.
— *No. I think Dilan is good.*

Mina is quiet. *Please don't say Kaethe. Just your grandmother. Not mine.*

— *I didn't have any names in mind, you know.*
— OK. It's OK. Dilan.

Mina smiles. Rests her hand on the back of Micha's neck.

— Dilan Lehner.
— *Dilan Lehner.*

———

Micha hates being alone.

The journey to work and back is the worst part of each day. He takes books to read on the train, picks up discarded magazines, newspapers, scans the adverts above the other passengers' heads. For a while, he tries a Walkman; has the music up so loud that his fellow commuters stare. Nothing helps. Micha can't concentrate on anything else.

I have the photo. I can say: that's Askan, he was my Opa. Married to my Oma, even then. And father to my mother, and later my grandfather. And all the while a murderer, too. How do I know that? I was told by a friend. Where is my proof? I have no reason not to believe it. There are no pictures of him holding a gun to someone's head, but I am sure he did that, and pulled the trigger, too. The camera was pointing elsewhere, shutter opening and closing on another murder, of another Jew, done by another man. But my Opa was no more than a few paces away.

At home he does his marking in the kitchen, in the living room, wherever he can be with Mina and the baby, too. Lying on the blanket next to Dilan, pens and exercise books spread out over the floor.

– She's sleepy. I'll put her down.
– *I'll do it. Can't we just wait a bit?*
– She needs a routine, Micha.
– *We could go for a walk. You and me. She can sleep in the pushchair.*
– It's dark.
– *That's OK.*

Mina looks out of the window.

– OK.

—

– How is she? Dilan?
– *Great. Beautiful. Putting on weight.*

Micha and Luise meet and eat lunch together every other day or so now. Without discussing it: it just happens. A regular time, after school, in a café near the hospital. Luise always in a hurry, but always there just the same.

– You OK?
– *Yeah. You?*

They sit in a window booth. Glass steam-edged against the cold spring days outside.

— I really don't think we can ever know.
— *So you keep saying, Luise.*
— Yes, I know. But what I mean is that we won't get anywhere. If we just keep asking that question.
— *You're the one that's still asking. I know what he did. I want to know if he felt guilty about it.*

Micha clears his throat, irritable.

— *I'd like to look at the photos again.*
— Oma's?
— *Yes. Before and after the war.*
— So. You'll have to go to Oma's then.

Micha doesn't answer. Searches through his pockets for his cigarettes. Hasn't been to see his Oma for over eight months, now.

— Yes. Well. No point anyway.
— *What?*
— I looked at them. You can't see anything.
— *When did you look at them?*
— After you came back. After you told me.
— *With Oma?*
— Yes, of course with Oma.
— *She saw one was missing?*
— Yes. From the honeymoon pictures. We looked all over the flat for it.

– *I've got it.*
– Oh. Right.

Luise stirs her soup.

– Anyway. They don't show anything, the pictures.
They're family shots, you know? Celebrations. Always
happy. You can't see anything.

Micha stares at Luise. Doesn't know whether to believe
her. Doesn't want to believe her.

– *He always looked away from the camera, though. Did you
notice that? After the war.*
– So?
– *Doesn't that say anything to you?*
– No. I don't think that's true, anyway. I'm sure there are
pictures where he looks at the camera.
– *No. Name me one.*
– Micha. God. Wedding anniversary. The thirtieth. Oma
and Opa together in the Kirchenweg. In the garden.

Micha tries to remember it. Still thinks Luise is wrong.

– *So you don't think he felt guilty?*
– No. I mean I don't know. We can't ever know. I'm just
saying maybe he never really knew what to think himself.
– *He killed people.*
– OK, Micha. Just listen. Maybe that's true. People do
terrible things. It was war. I'm not excusing it. Not at all.
But it was war and it was cruel and confusing and he
couldn't tell right from wrong any more, and he did

something terrible.
— *Yes.*
— So when people do these things. Maybe. I don't really
know, of course, but maybe sometimes they believe in
these things, or they become them, or maybe sometimes
they don't. They just do them and then they go on.
— *That's it?*
— What do you mean *that's it*? You haven't even thought
about what I've said.
— *I don't want to.*

Micha tries to remember the photo again. The
Kirchenweg garden. Can almost see it. Can't see Opa's
face.

— I'm just trying to help. Both of us.
— *I know.*

———

Mina goes back to work: part time, see how it goes, she
says. They time it to start at the Easter break, so Micha can
be at home to get Dilan used to the crèche routine. At first
for an hour or two, building up to lunchtime, and then
early afternoon, ready for when Micha is to come and
collect her after he finishes at school.

After he has settled her in, Micha waits in a café opposite
the kindergarten, not wanting to go back to the flat alone.
There is washing to be done, tidying, shopping, but he
will do it later, when Mina comes home, listening to her

talk about her day. He reads his way through the morning, eating, drinking, watching the waitresses chat behind the bar, the other customers come and go. It is a relief to pick Dilan up again, wrap himself in her smell.

Micha wonders if his Opa took comfort in his children, and then his grandchildren, too. *Mutti and Bernd. Luise and me.* Micha remembers Opa's arms, his lap, his soap-cigarette smell. Dilan shifts in the sling strapped to Micha's chest. He pulls her sock off, inspects the small toes and smaller toenails, rubs the foot, pulls the sock back on. *He didn't deserve to feel comforted*. Micha thinks it, and it feels right, but it also feels impossibly cruel.

The week passes and the day comes that Micha is to leave Dilan until after one. Walking from the underground he changes his mind. The too-long morning ahead, he turns the pushchair around, carries it back down the steps and runs down the platform to catch the departing train. Dilan blinks at him, dark-eyed, as he takes them past their stop, and on into town, where he changes trains and leads them to the main-line station.

He buys pretzels from the kiosk, changes Dilan's nappy in the women's toilets, and gets them on the first available train to Hannover, even though it means a change at Kassel and a twenty-minute wait.

— *I'm looking for the Steinweg.*

Micha tells the taxi driver above Dilan's screams. She is

hungry, and he's already given her the bottle from home. The driver takes them there, driving fast along the wide streets of the centre, and the unfamiliar suburbs, post-war housing blocks.

Micha stands on the pavement with Dilan propped on his hip. He has never been here, only seen photos. Knows the house number just like he knows so many other, cluttered details of his family's past. *Not the bits that matter.* He has no idea now what he hoped to gain from coming here; his Opa's first home after prison. *After his crime.* The house stands solid, respectable, suburban, impassive. *Lived in by somebody else.* Micha stands outside, confused, afraid, his hungry daughter screaming in his arms.

The childhood times he remembers are all good. Even when the drunken rages are included; the letters Opa burnt; the photos in which he looked away. Even now, with all his certainty about what Opa did, where he did it, the faces on the museum wall he might have done it to, Micha tries, but he can't make it all add up to anything. Guilt, remorse, pride, defiance, shame. Nothing definite. Nothing for Micha to pin everything to.

Facts, events, places stand separate, distinct, and Dilan screams.

Micha straps her into the pushchair, walks away from the house in search of a shop or a café, a place to buy water, some formula, somewhere to warm it all up. Dilan won't stop crying and he is afraid. *Over two hours home on the train.*

The streets are just one house after another and Micha can't forget Kolesnik's bleak answers. No guilt and no forgiveness either. *No point in sadness.* In any small, human emotions. *What did Luise say? People just do it and then they go on.*

Micha walks, Dilan cries, he finds no shops.

All this time. Since the start of it all at the family dinner, on Oma's balcony, in the library, reading and writing things down. Micha has thought for months now that there might be an end to this, but here in this unfamiliar suburb with his hungry, angry child, he knows that for all these months he has been wrong.

—

– *Even when I cry about it, I'm crying for myself. Not for the people who were killed.*

Mina frowns for a while, dangles the bright starfish over her daughter's face. She is still angry about yesterday, the fact that he went away without saying anything, without food for Dilan, without proper thought. Micha can see Mina collecting herself.

– That's OK, isn't it?
– *Do you think so?*
– I don't know.

Dilan's hands reach, fall away again. The red and yellow starfish jangles, tiny bells on each of its points. Soft towelling body squashed between Mina's fingers. Nails bitten to the quick.

— *Who do you cry for?*
— When I see things about the Holocaust?
— *Yes.*
— You. At the moment. Me. Her. I'm going to walk a bit, get her off to sleep.

Mina moves slowly back and forth along the path in front of the park bench, with the baby leaning on her shoulder. Micha looks at the small face lying against the soft wool of her mother's coat. Cheeks pink in the cold morning air, lashes like black ink lines on her skin.

— When I was young I used to think it was awful, all the children who lost their parents. You know that photo? The little boy running along the road in Belsen when the Allies came? All alone.
— *Yes.*
— Now I think about the parents who lost their children. Children were killed first in the camps, no?

Micha nods.

— I think how terrible that must be. To survive after that. To have to live without them.

The baby is asleep. Micha wants to hold her. Knows it would wake her. Mina stops walking, starts swaying gently, side to side.

– You look at things differently. Everyone does. You loved your Opa. You found out something terrible about him, maybe you feel like you can't love him now. You have to cry about that.

Mina lies the baby down in the pushchair, and Micha rocks it with his foot, tucks the blanket over his daughter's feet.

– I know that's all very logical.
– *Yes.*
– Difficult to be logical.
– *Yes.*
– He still did all those nice things you remember, though. He still loved you.
– *I can't think about that, Mina.*
– No.

She pulls the bag off the pushchair handles, searches for something among the pots of cream and bundles of nappies.

– *What would you do?*
– What do you mean?
– *If it was your Opa.*
– Honestly, Micha. I don't know. I'd maybe piss on his grave. Sorry. I don't know. I probably wouldn't want to think of the good things, either.

You look at things differently. Micha repeats Mina's statement to himself, but it makes no difference. Doesn't make it easier at all. He thinks about himself, this is true. *Selfish.* But what Micha finds far more difficult are the others he thinks about, too. *Opa, and Jozef. What they did, and they each lived a whole life afterwards.* Micha always finds them in his mind's-eye maps; replays the choices they made; follows the unravelling lines. *Years and generations. No way to change it. Never enough sadness and no forgiveness.*

It revolts him that he thinks of them. Doesn't tell Mina because he knows it would revolt her, too.

—

It is late. The baby is asleep. Micha stands in his pyjamas in the dark hallway and answers the phone.

There is an echo on the line; long distance. A voice he doesn't recognise speaks in halting German. A familiar heavy accent.

– This is a telephone call from Elena Kolesnik.

It is a woman's voice, but not Elena's. Micha hears Elena speak in the background. The voice on the phone translates.

– Am I speaking to Michael?
– *This is Michael. Is that Elena?*
– Yes, she is here. She wants to tell you something. She says you should sit.
– *Yes.*

Micha stays standing.

– Elena says that her husband has died. She is very sad for you. For herself, but also for you.
– *Kolesnik?*
– Yes, Jozef Kolesnik. He died in his sleep and she laid him to rest today.

Micha hears Elena repeat his name. She is crying. Her voice sounds closer now, she has the receiver. Elena Kolesnik speaks to Micha in Belarussian. He only understands her husband's name. She breathes deeply and Micha can feel how sad she is, can see her standing in the narrow hall, holding the telephone and crying.

– *I am sorry Elena. I am sorry about Jozef.*

But the other woman is on the phone again now.

– Elena says she would like you to come. She would like you to see the grave.

Micha can feel Elena's silence, can picture her in the kitchen doorway, waiting for his reply. He thinks of a thousand reasons to say no.

– *Please tell Elena I will come.*

The woman translates. Micha imagines Elena Kolesnik listening, wonders if she is smiling, what she is feeling.

– *I will come in a couple of weeks. I will book a train and write to her.*

When Micha goes back into the bedroom, Mina is

dozing, and the baby is lying next to her, arms flung over her head. He watches them a while, and then whispers, careful not to wake them.

– *Jozef Kolesnik is dead.*

He will tell Mina in the morning. *That will be soon enough.*

Belarus, Spring 1999

The journey is familiar now. Micha is prepared for the waiting, the slow trains and the crowded bus. It is not difficult for him to remember that Kolesnik is dead, that he won't be seeing him, and he is surprised at that. Micha thought he would expect the old man to be at the bus stop, that it would be a shock to walk to the house on his own, but it isn't.

Elena Kolesnik is on the porch, waiting for him. She waves as Micha comes round the corner, and he waves back. There is another woman with her, a younger woman. Micha thinks she was probably the voice on the phone.

Elena Kolesnik offers Micha her bedroom, hers and her husband's. Micha declines, but the neighbour says Elena wants it that way.

– She will sleep in the kitchen, that is the way she does it with guests.

Elena slams the plates on to the table, cuts the bread in huge slabs. She is angry with Micha. Can't understand why he won't stay for longer. He asks the neighbour to tell her that he must work, he has taken leave.

– *They only allowed me two days. I have to leave tomorrow. I am sorry.*

He unpacks the photos of Elena and Jozef from the top of his rucksack, and Elena stares at them while they eat. Micha knows he should have sent them months ago. Before Jozef died. He apologises again, through the neighbour, and Elena nods, but is not really listening. Absorbed in the images in front of her. *Jozef looking at her, in the next room. Just a few months ago.*

After they clear the plates, Micha shows the women pictures of Mina and the baby, and Elena smiles again, but she is still hurt. Micha knows he should stay longer, but he doesn't want to. He doesn't want to sleep where Kolesnik slept and where he died. He wants to tell Elena that he was not her husband's friend, not even her friend, but the words won't come. Too cruel, too ungrateful.

The neighbour says goodnight.

– Elena will take you tomorrow to see the grave. In the morning she says, when you get up. You can walk from here.

In the bedroom, Micha pulls the blankets back off the bed, messes up the sheets a little and dents the pillow. Then he lays out his sleeping-bag on the rug under the wide windowsill and rolls his jumper up under his head.

—

In the graveyard Elena smoothes the new grass with her fingers. There are fresh flowers laid next to the grave. Not from Elena, not from Micha. *Jozef Kolesnik is mourned.*

Micha is not sure what he should do. The morning is warm. Bright sun through the few clouds. He is still half-asleep. Tired from the journey and the night spent on the wooden floor.

No headstone yet. Nothing to mark Kolesnik's grave but the high mound, the fresh turf which Elena presses down, kneeling on the ground next to Micha, silent, laying her cheek, her forehead on the ground. Micha looks away, down the slope towards the village and the river. Trying to feel something; failing; wanting to go home as soon as he can.

Micha expects to go back to the house, but they walk in the opposite direction, out of the village. South towards the marsh and then, after ten minutes or so, east towards the forest. The neighbour is not with them, so Micha can't ask Elena where they are going. He just walks with her in silence, and follows her into the birch trees, waking up, taking in the landscape now, the beautiful day. Clear, strong sun through the leaves. Light falling in shafts on earth and grass. He walks with Elena in the birdsong and cool forest smell.

Elena takes hold of Micha's elbow, and he sees the tears on her cheeks. Wet, sudden, Micha is shocked; that he was distracted, paid so little attention. That she should cry, and he shouldn't see.

– *Frau Kolesnik.*

They are still walking, Elena slightly ahead, pulling Micha with her. He reaches for her hand, but she pulls it away, points further into the trees. Up ahead, further along the forest path, Elena keeps them moving, pointing towards a clearing; bright and green through the dark and brown of the trees.

Micha looks and then he sees it. It's like a blow to the head.

He stops walking and Elena turns round. She looks at him, tears flowing now. Micha puts his hand to his mouth; feels the wet breath on his palm; the hot, spinning feeling that comes with it. Elena raises her arms, one hand at her shoulder, the other a fist in the air in front of her. She mimes shooting with a rifle, but Micha already knows.

He shouts. She makes the bullet noise, a puff of lips and air.

Micha squints. The sun is loud and bright on the leaves. He sweats, and the salt stings his eyes.

Elena stands ahead of him. Micha squeezes his lids shut.

There is forest around him, a thudding pulse in his stomach, and blood hot and black behind his eyes. She is waiting for him, but his legs have turned to water. He doesn't want to be here. Wants to open his eyes and be back at the house, back at home, in the kitchen, with his daughter on his lap. Elena mimes shooting again and he shouts at her. That he knows; that she should stop.

– *Please. Stop.*

He holds his hands up, covering his eyes, and she lets her arms fall to her sides. She stands there, small and sad, and Micha hears the faint, dry noise in the back of her throat, thinks, *She has lost her husband, her Jozef.*

Elena wipes her face with her sleeve, but her tears only wet her cheeks again. She walks on. Narrow back, stiff shoulders turned to Micha, sun falling full on her head as she walks out of the trees on to the wide, bright grass.

Micha stands on the edge of the clearing and watches her. Feet on the boundary where forest floor gives way to grass. Fists, teeth, stomach clenched. The old woman moving ahead of him, across the broad, flat space, in the bright light beyond the trees, dropping to her knees.

Micha waits. Elena kneels. Shoulders shaking. *Crying.* He can hear her now. He moves.

Walks across the clearing that is also a grave.

Elena wipes her tears and strokes them into the ground.

Micha's head swims. He tries to, but he can't stay with her. Can't stand here on this soft ground, on this grass and moss. He turns away again, leaving Elena in the bright sun, crossing the damp ground to reach the dry cinder track through the trees. He doesn't even want to wait for her now, but he does.

They walk back to the town in silence. The sun high in the sky and hot. Micha still feels faint, sticky. Can't wait to get away.

Elena rides with him in the bus to the station. Dries her face on a large grey handkerchief; angry with him. He knows he has ruined it for her; her day for honouring the dead. They don't talk. Micha can think of nothing to say. Furious, too. Fighting his anger down.

She has no children. A young woman in an empty village, she told me that. She knew how many were killed. And when he came back, she loved one of the murderers. Had no children. Found her measure of blame and loved him.

The train pulls in and they stand together and wait for the guard to open the doors. Elena pulls bread and fruit from her bag for Micha to eat on the journey home. He thanks her and climbs into the train. He puts his bags on the rack and goes back to the door, which is closed now, but Elena is still there. He pulls the window down.

Elena speaks now, and Micha doesn't understand anything. The few words he might have recognised are smothered by her tears. She speaks and speaks, gripping Micha's hands, knowing he doesn't understand. She doesn't seem to care. The words fall on and on and on until the guard slams the remaining doors.

Elena keeps hold of Micha's hands until the train moves off. Then she drops them. Silent now, she walks with the train, with Micha, to the end of the platform, and then she waves and Micha watches until she is out of sight.

It is dusk. The train rolls away. The bright leaves around the clearing are still in Micha's head, the soft earth. The terrible thought catching up with him, through the day of sickness and sunlight and Elena's voice and tears.

Opa. Jozef.

Micha knows why she did it; why she took him there.

—

Micha is alone in the compartment, and the moon is high outside. He keeps the light off and the curtain open, watching the passage through forest and marsh. Black shapes, white-edged. Sharp outlines framing the dark.

I didn't go to Opa's funeral. Luise went, but Mutti said I was too young. I think I spent the day with a friend. I don't remember.

Later, Mutti took me to see the grave. Perhaps two or three years later. I remember all the dark yew trees, and walking along the rows of gravestones. Some had fresh flowers, and others had bunches that were fading. Dried up. Rotting, even. Green water in the tall vases. It was hot.

I don't remember expecting to see Opa, but when he wasn't there waiting for us, I cried and cried and cried.

Home: Spring

Dilan walks next to Micha on a blue day. Bright and warm. He has her jacket tucked under his arm, and her discarded hat in his pocket. The walk from the bus stop runs through the landscaped grounds, and Micha takes small steps so his daughter can keep up; their pace matching that of the residents out enjoying the day, crunching slowly arm in arm along the yellow gravel. The trees are fuller and taller than the last time Micha was here, but otherwise he thinks that nothing has changed. White building, green lawn, grey car park; the cloudy, empty uncertainty inside. Dilan trips and falls and cries briefly until he picks her up.

– *No tears today.*

He brushes away the gravel that has stuck to her hands, checks the skin for punctures, kisses the tiny blue-black dents in her palms. She wipes her eyes and smiles. Small teeth. Dark cheeks. *Like Mina's.*

Micha doesn't go straight in to the entrance, but carries Dilan beyond the block to the edge of the car park and she hums as they walk, small fists tucked into the folds of his coat. When he gets to the kerb, Micha turns round and looks up; eyes to the top of the white high-rise block.

— *See, Dilan?*

He points for his daughter, and she follows the line of his finger to the sky, still humming, squinting in the sun.

— *If we start with the top right corner, then count eight windows down. And then one, two, three across. That's where Oma Kaethe lives. That's her bird's nest. And if we're lucky, she'll be out on her balcony waiting for us. Can you see?*
— *Oma Kaethe?*
— *My Oma Kaethe. Can you see her?*

Micha looks into his daughter's face, watches her accept another family member without a flicker. Her family map spreads out; unproblematic, curious, unhesitant. Painful for Micha to see. He lifts Dilan on to his shoulders.

— *Is she there?*
— *Where?*
— *Wave. If you wave, she might wave back.*

Dilan waves. Micha can feel her weight shifting gently against his neck. Lets himself enjoy this moment, down here with his daughter, humming and waving, steadying herself with a small hand pressed on the top of his head.

— *Is she there, Papa?*

Micha's eyes smart. Watery. Blurred vision against the

blinding sky.

– *Yes. Can you see?*
– Yes.

Dilan doesn't sound too sure, but she keeps waving, and Micha keeps his eyes on the tiny speck of movement which comes in reply.

BY RACHEL SEIFFERT
ALSO AVAILABLE IN VINTAGE

| ☐ | **Field Study** | 0099461781 | £6.99 |
